BECAUSE I WAS LONELY

Because I Was Lonely

Hayley Mitchell

RedDoor

Published by RedDoor
www.reddoorpublishing.com

The right of Hayley Mitchell to be identified as the author of
this Work has been asserted by her in accordance with sections
77 and 78 of the Copyright, Designs and Patents Act 1988

ISBN 978-1-910453-29-2

A CIP catalogue record for this book
is available from the British Library

Cover designer: Anna Morrison
www.annamorrison.com

Typesetting: WatchWord Editorial Services
www.watchwordeditorial.co.uk

Printed in Great Britain by
Bell and Bain Ltd., Glasgow, UK

For my family:
you are my everything x

part one

their lives

Rachel

Rachel sat at the top of the stairs, hands rolling around the overlap of wood on the step, rocking back and forth. The movements were slight but rhythmic. Her fingers were splayed, gripping deep into the pile of the stair carpet, knuckles white with the force of her grip. She gasped for breath, her face pale except for anxious flushed cheeks and dark circles that filled the hollows under her eyes. Sleep deprivation and anxiety left a confused mind. Her thoughts, which were often random and incomplete, now needed a mind that could focus.

What had she meant to do? All she had wanted was for the noise to stop.

The muslin cloth was on the stairs, dropped there as if it was a weapon, the puckered, once-white material frayed a little at the edges from endless washing. Jamie was still just a baby, but the crying was endless: a constant whining, whinging cry. Milky sick had dribbled from his mouth. She had shoved the cloth under him, expecting more to follow, unable to face changing the sheets again. The persistent wail had just risen higher and higher from that tiny mouth.

Rachel held her hands tightly over her ears; just wanted it to stop. Burping Jamie for longer would have helped, patting the tiny back until the air escaped; impatience had not. It was her fault, but this was supposed to be naptime. *Get a better routine, be firmer. Leave him to cry a little.* The same monotone drivel of the health visitor each time Rachel was desperate enough to reach out for help. Only it wasn't help. When you were that tired, you needed real help...you needed time to sleep.

As the dribble was wiped from the tiny mewling mouth, the sound had been muffled by the cloth. Held in place for just a moment too long, the noise had stopped. She hadn't wanted to hurt Jamie. This mess wasn't his fault; this was grown-up mess. When the noise stopped and all went quiet Rachel had fled, and, instead of the long hot shower she had been imagining all morning while a contented baby snoozed, she was here, sitting on the stairs, hair still greasy, rocking, and praying to a God in whom she had no faith that her baby was still breathing.

Rachel loved her children. She'd thought she would love her perfect family. Rachel and David, James and Maisie. But James had become Jamie and Rachel felt she had gone mad.

She was rooted. Her fingers were rigid, gripping at the pile of the carpet. Nails raked back and forth until one split, causing it to bleed. Unaware she was rocking, oblivious that blood from her finger was staining the carpet, Rachel felt her breathing become more rapid; gasping in, she seemed unable to exhale. She had a sensation of falling backwards, out of control, slipping, unable to hold on...the white walls of the stairwell falling towards her...they blurred and she held her breath.

She had to get a grip. *She needed to check the baby*. She felt sick, rotten in her gut. *She had to check the baby*. She wished she could die now. *She had to check the baby*. The pain in her chest was overwhelming, crushing. She knew she had to get a grip. *She had to check the baby*. She needed to slow her breathing. She had to control her breathing.

She couldn't control her breathing, and the bile of panic rose into her mouth, the taste acrid; her throat constricted, she retched. Breaking free from the hold of the stairs and running to the bathroom, gagging and heaving again and again as vomit gushed. Hot, uncontrollable tears streaked down her face, falling from red, swollen eyes. Her head hung and she didn't care that her long hair was dangling inside the toilet, the ends touching the sick that floated like lily pads. As she held tight to the edges of the toilet seat, clinging to it, her breathing started to slow. She could feel her heart still hammering, the rapid bang, bang, bang, pumping blood so fast it made her head spin. She sat back on her heels, her knees aching and stiff...pushed herself up and tried to stand, feeling old and tired; oh so tired. Her cold, numb feet made any movement difficult. Rachel didn't know how long she had sat there. If it was possible she was more exhausted than before, drained, wrung out. If age did this to you, she didn't want to get any older. If life did this to you, she was happy for it to end today.

Holding on to the basin, she turned on the cold tap and water trickled through cold fingers, splashing on to waxen cheeks and rinsing the vile taste from her mouth. Calm now, she needed to check she hadn't hurt Jamie.

Taking the few reluctant steps to the nursery, Rachel hesitated at the door, steeling herself to open it; afraid, expecting the worst, expecting a small pale lifeless body, tucked up tight in his little blue sleeping bag with the yellow ducks across the front. With a furrowed brow and a body wet with icy sweat that drenched her back and underarms, she looked, eyes just half open, as if this would somehow offer protection from the atrocity she might have committed.

The creases of her brow unfolded as relief flooded through her. Almost smiling, she watched the slow rise and fall of Jamie's chest. For a few moments she gazed at the little sucking movement of his mouth, contented in deep sleep. Taking a few steps into the room, she leant her back against the wall; too tired to stand up, she slid down it, then sat on the soft rug, numb with cold and unbearable fatigue, curling on to her side. Her shoulders shook with quiet sobs of relief. *She hadn't hurt him.* Yet she wasn't sure if, just for a moment, she had wanted to.

As the tears dried, Rachel lay there looking at the little yellow ducks as they waddled up and down the white walls. They had been placed there with such optimism, such delight, Rachel and Maisie singing 'Five Little Ducks' and counting as they carefully sponged them on to the walls. Rachel fixated on the one nearest to the top of the skirting board, torn a little at one edge where Maisie had been too enthusiastic with the damp sponge.

She fell into a deep sleep. She was woken by the abrupt sound of the alarm, ringing loud and shrill from her bedroom; it was set for 2.25 every weekday afternoon, just in case Jamie napped and on the rare chance she did as well. She groaned, aching, cold and awkward on the floor. When that alarm sounded there were five minutes until the next round of intrusive ringing began. Late was not an option; it took thirty minutes to get them both to the school gate.

She lifted Jamie from his cot. He was already stirring. The naps were new, a pattern of sleep beginning to emerge after almost ten months of non-stop crying and feeding, crying and feeding. The endless monotony of walks just to stop the constant wailing that now seemed to echo from the walls even when he was silent. He snuggled in to feed for the allotted ten minutes. Ten more minutes would make them both presentable, an outward show to the school that all was well: change his nappy, strap him into the pushchair and speed-walk to pick Maisie up from school. At the school gate Rachel would engage in inane conversation about how gorgeous Jamie was, and how much he had grown. Often, as her mouth moved, uttering acquiescent banalities in reply, she would wonder if they would like to take him home and enjoy the obvious pleasure of his company...a day would do. Only they didn't have breasts filled with milk, and Jamie refused to take a bottle. Ten minutes of letting him suck at her breast now would stop the crying later. She hated breast-feeding but it was 'best for baby' She leaned dutifully back against the chair as he latched on with a greedy suck. She hadn't hurt him; he was OK. She was OK. It would all be fine. They would sleep better tonight. They would, she was sure.

Rachel rocked Jamie as he cried. The health visitor said she needed to be stronger, to leave him longer, let him learn that he had to sleep. But the crying would wake Maisie, who was tired and cranky; she had to go to school, and it wasn't her fault they had decided to have him. Rachel looked at the clock. Six hours of possible sleep. That wasn't too bad: she could cope well if she had six hours of sleep.

Her arms and back were aching by the time Jamie's eyes began to close. Rocking him until she was sure he had gone off, she laid him in the cot, creeping out, making her way back to her room, her tiptoed footfall almost silent on the carpet. Just as she pulled the quilt over her head with a sigh of relief, he cried, at first intermittent sheeplike bleats, soon followed by a full-on wail. She left him for five minutes then went through to the nursery and shushed him with a reassuring light touch to his cheek. She did this three times, then, afraid he would wake his sister, they swayed together, Rachel burrowing her nose into the warmth of his neck and sniffing the slightly pungent yet reassuring smell. The crying ceased; she would try not to feed him. The dread came in the next moment, the look at the clock: five hours, ten minutes of possible sleep.

Rachel lay in bed, awake. If she just went to the toilet then maybe sleep would come. One visit to the loo had already been made straight after she had laid Jamie back in his cot: time had tick-ticked past since then. Digital red numerals like bloodshot eyes moved time on and on through the night. A second visit to the toilet, taking care not to wake anyone; back to bed, feeling her way across the room in the dark, afraid the sudden cast of her bedroom light would disturb one of them. She was cold now; Jamie had slept for an hour already. Rachel had stared at the ceiling then the clock and the ceiling once more. Cold feet always kept her awake. She pulled on a pair of black socks; she would regret that in the morning when her sheets were covered in black fluff but they were the first out of the drawer and rummaging was noisy. She moved her pillows and lay there, mind numb. A noise outside made her jump; she had been drifting, sleep had been reachable; tears welled but didn't escape…so unfair. The drift into sleep had been so close: sleep, precious, precious sleep. She lay still again; nothing. Awake, she turned to the clock: two hours, fifteen minutes of possible sleep.

The radio blurted out some cheerful song; the DJ spouted out some crap. Rachel just wanted to sob into her pillow. She hit snooze. A love ballad, big notes, big song, voice far too big, too many screeching high-reaching notes for a banging head. She hit snooze. The DJ spouted out a cheery good morning. She hit snooze.

David came in. She had no idea why he was shaking her arm – couldn't he see she was asleep? There was muttering she couldn't make out, comments about lying in bed when the kids needed sorting. David had *it* in his arms; it was crying. Rachel felt like a failure – in fact she knew she *was* a failure. Other people did this with far more kids, David told her that all the time. Why couldn't she? She hadn't heard *it* cry. She glanced at the monitor. The mute button was flashing; she must have turned it to mute when *it* was crying in the night and forgotten to turn it back on. It was bad enough listening to the crying, let alone having the sound in amplified stereo.

Rachel sat up, unwrapped her swollen breast and snuggled Jamie in. Maisie appeared at the door, hair everywhere, pink pyjamas halfway up on one leg and wound round her torso; her bed would be a mess as usual. Maisie twisted and turned through the night; Rachel worried that it was because Jamie disturbed her so much. She was sulky, sucking her thumb, not speaking, knowing she had to go to school when Jamie had the pleasure of staying home with Mummy all day. Rachel wondered why anyone would want to be trapped in the house with her all day. Where was the pleasure? Perhaps it was in the pervasive smell of shitty nappies and endless cleaning up of food thrown at walls. Bowls that were upturned the moment she glanced away. Maybe Maisie thought there was endless joy attained from wrestling with huge piles of infinite washing. Then there were the happy noises of crying; the endless crying. Jamie then Rachel. Rachel then Jamie. Sometimes, just for the hell of it, in unison.

Conversations were taking place, but Rachel wasn't sure who was saying what. She smiled at her daughter, a smile that reached her eyes for a moment before dying at the same moment it died on her lips. She didn't show her teeth when she smiled any more. David was ready to leave for work. Rachel wondered how she hadn't heard him shower and dress. David made noise and was not altruistic by nature and had no qualms about waking her every morning. He seemed oblivious to the dark circles that perfectly underlined the thousand-yard stare. Rachel looked at the clock. It was 7.50 a.m. – no more hours of possible sleep.

If David would just say, 'Stay in bed, I'll see to them,' then she could sleep. She savoured the imagined words... 'Don't worry, my darling, just sleep. I'll ring in sick.' If she was awake too long, if there was too much interaction, then there was no chance of any more sleep. In her mind she begged him just to take them away.

He was speaking to her. She looked up; he was waiting for a response.

'OK,' she guessed.

'I'll be home at the usual time,' he said. 'You need to hurry up, you'll be late. Did you have a bad night?'

'Not great.' Rachel smiled her vacant smile.

David kissed her cheek. 'Try and get a nap, then. See you later.' He popped his head back round the door. 'Oh, and we need milk and bread. Can you pop out?'

Popping out and napping – they were just so easy, weren't they? And he was gone, and the day started again.

Inside, Rachel was screaming, a high-pitched, angry, wailing, uncontrollable scream, louder than she had ever screamed, or imagined anyone was capable of screaming. Outwardly, she was silent and ashen. Her skin prickled with fear; she felt herself fighting, adrenalin pumping; there was nothing tangible to fight. Every muscle was taut. Sweat soaked her back, ran between her breasts; hair clung to the sides of her face and she pushed it back again and again, her fingers and the palm of her hand now damp, but still it kept clinging, driving her mad, itching, irritating. Shallow, fleeting breaths left her lungs before they had filled, making her gasp for more air, gulping it in with a greed that was not satisfying her need. Taking hold of her own wrist, she felt for her pulse: too quick, it was much too quick. If her heart gave out now she would leave the kids – the kids would be alone. She had to control her breathing. Slow it down, slow it down, slow it down.

She wanted to run, run anywhere; she ran downstairs. Sitting on the edge of the sofa, she kept moving, rapid, rocking, jerky movements, the phone gripped in one hand; if the crushing pain in her chest started she would just dial 999. Then at least if she died someone would get there for the kids; they wouldn't be alone for too long. She felt faint; the room was spinning. The walls were falling in and the floor was rising up. The room was closing in, then rushing away from her. Solid became fluid. She stood, unsteady, but trying to walk back and forth to distract herself. She told herself to keep moving – distraction; if she could *just* control her breathing...

Inside she was screaming but she didn't tell anyone; there was no one to tell. He was absent. His physical presence sometimes remained in their home, but he was an emotional void. 'He' with whom she had once been so happy to share every emotion, every feeling, every mistake. 'He' to whom she looked for sympathy and understanding, for laughter and love. 'He' with whom she had shared her wants, her desires, her body. She had thought him so emotional: he cried at books and welled up at sad movies, embarrassed to leave the cinema, blowing his nose and blaming allergies and dust. Now she realised that the only desperation he was capable of crying about was fictional.

David was sleeping in a hotel...sleeping, undisturbed sleep. Even when he was at home, when she needed him he seemed a million miles away and yet, at night, he slept no more than one hundred of her steps away. She knew it was one hundred steps because she had counted them. He slept in his study, because he needed to be fresh for work and the baby's crying kept him awake; yet David slept there whenever he was at home, even at the weekend. Sometimes, unable to sleep, she padded barefoot down the stairs and listened outside his door to his breathing, checking he was still there. Wanting to be sure he hadn't left. She understood about the week nights, but just sometimes, at the weekend...maybe...he could...maybe he could just try for a night...again.

Once, just once, David had tried to see to Jamie in the night and it had been a disaster. He just kept wandering in, telling her he didn't know what to do, as if somehow Rachel's gender gave her all the answers. David said the crying was hurting his ears. David moaned that the rocking was hurting his back. He missed the whole point of what they were trying to do, and after an hour he was begging Rachel to feed Jamie so that he would settle. He had looked like a lost and petulant child. Rachel had given in, feeling like a mother to all of them. David said he was exhausted even though it was only just after 1 a.m. and he still had six hours of possible sleep.

If he did a whole night, just once, Rachel would make sure that they didn't wake him in the morning. He could sleep until the afternoon if he needed to. If she could sleep a night through, just once, then maybe the three of them could go out in the car together; she would feel safe to drive. Just Maisie, Jamie and Mummy out on a little adventure, the way she used to with Maisie all the time. Rachel and Maisie had been so close, their time together so natural, so easy. The three of them could all go to the big park in town, the one Maisie used to love, with the bright red, blue and green climbing frame. The one Jamie hadn't been to yet. Not the one just up the road in the village; they were all bored with the one just up the road. David was a grown man, couldn't he figure it out…just once?

Rachel's thoughts were muddled in her head most of the time. She was the one that wasn't coping, wasn't she? David kept telling her she couldn't cope. Maybe he shouldn't have to help, but Rachel heard others at the school gate talking about husbands, grandparents and sisters who came and rescued them, helping them get some sleep or just a long soak in the bath. If she had time for her head to clear then she might not feel as if she was trapped in this eternal fog.

Tonight he was away for work. He was away much more since Jamie had been born. Rachel was calm. The panic was over and the need to sleep overwhelming. The stairs to her room seemed endless. Damp pyjamas clung to her and she sighed, not caring if she stank of dried sweat by morning; there was no one to cuddle up to, after all. Crawling under the quilt, she glanced at the clock: three hours, fifty-seven minutes of possible sleep.

She lay alone in a world of grief and confusion…*awake, so awake, so very awake…now even when Jamie sleeps I'm awake, so awake, so very awake…* The same words went

13

round and round as she tried to sleep...*awake, so awake, so very awake.*

Sleep...

How long? *How long?* The clock told her two hours, just two hours. She felt sick to the stomach with the need for more but Jamie wanted to feed. It was almost morning: Jamie had slept well even if she had not. It would be churlish to make him wait.

The health visitor told Rachel that Jamie should have stopped feeding at night by now, but she said it with a girlish giggle, in a way she believed was reassuring to mums but which in fact was a nerve-jangling annoyance. Then the health visitor said, in the knowing way of someone who had no idea what they were talking about, that all babies were different. She almost sang it – *all babies are different.* It was practised, the echoing melody said to every distraught mother who walked through that badly painted door.

Rachel wanted to beat the health visitor repeatedly about the head with one of the big baby manuals that sat covered with dust on her desk. Didn't she know babies didn't come out attached to an instruction book? They came out attached to a placenta. Rachel wanted to see the health visitor slump on to the desk, blood oozing from the back of her stupid head, her lifeless eyes looking back at Rachel. Within those eyes, Rachel wanted to see her own reflection frozen in the moment of death. In that reflection, Rachel knew that she would look smug with the knowledge that she had saved some other poor unsuspecting, exhausted mother from wasting her time listening to the woman's diatribe of vitriolic crap. The health visitor didn't have children. Rachel remarked on this to herself as she left the clinic. She muttered under her breath, 'She doesn't have children because nobody in their right mind would fuck the sanctimonious, self-righteous, insincere, ugly bitch.'

Rachel collected Jamie from his cot. Why on earth I let him continue to suck the life out of me, I don't know, she thought; he's like a parasite, a torturing, indolent leech.

She silenced his crying, holding his tiny body to her. Jamie was warm, his chubby fingers clasped on to her thumb. Rachel knew it wasn't his fault. She stroked his cheek. It was soft and smooth and he was innocent. Her anger was misplaced. It should have been easier this time, now she knew what she was doing. In the hospital there had been envy from the first-timers as she'd handled him with ease: nappies, feeding, burping and they soon went home. Those first few weeks as expected, tired but not exhausted, but now…dear God, now!

She fed him, he burped and, satisfied, he dozed. She rocked him, then they cried until dawn when they finally fell asleep, his tiny body tucked into the curve of her tummy.

'Mummy!' Maisie tapped her on the arm.

How long? *How long*? How long did she sleep? Thirty minutes! Just thirty minutes! Only thirty minutes! Time for school now, no time to sleep. She wanted to weep and weep and weep. She wanted to sleep. Another day of torment began.

The first boy Rachel ever had sex with killed himself when he was twenty. He parked his car in a remote country lane, attached a hose to the exhaust, ran it in through the car window, taped it up and ran the engine until he died.

His death had nothing to do with Rachel. At the time she didn't think it had much effect on her. It happened a long time after she had known him. She had, however, known him intimately: part of his body inside her body. The sexual act itself had been a hurried, emotionless event. It was furtive, and Rachel felt almost passive, observing the event from where she lay. The loss of her virginity took place on the grass behind a village hall, where a friend was having her sixteenth birthday party. From time to time Rachel thought about his suicide and wondered why he had wasted his life. She wondered why he didn't just wait it out; death was always so close at hand.

The whole event of losing her virginity was not something that impacted on her until later in life. It was one of those regrets stored in the deep recesses of memory, put away to be dusted off and revisited. Now in her forties, unable to sleep, Rachel wondered about that first sexual encounter, realising it should have been special or at least memorable. The penetration had lasted less than a minute, caused a grass stain on her favourite dress, left her feeling sore, uncomfortable and smelling of rubber: job done. She would talk to Maisie when she was older, explain the right way to go about it.

Rachel sympathised with that boy now, realising the pressure on him, a sign of the times, to keep up with your friends and make sure you had 'shagged someone' at least once by the time you were sixteen. Tonight, though, more than that, she understood why he had not sat it out, why he had not wanted to wait for death to arrive at a natural time; and, whatever had happened to him, she now understood that overwhelming need to feel the exhalation of that final breath.

David had made love to her last night. While it was happening, Rachel had been overwhelmed with love and desire for him, the solid warmth of another full-sized person, lying next to her, stroking her, kissing her. His touch designed to give pleasure. As she came, she pulled him harder into her, digging her nails in until he shuddered and cried out. Slumping down on top of her, he kissed her, before sliding off her body. They held each other for a while, lying side by side. Semen ran down the inside of her leg, leaving a wet, uncomfortable patch where she lay. David left soon after, kissing Rachel again and muttering something about having to be up at six. Strange how physically they could be so close together and yet…she had moved on to his side of the bed, leaving the wet patch to dry.

Later, as Rachel lay alone, unable to sleep, waiting for Jamie to wake, she had felt adrift on an ocean of expensive Egyptian cotton, miles from anything that mattered. Jamie slept all night that night, the only time that year. Rachel stayed awake until 5.30 a.m. She looked at the clock momentarily before falling into a deep sleep, realising she had an hour and a half of possible sleep.

The noise at the window sounded like someone trying to get in. Rachel sat for a while, frozen with fear, sure she had been asleep. The clock said five hours, nine minutes of possible sleep. At first she thought it was a dream but now she was sure someone was trying to get in. Panic made her stay where she was. Going downstairs to fetch David would mean she would have to leave the kids, and whoever was trying to force the window might get to them before she could get back upstairs. It was only one hundred steps; if she ran she could make it. Breathless, she opened the study door, shook David, shouted, 'Get upstairs!' and then, not waiting for an answer, she took the stairs two at a time. She checked both kids on the way back up. They were fine.

Sleeping peacefully. She sat on the bed, waiting, ready to fight whoever or whatever came through that window. She would protect her kids.

'Rachel, what the fuck?' David hissed.

'Someone, at the window,' she whispered with a frantic hiss, pointing at the window despite the fact that it was the only one in the room.

'Not again! It's a dream, Rachel. Go back to bed.'

David left. And Rachel sat there all night ready to protect the kids, whatever the cost. Watching the clock as the hours of possible sleep disappeared.

When Rachel's mother died, she felt as though she had lost both her parents. After forty-nine years of a difficult marriage, Rachel's father gave up on life. It seemed he valued her mum in death more than he had ever done in life. For a few weeks it seemed Rachel's dad would be OK, but then he just took to wandering around the garden. Whatever the weather or the time of year, he would be in the garden. Rachel thought he wasn't able to be in the house without her mum. Mum had died from a massive heart attack while she slept; she might have felt it – they would never know. There were no last words, no time for goodbyes, no time for Rachel to tell her that she was expecting another child. Instead, Rachel told her mum's lifeless body, when she went to see it laid out at the funeral director's. Rachel didn't believe in an afterlife or any God. Despite this, she wanted her mum to know. Rachel wanted those words, 'I'm having a baby', to vibrate on eardrums that would never hear again.

When her dad could no longer cope alone, he went to live with Rachel's older brother; when her brother couldn't cope, her dad went to live with Rachel's younger sister. The resentment towards Rachel for living far away and having young children caused the family rift. Jamie was born six months after her mother died.

Apparently, walking up and down the street in your pyjamas and socks when it was raining and well after midnight was not acceptable. David put Rachel back to bed; after making sure she changed into dry pyjamas, he dried her hair with a towel. Rachel was reluctant to take off her socks, but David insisted and she was too tired to fight. Jamie now slept in four-hour slots and was almost eighteen months old. Rachel slept for four hours and then put him straight back to bed, as the health visitor had said. After he settled, Rachel watched the hours of possible sleep disappear until morning.

The dripping tap in the kitchen made Rachel cry; she couldn't stop it: drip, drip, drip. The clock in the kitchen with its tick, tick, tick drove her so mad she threw it in the bin outside. Jamie chewed plastic bricks while sitting on the rug in the lounge, the frantic chew of a teething child, drooling down them and on to the bib placed there to protect his clothes. Rachel removed the bricks one at a time, washed them in hot soapy water, dried them and took them back. She swapped them every three minutes; she timed it on her watch.

Rachel had loved everything about being married. First of all there was sex more or less whenever you fancied it. Then there were friends popping round for supper and drunken parties. There were shopping trips to buy co-ordinating sofas and rugs for the house. There were colour charts and decorating and sex on bare wooden floors covered with dustsheets. There was sex in every room in the house; David said they had to christen them all. They had drunken sex in the garden under a blanket, so the neighbours couldn't see, at night, and once on a drunken Sunday afternoon but the neighbour had complained about that so they hadn't done it again. There was a lot of sex, a lot of drinking, and a lot of fun. The first big argument was a bit of a shock. The making up involved a lot of sex and a lot of drinking but the fun seemed tainted.

The doctor seemed kind. David had insisted Rachel go. In fact, David had made the appointment without even telling her and he had come home from work. This was unusual. What was even more unusual was that he had insisted on going with her. The receptionist ·took Rachel straight through, and handed her husband a box of clinical-looking tissues; at home Rachel bought the small square boxes with the pretty patterns on. Here the tissues were in a white rectangular box with large navy blue block writing; they were rough when Rachel blew her nose. She was worried about the tissues; there was going to be bad news. She was unaware that she was crying.

The doctor was rather good-looking. Rachel tried her best to smile at him. An affair would be interesting: a reason to dress up, take her time in the shower, shave her legs, do the things she used to do. It would be an excellent way to have some 'me' time. She stifled a laugh. David glanced at her, a stern look on his face. Then Rachel thought of her baggy belly, stretch marks and hideous saggy breasts. Even her husband wasn't fond of those, so why would a stranger want to touch them? Being touched intimately would be nice, though. Her smile faded.

The doctor was talking to her husband. Rachel tried to listen. She knew they were here for something important. As a family they never really went to the doctor; they coped. The room distracted Rachel; it was clinical but shabby, in need of a makeover. She imagined the walls painted white. That strange examining table in faux brown leather with the roll of blue tissue that sat at the end was horrible. Nobody in his or her right mind would want to be examined on that. They should re-cover it, make it pretty and inviting; perhaps some cushions and a throw. Cushions always made a place look better.

David touched her arm and then he left. Rachel watched him leave and noted that Jamie was with him. She hadn't remembered putting Jamie in the car. Rachel was alone with the doctor; an uneasy knot formed in her stomach. What if the doctor wasn't all that nice after all – should she be in here alone? She presumed she must be the one who was ill. She wondered what was wrong with her. She looked at the empty chair; she counted three chairs, three pens on the doctor's table, three light bulbs in the light fitting. *Three blind mice, three blind mice, three blind mice...*maybe she was going blind. She could go for a run; maybe some fresh air would make her better. Mum always said fresh air would make you better...cutting off their tails was a bit barbaric; no wonder children grew up so screwed-up. Maisie loved that rhyme; she should sing it when she got home.

Rachel wondered where Maisie was; maybe she was in the waiting room with David. Rachel couldn't remember seeing Maisie but then she was surprised they had Jamie with them. School, she remembered – they took Maisie to school in the car that morning. They never did that; they always walked. Maisie had cried; she hadn't wanted to go to school. She said she didn't like school any more. She was almost six now, though, too old to be making such a fuss. Rachel would sit and have a little talk with her later. She could role-play with the Barbies; that would be fun. Maisie could pretend to be the teacher and Rachel could pretend to be Maisie – they would sort it out.

'Sometimes,' Rachel replied; she had no idea what the doctor had just asked. She presumed he had asked how often she wanted to kill the children. Anyway, she was never sure if she wanted to actually kill them – it was hypothetical. If someone would just take them both away and she could have a break from the noise, that would do just as well. If he was asking how often she wanted to die, she would have answered 'all the time'. She watched as he typed some notes into his computer.

'Have you ever thought about hurting yourself or the children?'

Rachel decided this was a weird thing to ask, when he had already asked if she wanted to kill them; she'd have thought he would build up to the killing question, killing your children was a big no-no, but he seemed to be working backwards. Perhaps it was an interview tactic: go in with the worst possible outcome, then soften her up, gain her confidence and then back in with the big question once she was off her guard. She would have to be more astute and watch that. She counted the three chairs, the three pens and checked there were still three bulbs in the light fitting.

'No, never. Sometimes I think I'd like to leave them somewhere.' She laughed.

'What stops you?'

'It's cold out; they might not find them.' Rachel stated it as a matter of fact, and then thought maybe it would be

OK if she just popped a couple more blankets on Jamie's pushchair, and a big coat on Maisie. She could even tie them to a gate somewhere, the way people did with unwanted Christmas puppies, but she supposed children were really for life, unless of course Social Services took them. Maisie had a very bright pink coat. Someone would see them. If she did it, though, she must be sure she had removed all the name tags from their clothes…it would be a bit embarrassing to get them back.

The doctor made more notes. He typed so much for what she had said. Rachel was unsure of what she had said – always talking too much, that was the problem…well, it had been until she had become quiet; now she worried that she wasn't quiet; maybe the thoughts left her mouth.

Rachel was content that the doctor wasn't going to use one of the pens. She watched his hand; no, he was staying with the keyboard. Her husband came back in, sat on the empty chair. To Rachel it felt complete now: three chairs, three people, three pens, three bulbs in the light fitting. She watched sunlight dance through the slatted blind on the window, a light wind moving a tree backwards and forwards periodically, making her husband appear to glow. His back was to the sunlight and he didn't notice; he stared back at her, a half-smile on his lips, unsure, looking at her as if she might speak.

Three blind mice, three blind mice, three blind mice…will they tell me the bad news now?

The doctor sat back in his chair and turned towards them both. She noticed a little paunch on his belly; perhaps he was not as attractive as she'd first thought. She also noticed the wobble under his chin: too much sitting. She thought she wouldn't bother with the affair after all.

'Your wife is a little depressed,' he said. 'She needs to get more sleep. I've written a prescription for some anti-depressants and I will need to see her again in two weeks. To see how it's going.' He smiled to reassure her husband, her husband smiled to reassure her, and Rachel smiled to complete the pattern. Three smiles, three chairs, three people, three pens and three light bulbs in the light fitting.

David made sure she took the tablets for the first four days; they made her feel sick and vacant, and by the fourth day she felt that just for a moment she stopped functioning – a gap – then she carried on – then a gap – then she carried on. On the fifth day, she started wrapping the tablets in Sellotape and popping them in the wheelie bin outside.

Rachel made coffee, and watched the sunlight fade behind the trees. It was dark by the time Maisie pulled at her arm, and she was stiff from leaning on the oak worktop. She remembered choosing it, caring what her kitchen looked like, using oil to keep it in tip-top condition. She would polish Maisie's sticky fingerprints off the front of the white cupboard doors, all shabby chic, Rachel's dream country kitchen: a warm, cosy family house, the kitchen the heart of the home…her arm was stuck in something which might have been jam.

She turned to Maisie. 'What's the matter, darling?' Rachel scooped her up in her arms, hugging her close, breathing in the essence of young life, and a faint smell of school dinners. Touching the soft uncreased skin on her face, and running her hands through her curls.

'I'm hungry, Mummy, and Jamie has been crying for ages. He stinks.'

Rachel looked at the clock. Two hours until bedtime. David was late again; he'd said he would be home by 4 p.m. today.

'Do you want beans on toast?' She kissed her button nose and stood her down on the floor.

'Again?'

'Cheese, then?'

'With loads of tomato sauce, but Mummy, Jamie stinks.' Maisie screwed up her nose then pinched the end with her fingers.

'OK, poppet, in a minute. I'll do your toast first; he won't hurt for another minute.'

'He's crying, Mummy.'

'He's always crying, Maisie.'

David was home. Rachel sighed.

'Hi, I'm home,' he shouted from the door.

'Nothing like stating the fucking obvious,' Rachel muttered under her breath.

Maisie ran to him as he swung her round in a big hug; she laughed. Rachel thought she hadn't heard her laugh for days.

'Christ, Rach! Jamie is screaming the place down. He's crapped his nappy; it stinks in here...can't you smell it? Do you not think it might be a good time to start potty-training him? He's almost two and a half! It's not a great scene to come home to, is it?'

'Babies shit in their nappies.' Rachel picked up Jamie. 'He's half yours, why don't you change him? I'm cooking dinner.'

'Something on toast again,' he snarled, taking Jamie and marching off. 'For fuck's sake, what the hell do you do all day? This place is a shithole. It might be nice just once to come home to a clean house, the kids bathed and ready for bed, and a decent meal.'

She heard him but didn't respond. She poured juice for Maisie.

Rachel had enjoyed life. There was no doubt about it, life had gone well. Her childhood was emotional, however, and she had clashed with her parents at times. From the outside her family had looked happy and secure: a close-knit family where any occasion was an excuse for a party. Yet there was often huge emotional turmoil. Rachel was the middle child and often felt forgotten; she often wondered if maybe she was a foundling they had taken pity on. She never felt she quite fitted. This caused anxiety and deep-rooted insecurity. She loved her parents: as a couple they were very close and yet they could argue as though their marriage would have no tomorrow. Her siblings always seemed closer to her parents, and Rachel was considered difficult.

There were times, though, when Rachel did connect with her family, and after she married she became very close to her mum. Despite the emotional ups and downs of her childhood she did quite well at school, college and university. Work she found boring. The need to relieve the tedium gave her an excuse to go out and party. She didn't consider herself attractive, but she was never short of male attention. Rachel had a kind soul, a happy demeanour and an unusual, wicked sense of humour. She had a lust for life that made you want to be with her. If you were with Rachel then you had a good time and so did she.

It was on one of those drunken party nights that she had met David. Rachel had smiled at David, who was standing at the bar with a group of friends, and he'd smiled back.

She was surprised: he was out of her league. David was classically tall, with broad shoulders, dark and on the side of good-looking where Rachel would consider that she could look but wouldn't get to touch. When he caught her eye across the pub, Rachel laughed a little too much, holding his glance just a little too long; she threw back her thick dark hair and did her absolute best to let him know she was very interested. The next time she approached the bar, he appeared: he had already bought her a drink.

Right from the start of their relationship she had the feeling that this was all too good to be true. Her parents adored him, her friends welcomed him into their group without question or complaint, and within weeks it was hard to imagine he hadn't always been there. The relationship made Rachel insecure: the lust for life was replaced by a lust to be loved by him. She hadn't been aware of how unequal the relationship was, not until now. He was not lost without her but she was lost, a wondering, wandering soul, misplaced amidst an endless stream of mess and misery.

Amidst the tinsel and chaos of dismantled Christmas Rachel discovered Facebook, a diversion amidst the disillusion of the New Year. It was a link to the outside world other than the asinine conversation at the school gate.

It seemed to her that she was one of the last people in the world to discover it. She was hooked, fascinated, obsessed. Strange people whose names she had a vague memory of from school, college and university were sought out and accepted as 'friends'. Taking on the role of voyeur, trawling pages, staring in disbelief at youthful faces she remembered now older, fatter; steaming cups of coffee cold by the time they were sipped. Amazement often turned to wry amusement as lives were portrayed as an open book. She didn't comment, just read in disbelief the way others shared the day-to-day crap of their lives, noting on a daily basis what they ate – 'nom, nom' apparently had to accompany photographs of food...people photographed their food! They shared what they did, where they went. Some made political comment. Some deliberately courted controversy and enjoyed every moment of their warped need to be the centre of attention. She watched the people she considered to have solid relationships break up, and learnt not to trust the happy family photo. Then she watched with cynicism as broken hearts mended and followed the swift transition to a new relationship. She was never sure if the smug couple photos were posted to enact revenge on former partners or just because that was what they were: in love and smug.

After a while Rachel gained the confidence to post the odd photo of the kids, a pretence at normality she never felt. There were photos of Maisie starting school, posted long after the actual event. Jamie as a newborn baby, posted when he was three. She felt that she needed to catch up, to let the world know that she still existed.

In April, Maisie made Rachel laugh, and for the first time in years it was a laugh that came from her belly. A smile that made it all the way to her eyes and lingered on her lips. Maisie noticed and held her mum in a tight hug around her waist. Rachel swung her round the kitchen, still laughing. Jamie jumped up and down with excitement at this new game, sensing something was different; he took his turn being swung around until they were all so dizzy they pretended to stagger round the kitchen and fall dramatically on to the floor, both children leaping on Rachel where she lay, still smiling.

Now, at three, Jamie had a more regular sleep pattern. Rachel still didn't sleep well and would still dread bedtime. She viewed her bedside clock as an instrument placed there to torment her, enjoying informing her how many hours of possible sleep she had left in its large red digital numerals.

On a Friday in May, David informed her that he had an old work colleague who would be in the area that Sunday, who would like to call in to see them, so he had invited him and his family to lunch. David's suggestion was that he go out with the kids on Saturday morning and Rachel could make a start on cleaning up the house. Looking around her with a sense that a morning wouldn't even allow her the time to clean the bathroom, she started with a vengeance on Friday night, gathering toys into the empty boxes and baskets where they were supposed to be stored. She didn't sort them, just shoved them. After the kids were in bed, the bathroom was thoroughly doused with bleach, the bath and basin were scoured and, in a final despairing act, the shower was scrubbed. The toilet wasn't too bad; she kept squirting cleaner down that, and the ninety-nine per cent of things it claimed to kill seemed an accurate description. Lego bricks and hair were swept from the floor, and chalk and crayon scrubbed from the tiled walls. At midnight Rachel mopped the grimy floor and then stood in the doorway with a sense of satisfaction. It smelt of bleach and cleaner and the surfaces shone. She brushed her teeth, careful to rinse the foam from the basin and wipe down the surfaces again. She fell into bed, exhausted, and slept for seven hours; sleeping all the hours of possible sleep for the first time in three years.

Saturday morning was bright, warm and sunny. Rachel still had a lot of cleaning to do. David suggested she make a picnic for him and the children, which they would have in the park, the big one near town, the one with the coloured climbing frame, the one that Jamie had now been to, just the once. Rachel felt ill; the fear of David taking both children to the park and staying out until after lunch with them made her want to push him out of the front door and barricade the three of them inside for safekeeping. He hadn't taken them both together on his own before, and she was not sure he would cope. Rachel was not sure *she* would cope. But David insisted that they would be fine, so she had no option but to let them go. The kids clung to her at the door, both crying. David picked them up and plonked them in the car and drove off in a hurry. He sent a text twenty minutes later saying they were happy, already playing. Rachel had been pacing, stomach churning, waiting to hear they were OK. Right, so she had to get on. Cleaning 'this shithole', as David called it, was going to take a special kind of determination. Although, as she stopped to make coffee, she wondered why he wasn't there, helping.

Music – she needed music. She found old stuff on her iPod, tracks she hadn't listened to for years, Marillion and All About Eve, singing along with enthusiasm despite the ominous task of scrubbing, wiping, bleaching, vacuuming and mopping. At first when the music stopped she didn't notice, but after a while she realised she was listening to something near silence. It was creepy. On a normal Saturday the house would be full of noise – not necessarily happy, but always noisy. She thought about her mum; it was exactly what she had said when they had all left home. She had missed the bustle and noise. Rachel understood what she meant today: the clean house echoed emptiness.

Her mum; Rachel avoided thinking about her mum. She avoided thinking about the bad times they'd had, because those evoked feelings of guilt; and she avoided thinking of the good times too. She thought about her kids, she worried about her dad, she was upset at her siblings, but she never thought about her mum. It hurt too much.

Normality was drip-feeding back into Rachel's life. Most of the time she was tearful and her mood was low, at times angry, but the void had gone. Longing for the void seemed illogical, but the distant emptiness had in some ways been a safer place to live. In the days of her severe depression, the panic attacks, the confusion and the hallucinations, life had been unbearable, but the desolation of her reality now made the state of feeling almost nothing a sanctuary, a rock under which she could hide away. Now the pain leached into her mind; it was grinding her forever down. And as yet she was unable to deal with it, unable to find a way forward. She remained silent on the subject when what she needed was to articulate a path that led her to resolution. With no outlet for her emotions, she felt stuck, and the grief that she needed to deal with about the death of her mum seemed forever glued inside. To deal with the grief meant accepting that her mum was gone forever, and what was more terrifying still was that she had given life to children who would one day feel the same way about her own death. To give life and then, ultimately, to cause those lives you loved so much pain – that was too unbearable to even comprehend. It made her want to withdraw even more into herself, to remove her love from her children and in some way prepare them for her leaving.

When David and the kids burst back into the house, Rachel was in a deep sleep on the sofa, her arms tucked tight around herself. In her hand was a photo of her mum and her laptop was open on the floor, photos of her family slowly scanning across the screen. It was a long time since Rachel had allowed herself to look at family photos. The fact that she was asleep was positive, and David let her be. He ushered the kids back out of the door.

'Let's leave Mummy to sleep,' he whispered. 'Just look how lovely and clean the house is. Let's go and get an ice cream and perhaps some flowers for Mummy.'

The children seemed to sense that this wasn't a time to argue, and followed him silently to the door. David glanced back and wondered if he should cover her with a blanket – she looked so pale and cold. Her hair had been the first thing that attracted him to her and it now hung limp and greasy over her shoulders. It was hard to see the Rachel he had once fallen in love with.

Rachel was surprised how well the lunch went. Jack, the work colleague, she had met before. She had worried about meeting his wife, Sarah, but the woman was pleasant – uninspiring but pleasant. They had two children, girls, aged seven and nine. Maisie followed them round, at first a little overwhelmed by this sudden influx of visitors. They were well-mannered, happy children, though, and Maisie and Jamie soon had them bouncing around on the trampoline. The dads stood in the garden with a can of bitter each and Sarah helped Rachel with the lunch. Rachel almost laughed at the stereotyped sexism of it all, but said nothing.

Rachel had enjoyed cooking before she had the kids, but now it seemed like a chore, a constant reinvention of the hidden vegetable, so she didn't bother. Lunch therefore came courtesy of the supermarket deli counter, but nobody seemed to mind. They even opened a bottle of wine. Rachel drank half a glass but found herself feeling dizzy, as it had been so long since she had drunk – a far cry from her partying days, when a bottle of red wine on a night out followed by late-night cocktails had not been unusual.

Rachel had made an effort with her appearance: her hair was washed and straightened, and under all that grime it shone with some of the deep lustre it always had. She had noticed the odd strand of grey and far too many split ends; it was about time she did something about it. She had also applied make-up, and didn't look anywhere near as tired as she usually did. She tried a smile at her reflection just to check that the foundation she had slapped on didn't crack when her face moved. Her clothes were clean, the kids were clean and the house was clean. It all felt terribly civilised and terribly false. She could tell that David was tense. He was worried that Rachel would disappear into that vacant world of her own. As he chatted, she could see his jaw locking and unlocking as he ground his teeth watching her, casting glances just to check how she was doing. He relaxed a little after the food and they all sat in the garden, spring blossom still on the trees, the early afternoon sun warm and the coffee fresh and strong. The kids laughed together as they played and Rachel felt contented.

When they had gone Rachel started the clearing up. David was making his way up the garden with coffee cups and glasses. As she was wiping down the kitchen worktops, he hugged her from behind. She stiffened, unaccustomed to the affection, as lately they skirted round each other, avoiding touching, avoiding speaking.

'It was good today, wasn't it?' It wasn't really a question. 'You did really well.'

She felt like a child being congratulated for coming second in the hundred metres at school sports day.

'Yes, they were nice – easy people to be around,' she said without turning. David kissed the nape of her neck, holding her, pushing her against the worktop so that she could feel the pressure of his body the length of hers.

'Maybe we should have an early night.' It was almost a whisper, as if he was unsure of the response he would get.

She turned so she was facing him and smiled a non-committal half-smile and felt immense relief when she heard Jamie cry. Mopping the blood from Jamie's grazed knee, and applying a large Mr Bump plaster, Rachel realised that, when David had touched her, she had felt nothing.

In June, Rachel's unoccupied hours led her once more to her addiction to Facebook. She would scoot the kids out into the garden so she could sit at the kitchen table with her laptop in front of her. If she glanced up she could look through the patio doors and check on the kids but her eyes would leave the screen only for a moment. Her life had become vicarious – obsessed with the progress of the lives of others – as her own had come to a standstill.

By July, Rachel started to feel a little more normal for the second time that year. The fog of consuming misery began to lift and she ventured out into the summer sunshine with the kids more and more. But David seemed unreachable. He concentrated on work, the kids, the house…in fact he did everything and anything to avoid being with her.

As they stood in the kitchen together one day, she felt as if she hadn't spoken to him in days.

'I needed help, David, I really needed professional help.'

David avoided looking at her. 'I did my best, Rach. I'll take those drinks to the kids,' he said, grabbing the small plastic cups so quickly that juice slopped over the sides. Rachel watched him through the kitchen window as he hurried down the garden. He couldn't get away from her fast enough, as if standing too close for too long would make him catch the misery. She felt diseased, and the fog hung above her like low cloud.

Rachel had isolated everybody. Unable to deal with the everyday problems of the rest of the world, she couldn't cope with the deterioration of her dad's mental health as well as her own. With David unable to even stay in the same room as her, she had never felt so alone. The kids still adored her, though, and her response was to love them more than she thought possible. Their behaviour was deteriorating; she spoiled them all the time with small surprise presents and failed to check their appalling behaviour. Maisie was turning into a complete brat and more than one letter about her behaviour at school had already been sent home. Rachel burnt them in the fire, didn't respond, and didn't tell David. Jamie's constant crying had given way to tantrums, and to keep him quiet Rachel just gave him whatever he wanted. The dark suppressed anger, the panic and the confusion had left, but they had been replaced by complete listlessness. There seemed no point in anything any more. Rachel just wanted to disappear into her virtual world and leave her own reality behind.

The nights were the loneliest. Although sleep had returned to a degree, Rachel still slept alone. Sometimes she would reach out to the cold pillow beside her and bring it close, her arms around it, holding it in the same way that she hung on to a vague memory of hope from the past. The pillow smelt of washing powder, not of the warmth of a person. The room was dark, a blackout blind at the window to block out the warm orange glow of the nearby streetlight. Sometimes in the night Rachel would roll up the blind and sit and stare at the world outside; the occasional late-night reveller or early-morning shift worker would walk by, and she would watch them until they disappeared round the corner. At other times, she thought about shouting 'Help me!' out of the window, just to see if anyone would. When she climbed back into the cold sheets, what she missed most of all was the warmth of someone there. If someone had been there to touch, it might have stopped her never-ending circle of confusion. There was no one to reach out to. No one who would make a soundless whisper in their sleep: 'Hang on, it won't always be this tough.' Rachel missed being in love. When she couldn't sleep she wished she had an old-fashioned clock so she could count the ticking beat until morning.

By August things were a little better than they had been, on and off; the heat sometimes dissipated the fog of misery. Days no longer seemed eternal; the house was not much cleaner or tidier, but the shopping got done, clothes laundered if not ironed. The kids were OK, but they had suffered. Rachel now found it easier to hug, and they responded by clinging to her; she felt it was just in case she let go of them again.

The voyeurism of Facebook continued, less intense now but she still checked her newsfeed several times a day. She had started to make occasional comments on Facebook to people she knew well. In September, she made what she hoped was a humorous comment on a 'public' post made by a boy, now a man, whom she had once had a bit of a crush on. Well, actually a lot of a crush on. The boy, now a man, was called Adam, and at the time he had been a close friend. They used to talk and there had been an obvious connection between them, but Rachel had had a boyfriend, who later dumped her and for a brief time had broken her heart. Adam had had a girlfriend whom he said he would one day marry if she stuck around long enough or if he could get her drunk enough to accept his proposal. There were a few distant and blurry photos of the grown-up Adam on his timeline, some kids in the distance and an attractive woman who could have been the college girlfriend, even at a distance though she looked too young – maybe she was Adam's daughter, but time had made it hard to tell and Rachel couldn't for the life of her remember her name.

Rachel posted a photo of herself and the kids, and liked it so much that she decided to make it her profile picture. An hour later, he sent her a friend request, and from that day life became a little more interesting.

David

David sat in the pub looking at the pint of bitter on the table in front of him and tried not to think in clichés. Bitter didn't quite sum up how he felt about life at the moment; he wasn't sure that it went far enough. It was six o'clock, but what was the point of rushing home? Rachel would be there; clothes hanging off her, covered in various bits of food, hair hanging with grease. The TV would be on and the kids would be sprawled on the sofa. If they weren't sprawling they would be fighting and Rachel would be unaware of what was going on around her, staring at a screen or staring out of the window; whatever she was doing, she would be vacant and staring.

It was when he was stuck in traffic a few weeks ago that the pub had beckoned David in. Here, among the hand-pulled pints and the optics with the soporific smell of alcohol, there was at least a homely feel. David leaned his head back against the wall, stared at the yellowed ceiling of the once smoke-filled room and breathed. The pub had brought a vast improvement to his life, and he wondered why he hadn't thought of it before; work was done without the preternatural presence of Rachel, beer was consumed, and, while he could hear many a middle-aged man moaning, there was a complete absence of screaming kids.

At home Rachel would lurk with an unnerving presence. Outside his study door, he could hear her shuffling about;

the door handle would creak as she rested her hand on it, then creak again as she removed it. It was obvious that she wanted to say something, but David had no idea what. Sometimes, he would open the door and Rachel's eyes would fix on his face just for a fleeting moment, her lips would move, but then she would just shake her head and drift away.

David had forgotten quite how much he enjoyed a pint of bitter. The Crown was a proper old pub with cask ales. It had authentic atmosphere; the background hum was the chatter of the few that still called this place their local. The sound of voices and the occasional clank of glass was a pleasant change from the banging beat that chain pubs seemed to think you needed. This pub had 'Olde Worlde Charm' – it said so over the door – and the bonus: it was next door to a Starbucks so he could connect to their Wi-Fi. The art of conversation wasn't dead in this place, and voices rose and fell with intonation and inflection – emoticons not required.

Apart from the beer and the Wi-Fi, there was the view of Emma. She was young and pretty and David was trying very hard not to make a move on her. He had never done that, not since he had been with Rachel. Their marriage might not be all it should be right now, but he still hoped that things would come right, some time. That was what the doctor had said she needed: time. But David had to carry on regardless. The mortgage didn't take a break just because you had emotional trauma.

This bitterness led to the inappropriate objectification of Emma's ass. They were just thoughts; to act on them would be a sybaritic betrayal of the sanctity of his marriage. David wouldn't betray Rachel, he told himself this every time he set foot in the pub. The idea of Emma was appealing, though, very appealing. Tonight, in that very tight black T-shirt with the pub logo stretched to its limits...for fuck's sake, life was complicated enough. His warped justification was that Emma reminded him of a young Rachel. Not so much to look at, but the fact that she was so vivacious, so overtly sexual. Just watching her...and that hair, so like Rachel's hair used to be; just the thought of tethering Emma with that ponytail while he knelt behind her so he could objectify that ass... David shook his head and laughed to himself for a moment, a happy, indulgent laugh, which stopped as he downed the rest of his pint, lingering with his glass tilted upwards, letting the foam drain into his mouth and enjoying the last few moments of peace and sanctity. He had to go home.

As David currently had no virtuous thoughts, he delayed his return to the first circle of hell for a couple of minutes by calling his mother. Miriam was elderly, and his dad, William, was ill. David liked to give them a quick hello every day if he could. His brother and sister did it too, even though sometimes they all thought their mother was fed up with the attention. Miriam was a very private person: a good mother, but very reserved, very proper; there had not been much affection when he was young, and even less as he grew up. She would talk to them, ask questions about their day, and she had taken a close interest in everything they did, always encouraging them with their schoolwork. They were always well dressed, and birthdays and Christmases were always pleasant occasions, but fuss had been minimal. His childhood had been content, but hugs had been scarce; David's early years lacked the time for carefree lethargy and out-of-control laughter. They had fun, but it was organised fun. In fact, all their days were organised: mealtimes were set, schedules adhered to. Friends were allowed over to play, but home times were never extended on a whim. David could never remember anything happening on a whim.

His dad was a good, solid man, both physically and emotionally. William worked hard for his family, but he was always on the periphery. David realised, as he grew older, that his father was rather shy. William hadn't meant to be distant; he just didn't know how to interact.

Rachel had been the polar opposite of David's mum, always touching him. Sometimes the touching had been quite inappropriate; when they had dinner with David's parents, Rachel liked to watch him squirm. He would try to stay in control as she slid her hand into his pocket. Miriam used to give them both glacial looks across the table, but Rachel just smiled and carried on talking.

Also, Rachel had been loquacious where Miriam was taciturn. The clash when they met was obvious. Previous girlfriends of the same ilk as his mother had been approved of, and David had to admit he enjoyed his mother's disapproval of Rachel. For once in his life he felt as though he had veered a little off the planned route – a touch of the bad boy. A girl like Rachel would never have been scheduled in as a suitable playmate. As a child, a girl like Rachel would have been out of bounds; girls like that led young boys astray. What his mother didn't realise was that, being a good-looking bloke, David had no problem with the opposite sex leading him astray; but Rachel just took him that one step further, to a place he had never wanted to leave.

'Hello, Mum. How are you?' David asked the same question every time they spoke followed by, 'How is Dad?'

'We're both fine, David; you don't need to call us every day.' He was always David, never Dave – even Rachel called him David. The look Miriam had given Rachel the first time they had met and she had called him Dave had been enough to put the fear of God into even her, and she had never lapsed. His Mum's 'fine' was always definite, although David suspected she was relieved they all kept an eye on things…just in case.

Miriam's days were long, staying in with David's father most of the time. William's heart condition was worsening; the decline was slow but they could do no more for him. Miriam was still coping on her own, too proud to have strangers coming into the house to help, but David knew that this situation would have to change soon and his mum would have to accept the daily traffic of carers in and out of the house. Palliative care would be needed towards the end, to stop his dad becoming distressed, and it was his wish to die at home. Not in a hospital or a hospice, but in familiar surroundings with his wife by his side and his children nearby.

David's sister, Sarah, lived nearby, and would call in with the shopping two or three times a week after work, and she would stick around while William had a shower. Sarah made out that she didn't have time for a big shop and that it was easier for her to pop in with a few things at a time. It was her way of keeping a closer eye on them. Mark, David's elder brother, lived further away, but he would drive over every other Sunday with his family and they would get stuck in to the garden or help out with the cleaning. It was a strategy the siblings had worked out together. They were aware of the situation with Rachel and knew how much pressure David was under. One thing Miriam had taught them all was to be practical.

David sometimes wondered how he found it so easy to see what his parents needed, but at the same time he seemed to be failing Rachel. The physical illness of his father, the ageing of his mother, these were visual, but Rachel had just retreated into her own world, disconnected from anything within David's comprehension.

And yet, despite knowing what was needed, and being willing to give it, David was seeing his parents less and less, just at the time when they needed him more. The oxygen tank William needed made going out difficult, and he needed a wheelchair if they were to go very far. Miriam hid her increasing frailty well, but the wheelchair was too much for her on anything other than a flat, even surface. David's dad was a large man, tall and well-built like David, and in recent years all that sitting about had meant that he had gained weight along with the fluid retention caused by his heart condition. This made him bulky and difficult to move. Miriam's hands were riddled with arthritis, her joints bent and gnarled. David took his mum and dad out when he could, just to give them a break from the TV and looking at the same wallpaper, but since Jamie had been born it had become more difficult. If David went alone, Rachel resented the time he spent away from the family, and, if the whole family went, Rachel was so distant it was embarrassing. If they went to a pub or restaurant the kids simply ran riot and the disapproving looks from his mother were just too much. Often they would settle for a walk in the park and coffee and cake at Costa. The kids loved the warm foamy babyccino and would sit, contented, tired from running around, munching on cakes for half an hour. The pressure of it all sometimes made him wish he could just join Rachel in her abstract world.

In return, his mother worried about David. She had been brought up to keep her emotions in check, but nothing eventful had happened in her life to challenge this. She had instilled this in her children, not to be overemotional. 'Wait and see' was Miriam's motto; she was always telling them that things would sort themselves out. Only Rachel wasn't sorting herself out. Miriam had always thought there was something about that girl that wasn't right; she drank too much for a start. She also talked too much; her clothes were a little too revealing – and that hair! That hair needed a damn good cut and now Miriam was convinced things were living in it. Rachel looked as if she needed a good scrub. Then there was all that touching of her son in public. She didn't do much of it now, it was true, but before she had the children she was always hanging off him, hugging him and kissing him; when they were younger she would even kiss him just because he was leaving the room. The sliding of her hand up and down his thigh while they sat on the sofa had driven Miriam to snap. That sort of behaviour should be reserved for the bedroom and she had told them as much. When that little tramp had stifled a laugh instead of being embarrassed, Miriam had left the room. It just wasn't right, not in front of his parents; Rachel's future parents-in-law. Rachel lacked decorum, but then her whole family were a little out of control. Melodramatic and terribly loud, the lot of them!

Now it seemed Rachel had fallen apart. Miriam had to give the girl some credit: she had been a good mother to Maisie, and David had been very happy for a long time. It seemed, however, that Rachel just couldn't cope with the normal twists and turns that life threw at you. Miriam understood she had had a lot to deal with. Her mother dying while she had been pregnant was very difficult, and she knew they had been very close, but Rachel had young children; she needed to think of them, not herself. Parents died, and children weren't young forever. She was a wife and mother herself now, and she had to move on.

David bade his mum goodbye. Their conversations rarely lasted more than a minute or two. Once they had established that everyone was still alive, there never seemed much more to say. He knew that his mum and dad were aware of the situation with Rachel but they didn't like to interfere. His mother had once said that what happened in a marriage should stay in a marriage. She was a weird old fish, but he loved her – a bit stiff, but she was always there. David realised in that moment that her days were now shorter. He would miss her when she was gone. Not in that overriding emotional way that Rachel missed her mum – Rachel's relationship with her parents had been difficult and the process of grief abnormal. Unable to reconcile her mixed emotions, she had shut down: the pain was too much and David didn't know what to say. It wasn't just the loss of her mother that Rachel couldn't cope with, though – it was also the loss of a relationship she felt had never been fulfilled.

David's own upbringing had not left him equipped with the appropriate empathetic responses. His childhood had remained simple and uncomplicated; there hadn't been any upheaval or drama. Often he thought Rachel's family made their own drama because they thrived on it, but when he thought like that he felt as though he was turning into his mum, and banished the idea.

Miriam was slim, tall, and had an elegance the other mums had never had when he was a child, a serenity in both character and movement. She hadn't worked and had never left them as children. She had worked in an office for a few years before she had married his dad, but she had been proud to be a wife and a mother. Despite her correct manner and the lack of open affection, David knew that he had been deeply loved. On the day he had left for university she had told him she loved him and that she was proud of him. Until he met Rachel, that had been the most emotional moment of his life.

David was steady and confident, therefore; he didn't lack the insecurities of a lot of his peers. This confidence had always made him easy company, but one particular girlfriend, whom he regretted losing, had told him he was cold and broken up with him because of that. And she'd been right: that was how he was, until Rachel. In Rachel he'd found intense passion and love.

The thought of no mum and maybe sooner no dad gave David an involuntary shudder. He pushed himself into the car seat as if somehow the solid object could create a barrier against the inevitable pain of loss.

David was surrounded by a sense of loss at the moment, not just his parents but his marriage, his once stable and happy home. Rachel had become impenetrable in both the physical and emotional sense. He tried to talk to her in her moments of lucidity, but she was dismissive, saying there was nothing wrong, she was sad about her mum. 'Sad' didn't begin to describe the way Rachel behaved. He could barely remember the last time they had made love. There had been sex for a while but it was cold, free from emotion, functional. David needed the physical side of their relationship, really needed it, but it seemed the passion and desire from Rachel that had once overwhelmed him had drifted away along with her sanity. The days of Rachel calling out her gratitude to a deity were long gone.

David knew what Rachel needed was compassion and understanding, yet all he seemed to manage was disgruntled annoyance and irritation. Fear of confronting his own mortality had prevented him from helping her to grieve. When she was pregnant with Jamie she had had this innate fear that somehow all that emotion would hurt the unborn baby, but David felt that holding it in had hurt all of them more. Then again, he held everything in too, so who was he to tell her what to do?

Rachel's relationship with her mother had been complex and since her death Rachel had withdrawn from all her family. She blamed herself for the complete dissolution. What was that stupid saying about everything happening in threes…birth, marriage and death? Her sister had remarried the year before Rachel's unexpected pregnancy with their second child and then her mother had died. He suspected that in Rachel's illogical thinking this was conclusive proof that she was to blame for her mother's death. In one senseless ramble Rachel had also blamed her sister for remarrying and starting the chain of events. David had no idea what she blamed her brother and father for. She didn't speak to any of them any more. Once upon a time, when time had still been full of fairytales and possibilities, Rachel had been close to her sister. That relationship had become strained owing to her sister's trying to care for Rachel's dad and being unable to cope with the demands of work, kids and a new stepchild.

David started the engine and took the long route home. He was hoping for a traffic jam as he approached the main road but the rush hour had passed, it was later than usual and his way was clear. He longed to go home to the Rachel he had loved. He wanted the life they had before – the life before and after Maisie. Life before kids had been such a good time: no worries, plenty of money; work, fun, sex, drinking, more sex, parties and friends. Where were all the friends now?

David and Rachel had taken far too many holidays, gone to endless parties, gigs, clubs, bars and restaurants, so by the time Maisie came along, much later in life than either of them had expected, they had been ready to settle into family life. The unexpected pregnancy with Jamie should have been the sugar coating, but it hadn't been. Jamie was better now, though, much easier than he had been, and he slept more. Well, he did a lot of the time. David tried not to think about the sleeping – he could have helped more, he knew, but he hadn't, and he couldn't go back.

Sometimes, there was a glimmer of the old Rachel, a flicker of that vivacity in her eyes; the faintest glister of who she used to be. She spent far too much time on Facebook, or Googling things that were worrying her. In some ways it was positive: at least she was reconnecting with the world outside the brick walls she had built. But the reconnection with society was coming at a cost: a constant stream of parcels kept arriving. David had noticed the dramatic increase in the credit card bill but was loath to say anything in case this sudden interest in herself meant Rachel was starting to feel a little better. Washing her hair more often was a definite bonus. Miriam had joked about things living in that hair but sometimes it was hard to tell.

Often, Rachel would look right through David when she spoke, and sometimes he wondered if she even knew he was there. That comment, a couple of weeks ago – 'I needed help, David. Professional help.' Oh, how he had tried, but she'd just shut down. They had been to the doctor together, when Jamie was still small, many times, but Rachel seemed to think they had only been the once, when he was older. Together they had seen the same doctor, but no matter what David told the doctor he just kept saying it was mild postnatal depression; that these things sometimes took a long time to overcome. He would say that Rachel needed more sleep and time to herself, and that with medication and support she would get there... David had the feeling that Rachel just batted out the answers she thought the doctor wanted to hear, and, at the end of the day, that doctor sitting there in his prescribing chair didn't know the Rachel he had loved.

The words 'had loved' preyed on David's mind; he rolled the phrase round. *Had. Had loved.* Did love, he corrected himself, sure this was still the case. He just needed to find a way back in.

The first time David had taken her to the doctor had been the scariest. Rachel had looked insane. She'd looked dirty, with a deathly pallor and the darkest of shadows in the sunken hollows under her eyes, her long greasy hair scraped back into a tight ponytail, giving her forehead the tightness of someone who'd had an overenthusiastic facelift. He had thought they would have her committed. Her eyes were empty; a smile never touched them, not even close. She didn't speak at all about what was going on inside her head and her face was a book shut tight, pages glued. David wasn't the best talker himself and he just hadn't known what to ask or what to say to make headway into her mind. He had just thought the medication would work and then they could get on with enjoying life. Having family days out again. Perhaps finding a babysitter and enjoying an evening out together, a few drinks and laughter.

Rachel used to laugh; she used to laugh all the time. David had loved her intensity, the way she would watch him as if afraid he might leave without her noticing. It made him feel secure. Rachel's best friend Jo had said Rachel had changed after she met David. Jo had accused him of taking all the sparkle and confidence out of Rachel. She said Rachel was constantly living on a precipice of fear that David would be gone. Rachel, she said, talked about David non-stop and no longer went out with her friends unless he was coming too. Jo said she had become clingy and insecure and that he had destroyed their friendship, but she had been drunk at the time and upset because of a fight with her own boyfriend so David had just believed that it was a moment of jealousy and insecurity that her friend was moving on. Boyfriends and marriage had a habit of ruining close friendships.

He wondered if Rachel still had any contact with Jo. Maybe that was who she spent all her time on Facebook messaging. If it was Jo, he was glad they had become close again. The Facebook addiction had become a concern to him but then he guessed everybody was a little guilty of spending too much time messaging on their phones rather than talking to the people in front of them. Loneliness and isolation did that to you, and a need to compare your life to others – the need to validate your own circumstances and rate them on a scale of one to happiness. Photographs and brief comments could portray a falsehood, though; you only had to look at his and Rachel's pages. The 'happy family' photos would tell you a lie and he could tell the truth: the argument or silence behind every one of them.

David sat in the pub much later than usual on a very wet and humid August evening. He was desperate to go home and remove the shirt that was sticking to his back, the hot suit trousers and black lace-up shoes. This was his workday uniform of conformity and he hated it. He wanted a cool shower and to change into a T-shirt and shorts. Actually, what he wanted was to sit with his arm around Rachel, not talking, just being, a glass of wine each, with the patio doors wide open, watching the rain as it lashed down, soaking the leaves and removing the heat of the day. But instead he sat in the pub, his laptop closed, his phone off, and wallowed in destructive self-pity.

While he wallowed, David took refuge in thoughts of his past and the night he first met Rachel. They had met in a pub he never been to before. His friends had fancied a change to the regular haunts; they'd said they needed fresh meat, new prey. They had laughed when they said it – they were good blokes and most of them just wanted to have a steady girlfriend, but lately they seemed to have lucked out, and all bar one of them were single. David never had difficulty attracting girls; he just had a problem maintaining interest in them. He had a type: tall, thin and with neat hair. He realised that they always had the same qualities as his mother, and he felt a little disturbed by the thought, but then aloof woman were in his comfort zone. They were pleasant enough but boring, and his relationships had been short and transient.

The night he met Rachel he watched her for a long time before she caught his eye. She was fascinating. She was so not his type; she was quite short and nothing but curves, with a wonderful expressive face that was framed by a cloud of dark, messy, glorious long shiny hair. That feeling that let you know someone was looking at you kicked in and she turned and caught his eye, her huge, almost black eyes holding his gaze for a long time, confident; raising her eyebrows just a little and smiling at him. When she smiled he was hooked – it was not so much the curve of her lips or the flash of slightly crooked teeth but the glint of wickedness in her eyes. She only turned away when a friend, who he would later discover was Jo, tugged on her sleeve for attention. Rachel must have said something about him, because they had both looked in his direction and then laughed. He had smiled to himself, liking the attention but not wanting to show it too much.

David had kept a watchful eye on the bar, pretty sure Rachel would be on her way there soon, unless of course the friend went for the next round, in which case he would have to wait longer to offer to buy her a drink. He was very sure that he was not letting her leave without talking to her.

On the drive home David thought about their first date. Reliving the good times meant he didn't have to confront the misery of the state of limbo in which he was living now. That first night he had taken her to the pub. Dinner, she'd said, was always awkward and made talking difficult. With their incessant chatting it was surprising they had managed to get so drunk.

The memory of the morning after that first date always made him laugh out loud. David had watched Rachel as she tried to stand, her face tinged a rather off-putting green. She'd struggled to stay vertical and had weaved her way to the bathroom, rebounding off the walls of the hallway as she lost her balance. One leg of her jeans was still attached at the ankle; stepping on the loose leg, she had tried to free herself but the vomit was imminent, so she'd just shuffled along, dragging her jeans behind her. The delay of the jeans-tussle meant that she didn't make it into the bathroom in time and threw up half on the floor and half over the toilet. Crimson vomit seeped into the grout of the neutral floor tiles. The stain had still been there on the day David sold his flat. He wondered what the next occupants thought it was. Rachel's sick still smelt of red wine. David followed her to the bathroom to make sure she was OK, waited outside for a while, but when it went quiet he opened the unlocked door and found her where she had slid, face down, her forehead resting on the cool tiles. David put a large, fluffy white bath towel around her, and she crawled on to her knees and began an ineffective mopping, with toilet roll, at the red puddle on the floor. David stood behind her, naked and grey.

'It's just like a replay of last night,' he had joked. 'Only with the addition of puke.'

Rachel had laughed without embarrassment, then retched for several minutes, emptying the entire remaining contents of her stomach into the toilet. She was sweating and exhausted, with sick splashed on her face and little reddish-pink droplets in her hair. They shone in the bright lights of the bathroom and looked strangely pretty.

David hovered, helpless, until she had finished. 'You shower, I'll clean this up,' he said firmly.

She didn't argue, and managed to free her foot from the leg of her jeans. She dropped the towel on to the floor and slid behind the frosted door. The shower was too noisy for conversation. David came back with a bucket of hot water and bleach and set to work. Rachel just let gallons of water flood over her. She stayed in the shower until he finished cleaning up. David smiled as Rachel poked a hand out and asked for a towel to cover her body before she left the cubicle. He laughed as he handed it to her. The vision of her naked body might have been blurred in a drunken haze but he had already seen all that this woman had to offer. 'I think it may be a little too late for modesty,' he said, leaning forward and kissing the tip of her nose.

She gave him a serious look.

'When I'm drunk I may think I'm incredibly hot, but sober, I'm realistic enough to know I have the body of someone who has missed one too many Weight Watchers meetings.' She tried to smile as she said it, but went a little green and then closed her mouth, realising she had rancid breath.

They had spent the whole of the day cuddled up on the sofa, watching movies and drinking endless cups of sugary tea. By mid-afternoon they managed to eat toast, and at 9 p.m. David had reluctantly driven Rachel back home to her flat. As he watched her stand in the doorway to wave goodbye and blow him a kiss, he knew he had met the woman he would marry. He also knew his mother wouldn't like her one bit.

That had been the real Rachel, all curves and warmth, generous with her body and her mind in equal measure. The Rachel he went home to now was angular, cold and vacant. The real Rachel had faded so far from conscious reality that he wouldn't have been surprised if she failed to cast a shadow in sunlight.

David stopped off at the pub most nights for a quick pint before dragging himself home. Emma had started to chat to him when he took on the status of 'regular'. She flirted; he was sure it was part of the job description. The pub T-shirt that she had to wear for all her shifts had been chosen to make flirting unnecessary, designed to attract the gathering of lonely men and those slow to wend their way to unhappy homes. David noticed that Emma stayed and chatted to him until she was beckoned away to pull a pint, and instead of lurking at a nearby table with his laptop and phone he stayed at the bar to drink his beer. As a result he was behind with work and often had to work late into the night. Normally he would aim to arrive home just as Rachel was running the bubble bath for the kids; that way he could take over while she made dinner for them both. Rachel never ate anything these days, she just slid food around her plate and chewed a couple of unenthusiastic mouthfuls. Then, after clearing the plates, she would stand and stare somewhere near the dishwasher. Since Emma had started flirting, though, David had missed the bathtime deadline quite a few times and arrived just in time to give the kids a goodnight kiss. As an unfortunate consequence of this failing, he was also now eating rather a lot of beans on toast.

Emma kept him at the pub, because in Emma he saw that same spark that he had seen in Rachel, the same directness. Rachel had always been forthright: if she wanted something then you knew about it. Emma was starting to make it very obvious that she was happy to get past the barrier of the bar, and David was having increasing problems resisting. Going home did two things to him: when he saw Rachel sad and bewildered, his resolve strengthened to get through this, to be with the woman he loved; but when he went to bed alone in his study he despised her. Sleeping with Rachel was impossible; he had tried to sleep in their bed so many times, but she just didn't sleep, she tossed and turned and cried out. If she did sleep, the slightest movement from him would wake her and she would lose it, a surge of uncontrollable rage that left her lashing out at him and shouting abuse, the veins standing out on her neck as she railed at him, punching him and pushing him out of the room. When that anger was awakened she at least seemed alive, but totally out of control. Every feeling of pent-up emotion she had was released in the moment he prevented her from doing the thing she needed most.

He hadn't forgotten the time, a few months ago, when Rachel had flipped out to the extent that she ran out of the house in her pyjamas and socks. David had run to the door after her but she'd just turned the Yale lock and run out into the night, leaving him not knowing what to do. He couldn't abandon the kids…he settled for standing by the open door shivering in the cold, waiting for her to come back. He resolved that if Rachel didn't come back in an hour he would call the police. After forty minutes she wandered back down the pavement, head hanging, her arms wrapped around herself and sobbing audibly. David had made his way to meet her, took her upstairs, cleaned her up and dried her, comforting her like a child while he helped her change into fresh pyjamas. Rachel's feet were frozen and he warmed them in his hands before sliding dry socks on. He held her while she cried, and stroked her hair until she fell asleep. An emergency appointment at the doctor's was made the next day, but the doctor still said the same thing. Just depression, same prescription; she just needed time. The doctor suggested that perhaps some counselling would help. He would make a referral. David had suspected that when he left the room Rachel just made out it was an overreaction to an argument. He knew the counselling was pointless: she wouldn't go, and he just couldn't take any more time off work – he had already been called in for a talk about the importance of maintaining a proactive role in times of economic austerity. The message had been clear. He was exhausted.

The majority of the drama was over with Rachel, but now she was just there...and here was Emma; a potential consolation prize for everything he was losing. What would she be to him? he wondered as he stared at her behind the bar. A one-off fuck just to relieve the tension, a full-on affair, or maybe he would say fuck it all, pack his bags, leave Rachel and the kids and move on. Right now, he didn't know; he just knew he had to get home. He downed the rest of his pint. Every night he was tempted to just stay, to drink until he could drink no more. He wouldn't, though...the kids.

David sat on the edge of the sofabed in his study, wanking furiously. He felt somewhat furtive and needed to come before he was disturbed, but nothing was happening. He was not only wanking furiously, he was also furious with himself for turning Emma down. Rachel would never have known. It would have just been what it was...a fuck, a one-off fuck, pleasure in an otherwise miserable existence. The problem was that Emma was not Rachel, and he was furious at Emma for not being Rachel and furious at Rachel for...well, just furious at Rachel. If he hadn't said no he could have kissed Emma, touched those breasts, been inside her right now. He could have had her on all fours, grinding himself against her tight ass. God, he was an idiot, a total loser, a complete and, it had to be said, total wanker.

Emma had been in the car park, just leaving her afternoon shift at the pub. David was making purposeful strides towards the pub door, looking forward to his early evening respite before facing the crap at home – quite literally the crap. Jamie in a shitty nappy although he should have been potty trained by now. Used nappies, toys, juice cups, mugs, plastic bowls half-full of congealed food, piles of washing, clean and dirty clothes mixed together in an ever-increasing heaving, festering, tangled mass. Half-eaten biscuits discarded on the floor, which he trod on, working their way into the soles of his shoes. It was pointless worrying about treading them into the carpet – he couldn't see the carpet!

Then there was Emma standing in front of him: long brown hair, skinny jeans and the very stretched words 'The Crown' on her T-shirt, smiling at him.

'Hi, David, how are you?' She cast a downward glance then looked up, smiling, and he stared hard at her row of small, even white teeth. He avoided looking at her eyes, feeling shy and out of his depth; it had been a long time since he had wanted anyone but Rachel. For the last couple of weeks, as August turned to September, Emma had been flirting and David had been flirting back, but out here in the car park he felt exposed and had an overwhelming urge to run for the cover of the bar. He needed that physical barrier between them. Here he could reach out and touch her, kiss her, hold her close and suggest they take things further. In his mind she was already climbing into her car, telling him to follow her back to her house.

Interrupted from his own fantasy, he realised it was no longer just a thought.

'I was thinking,' she said, looking down, trying to look coy, as though this wasn't something she ever did, although her confidence made him think otherwise. 'Maybe, instead of going for your usual pint, you could come back to mine for a drink or a coffee?'

She had been standing just a little too close, her hand almost touching his. If he just moved a little, or shifted his weight on his leg, their hands would touch. Maybe he should let them, to see what would happen.

'Emma, I would love to,' he said, 'but I really don't have long and I need to get back to Rachel and the kids. Maybe some other time?'

'Yeah, maybe,' she said, turning towards her car. 'See you tomorrow.' The tone in her voice had made him think he had blown his only chance. Emma was not used to being turned down.

So he sat in his study, frustrated and angry, a chair jammed under the door handle to stop Rachel or the kids walking in. No matter how furiously he wanked, he could not make himself come; the erection that had not gone away since the moment he left Emma in the car park now died in his hand, and the only fluids to leave his body were the tears of frustration that tracked a silent path down his sweaty face.

He was wrong, of course, but he was wrong about most things these days. To Emma, who was indeed used to men saying yes to her, he was now a challenge. She had followed him home once – not intentionally, she just happened to leave behind him out of the car park – and he lived in a rather swish house, but then again anything was nice compared to her hutch-sized flat. He was older than her, but he was a good-looking bloke. She had fancied him the first time she saw him, but then she had been in yet another of her no-hope relationships. The last boyfriend had been arrested for dealing drugs and she hadn't been surprised: his car had been far too expensive for the estate he lived on and the job he'd said he had. David was different: nice house, good job, funny, and a marriage on the rocks by the sound of it. Emma was looking for a change, and David could be the catalyst.

David lay in his study. Bleak, endless hours; sleep was elusive tonight. Most nights he slept like the dead until morning. Tonight, however, he thought this was what it must be like for Rachel. He wanted to lie next to his wife but it was impossible: for her sleep had become an obsession, and the more she obsessed, the less she slept. He had to sleep, he had to work, he had to hold this fucked-up family together. Family – he almost laughed out loud at the thought. Fucked-up, yes, but family? Rachel did the basics, the kids were fine; on good days she even played with them. Days like those, when he came home and the three of them were laughing together, or cuddled up on the sofa watching TV, looking content, were the days that kept him going. They were all fed something and the washing was done, just about. The contents of the shopping trolley might have been a little random but nobody starved. Apart from that, though, the whole house was a shambles. Piles of stuff everywhere. David couldn't stand it; he stayed in his study to avoid it all. It might be a bit dusty but at least there he could walk across the floor without sticking to something or falling over a toy. He had started locking the door from the outside, with a small bolt he'd fitted, just to keep the kids out. Rachel thought he was hiding something. Chance would be a fine thing, he thought – then rethought: he might have had something to hide, if he had just had the balls to go through with it. What the fuck was wrong with him? Hot woman handing it to him on a plate and he put first the feelings of the woman who no longer wanted him. Insanity ran in this family and it didn't even need to be genetic!

Work was OK, it was his escape, but since the talk it had become more stressful. Rachel had said he stayed away more since Jamie had been born and it was true, he had; he just couldn't face coming home. He loved them all, but they were exhausting.

Maisie had been such an unexpected delight. David and Rachel had put off having kids; they had been having too much fun. David, however, had always wanted a large family, imagining a big old house and a scrubbed pine table. He thought he might have hung on to the image from his childhood of *The Waltons* just a little too much. He wanted happy, barely-under-control children, messy Christmases and smiling faces everywhere. A memory of a particular birthday party when he was a child had set this standard. A house that wasn't clean or organised. Too many cakes on the table for tea and not enough sandwiches; fizzy drinks and noisy party-blowers...the games had been chaotic and mostly they had run round the garden in total freedom, climbing trees and shouting. Oh, the joy of shouting! At home they didn't shout, they were calm and well-behaved. They laughed, but even that had an air of stifled control about it. The boy had not been a close friend and David felt that he had only been invited to make up the numbers. He had longed to be this boy's friend but now he couldn't even recall his name, just that feeling of joy on an afternoon that he had never wanted to end. When his mother had picked him up she had asked what they had for tea and had muttered disapprovingly when he related a list of cakes and mentioned the word 'Coke'. She also muttered about his torn shirt, grass-stained shorts and muddy legs. David hadn't cared; he had sat happily in the back of the family car, picking mud off his knees.

That was his vision of family: carefree kids with happy parents. The reality was nothing like this; instead of pulling in one direction, they were both pulling everything apart. The mess and the noise were getting harder to tolerate every day. The threads of David's life were unravelling faster than a jumper caught on a nail; sometimes he made a half-hearted attempt to stitch it back together but most of the time he just picked, making it far worse. Most of the time he hid away and hoped for the best, but the unravelling continued from the other side of his door, slower now, but unravelling all the same. How to stop it was now the problem; sometimes he wondered if he should just leave and see if the shock of it brought Rachel back to her senses. Or maybe he would simply watch her unravel until she was a long, winding thread on the floor, and let the professional she said she had needed wind her back together.

David's thoughts drifted back to happier times. Their wedding had been an amazing day. They had wanted to keep it simple but Rachel's mum was having none of that! The first daughter in the house to get married was going to be a celebration. This had been Rachel's mother at her best, loving and giving. Over one hundred guests had squeezed into the local church to watch them exchange their vows. The ceremony was simple, white flowers lining the aisle. Rachel's dress was stunning in its simplicity, with a headband of fresh white flowers in her long hair but no veil – she'd hated the idea of a veil. She didn't want to be curtained off on the way down the aisle; she wanted to see what was going on. The church ceremony might have been simple and understated, but the party afterwards was not. They had married late in the afternoon on the last weekend in June and partied into the early hours. He had thought he could never love Rachel more, until the day she had lain there exhausted, cheeks flushed with pride and effort, holding the tiny Maisie in her arms, looking like the most natural mother in the world.

Maisie came downstairs crying, holding out a small bag, which on closer inspection contained a tiny off-white tooth.

The almost transparent cloth revealed the contents that by now should have been absent and replaced by a one-pound coin. Rachel had forgotten. Maisie was very upset; she had great faith in the ability of the tiny fairy to turn up at the appointed hour, but she had failed! Rachel looked pale and guilty. David cast her a look of disapproval. He had offered to be the fairy but as usual she couldn't trust him, wouldn't let go of any of the responsibility for even the smallest thing for her children. She always called them 'her' children, not 'their' children.

'Did you check on the floor, sweetie?' Rachel asked, taking the small voile bag off Maisie as if to inspect the contents. 'She might have left the coin on the floor.'

'I looked, but she hasn't taken my tooth,' Maisie lisped, both of her front teeth missing. She ran her tongue around the gap, getting used to the unusual feeling. She sprayed a little spit as she cried, 'It's not fair!'

'It'll be OK, Maisie.' Rachel said, bending down to hug her daughter. 'I just need to pop to the loo.'

David knew the pound coin was still in the pocket of the hoodie she was wearing. He had seen her put it there before she went upstairs last night, assuring him that she wouldn't fall asleep. It had been 8.30 and Maisie hadn't long settled.

'Maisie,' Rachel shouted from upstairs, 'I think you need to come back upstairs, poppet.'

An upset and disgruntled Maisie stomped up the stairs, only to come running back to David, all smiles, moments later. 'Mummy found the coin,' she said, holding it out to David on the palm of her hand so that he could see it. 'It *was* on the floor. Mummy said I must have turned over in bed and frightened the fairy away; she says the fairy mustn't be seen or it ruins her magic. I have to put the tooth back under my pillow tonight and she will come and get it.' She beamed a gummy smile.

'That's wonderful, Mais. I knew the fairy wouldn't completely forget.' David wiped tiny spots of spit from his face. He kissed Maisie on the forehead and went to find Rachel. Just to let her know he would remove the tooth tonight. It was more for him to remember. Work was stressful enough without having to do every little thing in the house on top of it.

David went to the pub as usual on his way home. He realised that since the car park incident the pub was no longer just somewhere to hide. Now there was the draw of Emma, smelling of perfume, wearing make-up, jeans that were far too tight and that T-shirt. An involuntary lustful groan escaped his lips. He had been popping into the pub most days, but guilt about the reason for his visit today made him cautious and he kept a packet of mints in his car to disguise the smell of the beer on his breath. Not that Rachel ever kissed him these days. Now they just spoke when necessary, in a fault-picking monotone.

Emma was there, leaning against the bar, chatting to one of the regulars. The pub was almost empty at this time of day. Just those few sad souls, either single or feeling the way he felt. David liked it that way; at least then Emma had time to talk to him. Since he had turned down her offer of coffee she had been a little cold towards him, engaging in small talk but standoffish and no flirting; even when he tried, she didn't respond. It was driving him mad and he suspected she knew this. Today, though, she smiled at him, and as she gave him his change she touched his hand, lingering so that her skin touched his. That slight breath of a touch made his heart pound. Jesus, he wanted her; he wanted to run his hands through that hair. A momentary image of Rachel flashed through his mind, lying back lost in a moment of pure pleasure, dark hair splayed across the pillow. He dismissed the vision and smiled back at Emma, finding it hard to resist the urge to reach out and touch her hair.

'How's things with you?' She asked the same thing every time she saw him and he replied with the same banalities. 'I'm OK', 'I'm fine, how are you?', 'Yes, fine, thanks; it's quiet in here today'. Same old crap responses, but today he surprised himself.

'I'm good, thanks…but Emma, the other day, when you asked me back for a coffee…well…I'm really sorry I couldn't. I had to get home, stuff I'd promised to do with the kids…you understand? I wondered if you wanted to do it some other time?' The words just tumbled out. 'Coffee, I mean.' David flushed.

Emma looked at him for a moment as if trying to decide if he would be worth the effort. 'My shift finishes at six. I'm free tonight if you are.' She said it staring straight at him, daring him to turn her down again.

'That would be good,' he said. 'Shall I meet you in the car park in half an hour, then? I just need to finish some work if I'm going to be late.' He spoke with a confidence that belied his turmoil.

'Yes, I'll meet you in the car park,' she said, and turned to serve the next customer.

All David could think was condoms; it might have been presumptuous but he thought it better to be more Boy Scout than regretful! He left his pint on the bar and headed for the toilets. Thanking Christ there was a machine, he slotted in the coins and pocketed the packet. Flushed once more, he returned to the bar, retrieved his pint and set his laptop on a nearby table. He had a couple of emails to send, which he wouldn't be able to concentrate on, and he needed to text Rachel to let her know he would be late. How late he was not sure, but apart from moaning at him that he was not home to help put the kids to bed he doubted she would even notice what time he walked through the door.

David followed Emma's black and rather old Ford Fiesta back to her flat. Parking on the street outside, he was conscious that he was leaving his car in a very public place. The sun had that soft golden orange hue that you got in the early evening in September, an Indian summer as promised; it was still light; early dusk, it was light enough to see his car. He wondered if he should move it to some more discreet place down a side street, but Emma was already walking towards her door and desire overtook rational thoughts at a rapid rate. He really needed a shower. Now he wished he had thought this through, but personal hygiene hadn't really been on his mind. It was all a bit rushed; maybe he should just suggest he have a shower. Then again, what if coffee really meant coffee and he had completely the wrong idea? It was nineteen years since he had slept with another woman. Rachel had been more than enough for him; he had never wanted anyone else.

Emma was standing with the door open, watching him with a raised eyebrow. He realised he had just been sitting in his car, lost in thought. Opening the car door without looking, he caused a cyclist to swerve round and shout abuse at him over his shoulder. David shouted an apology but the cyclist just raised a middle finger at him and rode on. Emma was laughing. He slammed the door, deciding his grey Audi was so bland that it blended into the row of parked cars anyway. And Rachel never left the house at this time of day. She had too much to do with the kids. The kids…he put the thought out of his mind. This was just coffee.

Emma's flat was small but tidy. A little cold and modern, it lacked the warmth Rachel had created in their own home. David loved the big pine table in the kitchen, and the tatty old oak bench filled with woodworm holes. He had treated the bench with a chemical treatment that had to be painted on. The smell had made a pregnant Rachel gag, but at the time even toothpaste had developed an unappealing smell for her; she had terrible morning sickness with both pregnancies. The bench had to be left in the garden covered in a tarpaulin until the chemical smell faded. Rachel had found some solid pine chairs in a junk shop. She had painted them white when she had been heavily pregnant with Maisie: she'd been bored and Maisie was long overdue. He remembered teasing her about feathering the nest, standing behind her, his hands over the swell of their baby spending its last days inside her. She had dabbed paint on his nose and told him to go and make her another cup of raspberry leaf tea before this baby got any bigger and erupted *Alien*-style from her belly. That had been a wonderful time, full of excitement and anticipation, holding Rachel long into the night when she was anxious about the birth. Sometimes he just lay there, watching her sleep, wondering how he could love a child as well as her.

Emma interrupted his thoughts. He sighed – his subconscious was making a last attempt to sabotage his planned infidelity.

'Sit down, make yourself at home.' Emma was smiling at him. 'What would you like to drink?' He noticed in the bright light of the flat that she was not as young as he had thought – closer to her mid-thirties than mid-twenties – but she was still younger than he was.

'Coffee. Coffee would be great, thanks. Better not have another drink – I still have to drive home.'

'Milk, sugar?'

'Just milk, thanks.'

'Sit down, I'll be back in a minute.'

He sat. Then removed his phone from his jacket pocket, checking for a reply to his earlier text from Rachel. *Fine* was all it said. She was probably happy to put the kids to bed and have more screen-staring time anyway.

Emma came back with two steaming mugs, one blue and one pink. This struck David as amusing. He wondered how often the gender-specific mugs served coffee. Emma sat down next to him…right next to him. Her thigh touched his as she tucked her feet under her, causing her body to lean in towards his so that as he raised his mug to his mouth his arm brushed against her. It was becoming apparent that this was definitely not just coffee. He sipped his drink, but it was too hot so he placed it on the coffee table in front of him.

'Emma, I haven't done anything like this before – well, not in a long time, not since I've been married – well, actually, not since I've been with Rachel. I know that I've told you my marriage is not in a great place right now, but I have kids…'

Emma silenced David by kissing him, and not a gentle, compassionate, understanding kiss either. This kiss had one aim, and he had no doubt that it was working. All thoughts of Rachel left him and he kissed her back, with a lust that had been dormant for quite some time. Emma took the lead but David didn't even try to resist: he needed to get laid.

Emma took his hand and led him towards the bedroom. Neither of them said anything. Desire took over. Mouths, hands and tongues worked their way over each other's bodies. David kept telling himself it was just sex, it had no meaning beyond the physical. She was pulling him towards her, wanting him inside her. He scrabbled on the floor for his discarded trousers, needing the condoms from his pocket; he wasn't even sure he could remember how to put one on. With trembling hands he fumbled, trying to tear the packet. Emma the expert seductress took over.

David looked down at Emma, her hips rising up to meet his, fingernails digging into the flesh of his bottom, her hair splayed across the pillow, the way Rachel's hair always did, and for a moment as he entered her she had the face of Rachel; the hair was Rachel's hair. He wanted to bury his face in Rachel's hair and smell the glorious scent of her shampoo, but instead he closed his eyes and fucked Emma. He fucked her hard, shutting out the image of Rachel's face, Rachel's sad and vacant face, Rachel crying.

David opened his eyes for just one moment, but a moment was all it took. The face was wrong: it was pretty but hard, too much make-up. The body was wrong: the breasts were firm; those breasts had never fed his children. The stomach that lay beneath his was taut and flat; he didn't want that stomach beneath his, he wanted the soft, out-of-shape one creased with stretch marks and puckered skin where it had been expanded too far to accommodate the babies that he and Rachel had made together. The body he wanted beneath him was one that knew how to move in unison with his, instinctively. This was so wrong; Emma was so wrong.

Movement ceased. David held himself above Emma, looking down at her angular face. Her eyes were closed and they opened to look at him, wondering why he had stopped. He knew he had to get out of there. He loved his wife and he wanted to make love to her. He wanted to hold her afterwards and fall into a deep, satisfied sleep. He wanted to wake up with his arm numb and Rachel's head on his chest. What he wanted was to be at home with her, helping put the kids to bed, eating dinner and talking about their day. He wanted to laugh with her and to make all this pain go away. When David had said his vows he had meant every word of them, but he wasn't forsaking all others, he wasn't looking after her in sickness, he was just relying on the doctor and hoping for the best. Rachel needed him with her, to help her find a way out of her misery.

David looked at Emma's face, not knowing what to say. He couldn't have carried on if he had wanted to; his cock was limp and useless.

'What's the matter?' Emma looked at him, confused.

'I'm sorry,' he said. 'I am so sorry.'

He rolled off Emma and sat on the side of the bed, elbows on his knees, resting his forehead on the upturned heel of his hand. Emma sat up too but he didn't turn to look; he knew he needed to leave but some sort of inertia held him. This was complete insanity, but it gave him the clarity to understand what he had to do.

'It's OK, these things happen,' Emma said. Sliding forward, she knelt behind his back, her nipples touching his skin as she bent her head forward to kiss his shoulder.

David still didn't speak. Her touch was enough to startle him into action. He stood and grabbed his things. He dressed as he made his way towards the door, not responding or looking back as Emma shouted after him. He made sure he had his keys, phone and wallet. And then he slammed the door and made his way to the safety of his car. He stopped on his way home and sat in the supermarket car park, panicking and feeling utterly frustrated and useless. He planned his excuses in case Rachel asked where he had been and why he was so late. He knew one thing for sure: she would not tolerate infidelity, even in her current state of mind. That was the irony, though – all the guilt and none of the pleasure. Jesus, his life was a mess. He sat, breathing slowly to calm himself, until he realised how dark it had become, and how empty the car park was.

Showering as soon as he got home, he tried to be quiet, so as not to wake any of them. He checked on the kids; they were fast asleep, tucked up tight. The evening was cooler and the windows were slightly open, letting in the autumnal breeze. He thought about closing them, but when he brushed his hand against the cheeks of the children they were warm.

Rachel was asleep, her breathing slow and regular. David climbed into bed next to her. Sliding his arm under her, he pulled her towards him until her head rested on his shoulder. He held her so tightly he thought she must wake, but it seemed exhaustion had finally taken over, and she remained in a deep sleep. If maybe she could just sleep like this every night then life might start to be better.

'I love you, Rachel. I love you more than anything.' He whispered the words close to her ear.

Rachel was awake, but she gave no sign of it. Her thoughts were with someone else.

David didn't even close his eyes that night. He held his wife to him all night, unable to sleep for fear that he had lost her.

Adam

Looking around him, Adam had to admit that his prison walls were rather comfortable, but his freedom to move out of the confines of the perimeter was restricted all the same. A maximum-security facility would have suited him better, but these days it seemed voluntary incarceration was the four-year penalty for killing both your parents.

Julia, his wife for the last eighteen years, had left for work at 6 a.m. She had a long drive to escapism and career satisfaction, working away all week and returning home tired and irritable on a Friday night. Her five-foot-one-inch presence dominated the house and made Adam, who was well over six foot in his socks, feel dwarfed. On Friday she would arrive home, drink coffee, open a bottle of wine before dinner and proceed to find fault with Adam's housekeeping. He now had five long days to fill before her return.

The kids had caught the bus at 8.05 a.m., as they always did, and Adam had been alone for fifty-five minutes. All this time he had been staring out of the window. To start with he'd watched the kids walk down the lane to the wide, long gateway that served as a pull-in for the school bus, but now he just stood, staring. He had nowhere to be.

Adam did too much thinking. He also watched too much TV, spent far too much time on Facebook, watched too many films and spent far too many hours engaged in the fulfilling act of staring. He was broken, trapped. You didn't kill your parents and wake up a couple of days later fixed; that he understood. So much time had passed, yet he still felt raw. The overwhelming guilt built a wall that became higher each time he tried to climb over it, and stopped him dead. He might as well have been in prison.

It was time to stop killing time. Sometimes Adam's life seemed to him as if it was nothing more than ghosts and shadows glancing off the edge of a consciousness he perceived as reality. The ghosts visited with increasing frequency and left him with a feeling of restlessness. The ghosts told him he was blameless. If they had been able to re-form a link to the present they would have told him it was time to restart his life. He knew this was a good sign. It meant he was ready to move forward with his life, but it was the shadows that stopped him. The shadows lurked in the corner of his mind and sat at the back of the room, and though they were silent they were the presence that left him doubting his sanity. How could he, the killer and useless idiot, think he was worthy of joy and pleasure? The ghosts told him it was an accident: black ice. The shadows told him it was his fault.

That morning, staring out of the window, Adam was going over and over the events of the last almost four years, a pointlessly repeated exercise. The immediate aftermath of the accident should have been the hardest. It wasn't. The funeral had been a haze of prescription-drug-induced confusion. Julia and his brother, Robert, had organised everything, from the 'his and hers' coffins to the jolly good send-off at the pub.

Adam had been at the funeral but they might as well have put one more coffin out, as he was just there as one more body. His mind was still sitting in a field, in freezing fog, trying to understand the noises and the smells. Wanting to make sense of events that were senseless. It had been another six months before his mind and body became one again. When they did, the resulting bang of that collision caused such an angry and self-destructive impact that they locked him away with all the other fragmented souls.

At 9.30 a.m. Adam glanced at his watch, a TAG Heuer, a present from his wife on their tenth wedding anniversary. On the back was inscribed 'love you'. He had missed the fact that that particular anniversary was a significant one, and had purchased the usual bouquet of scented flowers, making sure they contained freesias and pink roses, as they had been in her wedding bouquet. He had booked a cosy corner table at Julia's favourite restaurant and taken her out for dinner. This, it seemed, was not enough for ten years of wedded bliss. *Apparently*, the leather strap on the watch had some modern-day relevance to a decade of wedlock. Julia had been expecting some significance to be sent her way. She must have been devastated by his failings, because she bore that particular grudge for quite some time before releasing it among a tirade of his inadequacies. The feelings had been bottled and stored from that one in the same way as you might preserve lemons. Julia had kept the lid on for some two years, and the un-bottling had come about during a rather feisty argument about socks.

Still, it was a nice watch. Still going strong eight years later.

At 9.35 a.m. Adam decided to stop thinking and clean the bathrooms. Of all the mundane tasks he now performed, cleaning the bathrooms was his favourite. 'Favourite' was a strange way to describe housework, but at least it gave him a small sense of much-needed satisfaction. They were the rooms where you could see and smell the difference. As he polished the top of the last chrome tap he checked his watch. Time for a coffee.

At 12.55 Adam woke up with a crick in his neck and an empty coffee cup in his hand. It was time for lunch. His appetite had returned to normal and he fancied a rather huge bacon sandwich. After the accident his eating patterns had become erratic: at times he would starve himself, the aching pang of hunger at least giving him something to feel, a focus, a distraction. Days of not eating led to light-headed euphoria: a drug from nothing. Food would sometimes be a comfort, and he would gorge on biscuits and bread, any number of sweet sugary carbohydrates until the point where he felt bloated and sick. Unable to stop, he would carry on until the enjoyment of the food became a punishment. Adam had no right to feel comfort.

Sleeping during the day was a recent addition to his daily routine, and he presumed it was a side-effect of leaving the medication in the packet. Most of the past four years had been concerned with fulfilling the basic physiological needs he was unable to deny himself and punishing himself for needing them. There had been little room in his mind for anything more. At first he hadn't slept well, the odd fitful hour here or there. When he did sleep, it was induced by the heavy consumption of alcohol or prescription medication and often both. After he came out of hospital he seemed to do nothing but sleep.

Over-reliance on alcohol had also been an issue, but Julia had put an end to that when she realised he had emptied the drinks cupboard; he had even attempted to drink a whole bottle of cream sherry one night, and he hated sherry, it reminded him of funerals. The apéritif served to ease the pain. He had tried doing the weekly shop online, for more bottled supplies, but then realised they didn't live within a specified delivery area for any of the supermarkets, and as at the time he wouldn't drive or leave the house his days of alcoholism were short-lived. He had considered ordering wine in bulk but felt that he would only get away with this once, as Julia did a regular sweep of the house to check for supplies, gliding round with a large glass of red wine in her hand. Watching Julia as she searched, Adam reasoned with himself that maybe she was right: he should stop finding solace in a bottle.

Cold consumed Adam most of the time, a deep, penetrating, bone-aching cold; it made him weary. He dressed in heavy black jeans, a T-shirt and jumper and thick socks, when everyone else was sweating it out in T-shirts because he had cranked up the heating so high. If Julia turned the thermostat down, Adam would light the fire and stare at the flickering heat until his eyes were almost too dry to blink.

At 1.15 p.m. Adam looked at the clock on the wall. Lunch was late. Cooking was done on the champagne-coloured range cooker, a compromise made by Julia, who had wanted a full-size Aga fitted. As the fat from the bacon rashers sizzled and spat, Adam leant against the solid oak kitchen cabinets, with the hand-painted cupboard doors, the perfect shade of off-white to complement the oak worktops. Crisp bacon slid from the cast-iron frying pan on to thick pre-sliced white supermarket bread, the sort of bread Julia hated. Adam smothered the bacon in brown sauce and bit down hard. He tut-tutted at himself, throwing in a quick eye-roll for good measure, in true Julia fashion, as the sauce dribbled on to his T-shirt.

By 2 p.m. Adam realised he was already late starting the vacuuming. Sucking the dirt from the wooden floors downstairs and the deep-pile cream carpets upstairs, trying not to bump into the immaculate neutral walls, he thought about how alone he was.

Missing interaction with the outside world was a result of the undeadening of his feelings as the deep fog of depression had lifted and the drugs left his system. Where were all his so-called friends? Had they stayed away, giving him the space to grieve, or had they hidden away in embarrassment after he spent time in the nut-house? Adam thought he had a couple of mates from work, but it was obvious now they were just colleagues. He had one true friend and he had shut him out. Matt had sent a card and tried to speak to him on the phone a few times, he had sent texts and messages, but over time these stopped. People were uncomfortable with death; Adam had been more uncomfortable than most. Maybe if Matt had driven over, sat and talked, not taken silence as a rebuff…now Adam needed to talk, and longed for something akin to the friendships portrayed in Hollywood blockbuster coming-of-age movies. What did they call them? Bromances? He wondered if those friendships existed in reality, or were they the stuff of make-believe, written in the first place by the souls lonely enough to sit all day at a keyboard creating a life of fantasy to replace the despair and loneliness of their own existences?

Hours of alone-time were not healthy. Friendships, like any relationship, took effort, and Adam was tired – worn out. When life had been going well he supposed he had done what everyone else did and just counted on people being there. Now his life had turned to shit, there was no one but Julia to rely on, and she was sick and tired of him.

His kids, his wife, his friends and his parents he was often guilty of taking for granted, not in a neglectful way, but in a presumptuous way. He had been the same with friends, never bothering to involve himself in their lives and problems that much, always remaining on the periphery. He was happy to take a mate out for a pint when they were a bit fed up, but if he'd found himself with the tables turned would he have gone the extra mile? He doubted it. Would he have become intrusive enough in their tragic despair to make a difference? He thought he had never been that close to anyone, except once maybe and she was a long time ago. It was a case of reaping what you sowed.

It was 3.30 p.m., time for another coffee. The vacuuming and dusting were done, and Adam slumped, mug in hand, on the big brown leather sofa. Leather was a crap material for a sofa: when it was cold, the sofa was cold, and, when it was hot, you were glued to it. Julia had liked the sofa, saying the leather was 'sooooo soft' in her little-girl pleading voice, with a slight fake lisp and big doe eyes for extra effect. The fakeness annoyed Adam because Julia didn't need little-girl pleading; if Julia wanted it, Julia got it…she paid for it.

Adam turned on the monotony of daytime TV. Flicking through the channels, he paused, his attention caught by the lowlife on TV who was sleeping with his best friend and her brother. If they weren't lying then they were sensationalising the events of their lives for their fifteen minutes. Why else would they be so willing to show off their dirty laundry in such a public way? It amazed Adam the way people were sucked into this perpetual round of banal crap. This was the voyeuristic addiction of the masses: too shallow and uninterested to do anything about the real problems of the society around them. Then again, he also had far too many hours in the day to dwell on everything and almost anything, and was guilty about his own failure to act. Adam liked to keep things in. He had let go that once. He wouldn't take that chance again. Next time, the bitch might keep him locked up for good.

Adam stretched and yawned, rubbing his grey-peppered, stubbled chin. He would shave in the morning before he went to the supermarket. Tuesday, the day he drove to town to buy food.

The silence of the house was overwhelming; music might lift his mood. He was wearing his almost faded to grey black jeans and his Wonder Stuff T-shirt. He dressed like this from Monday morning until 3 p.m. on a Friday, when he would change into his more 'age-appropriate' clothes. Julia thought he was too old to wear band-emblazoned T-shirts: slogans on T-shirts had him sent to his room to change. He did as he was told; most of the time he didn't have the energy to argue. She would roll her eyes with that fabulous 'grow up' expression she had perfected over the years. She also became arsy with him if the house wasn't tidy when she arrived home on a Friday night. No point being doggedly stubborn and biting the hand of the bitch that fed him. He felt mean for thinking of her as a bitch. She wasn't a bitch; she just had high standards. She had held the family together, kept the wages rolling in.

When 4.15 p.m. came he would move to the window to check the school bus had dropped the boys off. They would be wandering up the lane laden with heavy bags. They would arrive in the hall, drop their bags on the floor and empty the fridge, then grunt at him and head upstairs to stare at screens or start their homework. They were good kids, considering what he had put them through. Adam didn't feel any less lonely when they came home. He would cook, and they would grunt at each other over dinner. Then they slept and the day began again. They would repeat this until Friday night. Then Julia would join them; then they would sleep and generally the day would just begin again.

Adam did something he hadn't done for a while: he logged on to Facebook at 7 p.m. instead of 8 p.m. He had no idea why, but when he did he was surprised when he saw a comment on one of his posts by someone called Rachel. The mini profile picture next to the comment was too small to see; he called up her page – yes, it was her. She had just posted a new profile picture, of herself and two young children.

He sat and thought for ten minutes, just tapping his fingers on his leg next to the iPad that sat on his lap. For some unknown reason he went into his study and logged on to Facebook on his laptop. He checked his suggested friends list. Rachel had appeared among them. Adam sat staring into space. He let out what was a cross between a laugh and a snort, calling up a memory of a young girl with amazing hair. They had been so close once, but not for long. At 8.35 p.m. he sent a friend request and waited.

Sleep was difficult that night. He had stayed logged on to Facebook and checked several times over the course of the evening to see if Rachel had accepted his request. She had not. He woke early; it was 4.42 a.m. It was far too early to get up so he lay in bed thinking. Although he argued with Julia most of the time these days, he still missed her. She slept with a peace of mind unknown to him, her face always serene, her breathing quiet and regular. Julia had smooth skin due to the combined effects of lack of guilt and Botox. When she would lie like that, next to him, at weekends, he would feel a sudden surge of love and gratitude towards her; but when she opened her mouth to speak the warmth of his emotion would cool and he'd find himself suppressing the urge to slap her. He would never do it, of course. He was far too gentle for physical violence…well, apart from that once.

At a few minutes past five Adam checked Facebook again…nothing, no reply. He couldn't go back to sleep. His iPad rested on the bedside table and the monotonous cycle of trawling for new friends began again. His regular contacts had of late become humdrum, and reading down their random posts was now tedious. He needed more variety. He concentrated on new recruits from his old high school and college friends. Mix things up with a little old blood. Remembering their names was a big problem, though. Age and absence had a way of doing that to you. Tip-of-the-tongue syndrome. If he did remember their names when he looked at their profile picture he wasn't always sure it was who he thought it was, they had changed so much, although sometimes the photos made him laugh, as the faces seemed unchanged, just with linear additions and a tendency in his male friends for more jowl and midriff. Some of the female ones still looked good for their age, but then again so did Julia. She went to the gym most mornings, although Adam sometimes wondered if she just went to Jim. Not a thought he was going to have today!

Living in the past suited him at the moment. Music was another escape. He had been a big fan of the alternative rock band The Jesus and Mary Chain in the late 1980s. He had also noticed that they had been touring again and wondered if there would be a suitable date and venue where he could meet up with friend and fellow fan Matt; maybe it was time to rekindle their friendship.

Julia's constant comments of 'Really – you want to keep that old rubbish?' had depleted his music collection. She didn't see the point of harbouring his collection of albums and CDs when he had an iPod. A CD of *Barbed Wire Kisses*, a compilation album that he played over and over, had escaped the most recent cull. He did consider he was lucky to have a CD player – the record player and records had been consigned to the loft years ago. Then she had thrown them out without asking him if it was OK, in the big pre-extension clearout.

Barbed Wire Kisses she was not going to get her hands on! The title and raw degradation of many of the tracks suited his mood. The guitar feedback was an audible version of how his head felt a lot of the time. Screeching! The distortion seemed more apparent to him than most. When he played the music that he loved he kept reliving his past. Lost in thoughts of a time when he had been happy with his life, with the way he dressed, and when his hair was shaved at the sides and stood up in a half-hearted mohawk. He felt he had been inventing his own style. The memory was a good one. His girlfriend – and Rachel – had loved his unique style, or so they'd said. He had never pigeonholed himself like a lot of his friends. They had locked on to a particular genre of music they identified with and then donned the appropriate style to suit. Adam's musical tastes had always been eclectic and he liked to think he was 'alternative', although if he was honest he had been a carbon copy of Matt. When he looked back at old photos he realised he had just looked like a lanky twat.

When Adam had met Julia, in his mid-twenties, she had changed him. She told him he would get on better if he smartened up a bit. Julia had changed a lot about him, but there was something about her strength, her directness and ambition, that had attracted him. A need maybe that he hadn't been aware of: to keep up with his brother and gain the same respect from his parents. Odd, as trying to keep up had just led to a lifestyle they couldn't afford, debt, misery, and non-stop arguments about who was to blame.

He checked the watch that lay on the bedside table next to the alarm clock: 5.47 a.m. – still too early to get up. He turned his attention back to the friend-finding task. At first he had been quite offended when he sent a friend request on Facebook and the person didn't bother replying. Now he just sent them as a matter of course. It helped a little with the boredom. Scanning down the list of names from the college where he had studied for his A levels, he found his old college girlfriend: Andrea, the love of his life, the girl he was going to marry. He laughed to himself – he had been round the block a few times since then. God, he was even thinking in clichés now! He needed to spend less time watching daytime TV.

Andrea had been great, though, until she'd found someone better. It was not to be, and nor were the next five girlfriends either. There was Rachel's name again. 'Friend request sent'. Still no reply. He thought about sending her a message – for fuck's sake, this was Rachel – but something stopped him. Did he really have the confidence to just contact her out of the blue? He needed an excuse – no, not an excuse, a reason.

Adam had tried to keep in touch with Rachel when they left college and went off to university. They had met up once for a drink, when they were both home, but family and distance seemed to get in the way and they lost touch, something he had always regretted. In his loneliness he wondered if she had ever thought of him. The Rachel everyone knew had been self-assured and gregarious, but Adam knew a different side to her. She was insecure, often intimidated by people. She laughed all the time, which made everyone else think she was this happy, irrepressible person. What she confided in him was that the reason she liked to party so much was that alcohol gave her confidence. Before college she had always been outside the loop of the popular kids, mocked for her hair and the clothes she wore. When she'd started sixth form college she had reinvented herself. She worried that others didn't like her and was insecure about the way she looked. If she hadn't been so genuine, almost tearful when she had related this to Adam, he would have thought it farcical. This unexpected vulnerability had made him long for her even more, but they'd seemed doomed to have nothing more than an intense short-term friendship.

Following a bitter and angry break-up with the so-called love of his life Andrea, when he found out she was seeing someone else, Adam had gone on to have a series of one-night stands, short-term girlfriends and then five more serious relationships before meeting Julia. He was a good-looking bloke but very casual and understated; women seemed to like this about him, so he nurtured it. He was also kind, softly spoken, pleasant and very easy to be with.

Julia was nothing like his previous girlfriends. For one thing, she was very attractive. Julia also had a daughter, Amy, who was two when they met, the product of a drunken interaction at a post-finals party; for Julia, being Catholic, termination would have been unforgivable. Her parents, horrified at first, had done the right thing and supported her through the pregnancy, and they had looked after Amy when Julia started work. Adam had a feeling that even though on the surface she seemed close to her parents they never let her forget how let down they felt by her.

Career became everything to Julia, and when she met Adam, who had a good job and was malleable, it seemed that she decided he was husband material. He suspected that, if she was married, Julia's parents would be able to gloss over the facts and forgiveness might just follow her down the aisle. He wasn't sure he ever proposed; a drunken conversation about spending their lives together took place, but he never did the whole bended-knee thing. They shopped for a ring and before he knew it the wedding was booked and the plane was taking off to a warmer climate, where the honeymoon took place. He hadn't been involved in the preparations, but at the time he hadn't minded. In fact until the accident he had been happy a lot of the time. Julia had impressive organisational skills but he felt he had worn away all her compassion.

Seven a.m. – he could get up. Adam was desperate for the loo so it was a great relief. He was showered and dressed by 7.20 a.m., when it was time to wake the boys: enough time for them to meander to the bathroom, dress and fall out of the door in time to walk down the lane to catch the bus. Another day started.

Tuesday was the traumatic trip to the supermarket. There was a strict timetable to be adhered to. Today he had been distracted by checking Facebook one more time before he left the house. The car park deadline was 10 a.m. and that included parking straight and central, not skewed – wonky parking led to tricky exiting. The church that was situated at the junction where he turned left for the supermarket car park told Adam that it was already 10.05. He also knew that the church clock kept excellent time and matched his watch; flustered, he parked across the white line of the bay. Now he had to move the car forward then back again, manoeuvre it into the space, annoyed with himself – he should have got this right on the first attempt. His hands were sweating. He took deep breaths and tried again. It was 10.07 by the time he was out of the car. He grabbed the bags and headed off to get the trolley. The deadline to return to his car was 11 a.m.

At 10.59 Adam paused by the car for a minute, steadying his breathing, watching the second hand as it swept by and he unlocked the car at 11 a.m. He wiped away an anxious bead of sweat from his forehead. It was very warm for September. Humid, he told himself.

The drive home was always a little more relaxed. There was plenty of time until lunch; it was OK to miss coffee on a Tuesday.

One o'clock and the shopping was away and lunch was ready. On Tuesdays he made ham sandwiches with thick slices of tomato, on fresh crusty wholemeal bread. The loaf had still been warm when he took it from the rustic wooden shelves in the supermarket bakery. Thick white sliced bread was always placed in the trolley; he didn't like it, but it annoyed Julia. Tuesday afternoons were for pottering. Today he planned to finish putting his CV together, after he checked out Facebook one more time.

The passing of time was excruciating today. There was still no response from Rachel. He scrolled down the list of possible college friends once more. Eloise! Many a boy had been damned to lust after Eloise. Who could forget Eloise? He was happy to find her still out there and she looked good, from her profile picture. He looked at her page, but it was only accessible to friends. He sent her a friend request. She must have been online, as she accepted him almost straight away. He clicked to see what she had put about herself, wondering what she did for a living: retired pole dancer maybe. Barrister – Jesus, Eloise was a barrister! Maybe he had misread it – a barista maybe? He clicked back to her page: nothing much on it, just the profile picture of her smiling and a picture of her cat. There was one recent holiday photo of her and a man in the Maldives – he knew this because it said 'Amazing holiday in the Maldives'. Wouldn't want anyone thinking it was a sunny day in Wales. Adam stared in disbelief at the picture-perfect self-congratulatory selfie. Fuck! He dropped his iPad hard on the sofa next to him.

Old Adam would have been pleased for her, but old Adam had disappeared in a cloud of white powder and the smell of explosives on a very cold New Year morning. He felt more pissed off than usual. Maybe he should just send her a message for old times' sake, or perhaps a thank-you note was long overdue; she had always been good with her mouth. Even he had to admit to himself he was being a little peevish, but it was one of those days.

Adam's career had been going well. He had been a lecturer in business studies at a further education college, but just before the accident he had secured himself a job as a business development manager with one of those local authority/government offshoots. The salary had been better, along with good pension prospects, and it was a permanent position. He would have missed the long holidays, which had been very handy while the kids were young, but, as Julia pointed out, the kids were old enough now; they could divide up their holidays, and with friends and various holiday schemes they would cope. She had said it would be a shame to let holidays stop him from taking a job that had better prospects.

The accident had ended all that, and now he had been unemployable for almost four years, having ended up with one splendid long holiday in which to sun himself in the garden. Except the outside held little appeal; he preferred to stay indoors when he could – it felt safer.

It was time to start looking again, he knew; he even made a few tentative enquiries with old work colleagues. His CV was almost in order and he was working on his LinkedIn profile. He just lacked the motivation, and the confidence. Then there was the fear. The fear was like the shadows. It was there but he didn't want to admit to it: driving every morning, facing people day in, day out and breaking all those routines. It would all be out there, goading him for a response, the noise, the unpleasantness and the smells, those awful evocative smells.

Adam moved to the window to watch for the boys earlier than usual. He was fed up with checking to see if Rachel had replied. Starting to watch at 3.30 p.m. gave him an additional forty-five minutes of staring time.

The kids were OK with him now – well, most of the time. Sometimes they grew very impatient with him if they just wanted dropping off at a friend's house and he couldn't do it. He would go pale and start to shake because the destination was not on his familiar safe list. Alex was the worst, often shouting at Adam and calling him a freak. Tom was calmer, more understanding. They had both been old enough to feel devastated by the loss of their grandparents, but too young to understand the impact it had on Adam. To them it was just a terrible accident. They had no comprehension of how or why Adam would torture himself. He couldn't explain to them that, late at night, he believed he was pure evil. How could he tell his children that he sometimes believed he had taken deliberate action to slide into a telegraph pole so that he could inherit his parents' money and end his financial problems? None of this would make sense to them. It didn't make any sense to him. They were just teenagers who wanted a dad to taxi them to fun and mates and, for Tom, to his girlfriend's house. Well, this week's girlfriend, anyway. At sixteen Tom had already had a string of girlfriends; he was a handsome lad, he had his mother's striking good looks, and despite the crap of the last few years he was very outgoing. Adam had been very responsible about his son's behaviour. Sitting him down for 'the talk', he had also provided him with a generous supply of condoms. Julia had backed him on this, but then she would, because she didn't want the consequences of an unwanted pregnancy. Adam had no idea if Tom had used any of the condoms yet, but he was very keen on this latest girl and she had lasted well past the normal week, so he suspected something was afoot.

Adam interrupted his silent, vacant stare by turning on the radio. The murmur of the voices sometimes helped to soothe him in the silence. Wasn't that what you were supposed to do with dogs that you left at home all day, to give them comfort and company? The programme was about canoeing, some advocate of outdoor pursuits for young offenders, making a metaphor about capsizing and righting the canoe. Adam felt capsized. He needed to right his own canoe. He needed to find a job; it was time to get his life back on track. He also had to stop the current obsession with Rachel. Rachel was twenty-five years ago. Checking Facebook all the time was messing up his routines. Insanity did not provide him with clarity. Lusting after Rachel was not the solution to his problems, it was a distraction from them.

Adam stared out of the window, watching the occasional car as it wound its way down the country lane, disappearing into a dip and then reappearing in the spot where the hedges dropped down lower...he knew the landscape from the window very well. The gate was further along, where the passing vehicle would reveal itself once more. This was the first car he had seen pass today; others might have driven by but he had not been growing roots at his spot by the window all day. Ford Fiesta, he guessed. Sometimes he played this game for a couple of hours, but sometimes nothing went down the road in all the time he stood there.

It was a game they had played in the car as kids, invented by his dad and dads everywhere before in-car entertainment kept kids glued to a screen. It always had to be the make and model, never any half-measures with Dad. Next came a dark blue van, driving too fast. Adam wanted to run outside and shout at it: his kids rode their bikes down this lane. They would be walking up here from the bus soon. Twat! He watched the road for a minute longer as the boys came into sight. Then he wandered round his detestable idyll, picking up discarded clothes and dirty cups as he went. Bloody kids couldn't put anything away despite the amount of times he told them. Repeat until ignored. They had no respect for him and who could blame them? A dad who just disappeared into himself for hours on end then came out shouting. What exactly did he expect?

Thursday was the day for changing the bedclothes, doing the washing, and in the summer months mowing the lawn while it was all drying. This Thursday, however, Adam had a trip to the dentist; a 9.50 a.m. appointment, which made everything rather stressful. The break in routine was difficult to deal with. He wasn't quite sure how he was going to fit everything in. Adam left the house four minutes after the boys had marched off, last-minute as always, to catch the school bus. The drive to town took an average of twenty-two minutes in traffic, but he also needed fuel and to check the tyre pressures. Adam left plenty of time just in case; arriving in the car park with fifty minutes to spare despite heavy traffic, owing to a broken-down bus blocking a lane on the dual carriageway. After buying his car park ticket, he had to decide whether to sit in his car or go for a coffee. If he went for coffee he could use the Wi-Fi. Coffee it was, then.

Adam held the large white mug in his hand, letting the warmth soothe him. He stared into the foam topped with sprinkled chocolate powder as if it had the answer. He worried about the kids, afraid of the impact all this would have on them. It was a good job they had been almost old enough to look after themselves when the accident happened. At seventeen, Amy had been involved in her own life and friends. Another two years and Tom would be off to university, if Adam's lack of support hadn't fucked that up for him as well. Alex was eighteen months younger and already he had started his GCSE years. Julia had been around for a year after the accident; Adam had been too busy rocking and drooling to be left at that stage. Then came Julia's promotion, and it was a big promotion, almost doubling an already good salary, and with the house extension and the bigger mortgage they had needed the money, until probate was settled. She was supposed to come back after a year, back to the local office, to fill a new role created by her company's expansion plans. Then the economy went tits-up and planned acquisitions were withdrawn from and Julia was just relieved she still had a job.

Julia, Julia…he often wondered what he thought about Julia. No, Adam didn't wonder what he thought about Julia, because Julia would tell Adam what he should think about Julia. That was unfair: Julia had been amazing. She coped, she sorted, she got on with it. The kids had not suffered in that year because somehow Julia had kept them all together: she had paid the bills, taken very little time off work, kept the house together and even got home in time to talk to the builders as they finished the snagging on the extension. Adam had felt as though he had become her child; she would lie awake late into the night, holding him, stroking his forehead. After all that, how did he repay her? He resented her. He would try to justify it to himself but he couldn't. She had coped; he hadn't. Julia viewed life and death with distinct separation: life you lived, death you accepted and moved on. She had been there the same as he had; she had been bruised just as he had. Her arm had been broken, whereas he had just been concussed and bruised; they had both been on the driver's side of the car. Julia's mind remained intact – but they weren't her parents, they were his. She hadn't ended their lives, he had. She had been a passenger, just as they had been, entrusting their lives to his ability to steer a car around a slight curve in the road. He was the only one sober and yet…

Adam stirred his coffee and logged on to the free Wi-Fi. No response from Rachel. The coffee was cool now and he gulped it down, not wanting to be late for his appointment. He checked his watch: 9.39 a.m. He had eleven minutes to walk to the dentist.

At 10.33 a.m. Adam was back in the car and ready to go home. He edged out of his parking place, but somehow he misjudged the narrow space and just clipped the wing mirror on the internal pillar of the multistorey car park. Numerous people had done this before. The pitted black marks were the evidence. Most people would have just pulled in the mirror and carried on. Adam, however, reversed in a panic, bumping into the wall behind him before hitting the brakes so hard that he jerked forward in his seat. His phone, which he had placed on the passenger seat next to him, shot to the floor.

Adam froze, sweat forming in small beads across the bridge of his nose and across his forehead and lip. Anxiety flushed red across his cheeks, spreading down his neck like a rash. In his mind he returned to the memory of a New Year that was no longer celebrated.

New Year morning, a time to start the resolutions, try not to think about all those canapés, regret too much champagne and wallow in thoughts of blood, so much blood. Adam's dad wasn't a big man; how could there be so much blood? It stained and drenched, at first gushing and then leaking, spreading through clothes and soaking into torn upholstery. A huge stray splinter from the split telegraph pole had lacerated his father's thigh. Adam's hands slipped and slid in the sticky warmth. It would have been rather a pleasant feeling if it weren't for the fact that the blood was leaving his dad's body at a rate too fast to be stemmed. He tried pulling off his dad's tie but the older man's head and neck were jammed into the side of the car. Adam realised the telegraph pole was sitting directly above him. He tried to move his dad, but couldn't get his hand under his legs; they were wedged by the plastic surround and the part of the engine that had shifted to where the car seat should have been.

The fact that the telegraph pole had also hit his father's head so hard that he was already beyond saving had not occurred to Adam. The dense, freezing fog created an eerie mist, a white haze blocking all hope of light from the moon. They were in the countryside, miles from nearby buildings and streetlights, but if there had been light Adam would have seen that his father's head no longer resembled the symmetrical form it once had. Adam focused on the blood he could see and feel, the initial gush slowed as his father's heart stopped beating and his pulse stilled.

The full impact of the accident was on the passenger side, the seat forced backwards towards the rear passenger seat, where his mum was still talking. In reality she was just crying out and moaning, but to Adam's confused mind she was still issuing instructions to him as she would always have done. His mum always knew what to do in a crisis. But her injuries were too extensive for her to be lucid. Slipping into unconsciousness, she soon stopped making any sound, but Adam could still hear her telling him what to do.

She told him he needed to call an ambulance! He hadn't thought of that – why? He was confused, his head hurt so much, then he remembered: no phone signal. There was no signal – Julia had shouted this after she got herself free from the car, climbing through the smashed glass of the rear passenger window. The driver-side door was already open; he didn't remember opening it. She had taken her phone, limping up the road, desperate to find a signal. Where was she? He needed her. He needed her to see to his mum, while he tried to stop his dad from bleeding to death. Adam's head hurt so much he couldn't see straight. The smell of cow dung burnt rank in his nostrils; he was lying in a field, right next to the car, amidst the stench of fuel and shit.

He heard a disembodied shout from the darkness. 'Adam, Adam!' The voice was high-pitched and breathless. Julia arrived, high heels in her hand. He noticed the heel of one of the shoes was missing yet still she clung to them. Designer shoes, her pride and joy. She always wore bloody heels – what good were they in a crisis? She couldn't run in heels. She stood, her chest heaving as she sucked in the cold night air, misty fog dampening her lungs, making her cough. 'The police, ambulance, all of them, coming,' she gasped, holding her arm at an awkward angle. Her small, beautiful face pinched in pain, small gashes to her arms and legs, her expensive outfit in tatters.

Adam said nothing. He sat in the field, in the shit, in the freezing fog. Defeated.

Julia climbed into the driver's seat. Her father-in-law was dead. No doubt. Her mother-in-law was still breathing, but desperate inward breaths followed by the gurgling exhalation of someone drowning in their own internal fluids. Julia tried to reach out to touch her, just to let her know someone was there, just in case. Julia called to Adam, begging him to come to his mum, she was still alive, but, even as the words left her mouth, a desperate rattling last breath was followed by quiet. All quiet from the bodies, and just the hiss and occasional bang of the beat-up car as it settled in the night.

How long Adam and Julia sat on the wet grass in the freezing cold, neither of them knew. Julia heard the distant wail of the emergency vehicles approach and, as if to accompany them, the heavy, laboured sobs of her husband. She sat helpless on the ground next to Adam until the hive of activity and blue-flashing lights arrived almost en masse to fail to save the lives already lost.

His mum and dad's funeral happened. If the events hadn't been so brutal and so final, with their slow march and structure of conformity, Adam would have questioned whether or not they were real. The funeral was a blur of coffins and flowers. Words flew and drifted at various pitches around the church, but he was unable to catch them. The sounds reverberated off the walls and disappeared high into the rafters, echoing for a moment then dying away. That's what we all do, thought Adam – echo for a while.

'Always together even in death.' Adam listened but didn't hear as the vicar went on to spout his crap about eternal life. Somehow these few words lodged with Adam; he couldn't get beyond them. He could see the vicar's mouth moving but, even though he carried on and prayers were said and hymns were sung, and, even when the vicar stepped down and a close family friend read the poem that everybody read at funerals, all Adam heard was, 'Always together even in death.'

The church was alien to Adam and he was quite sure his parents hadn't believed in God. He didn't understand why they were there, clinging to a deity of false hope and comfort. His parents would have liked simplicity, not this big show of flowers and large black gleaming limousines.

Somehow they arrived at the crematorium where his parents' bodies were to be turned to ash. Adam wondered if it would be done in unison: 'Always together even in death.' He stifled an inappropriate laugh. His brother, Robert, couldn't even look at him. When the brief service was over they filed from their seats and Julia positioned Adam next to Robert. They lifted their hands one after the other like a repeating miniature Mexican Wave, heads ducking and muttering, 'Thank you,' as they touched the hands of those who had come to commiserate. Adam felt arms hug him and his cheek repeatedly brushed with soft lips. He wanted a shower; to wash away death.

Before the accident there had been the party. The reason they had been driving down that winding country road. They could have stayed the night in one of the cottages, but Adam's mum and dad had wanted to go back to their own bed. Adam had been glad to get away. He already felt that Julia had spent the night thinking she had married the wrong brother.

Adam's brother Robert had arranged a New Year's Eve party to celebrate his return to England from Australia, where he had been living for the last ten years, and to announce his engagement. Adam had suspected it was just to show off. The party had been at his new, yet very old, sprawling 'home'. One large and modernised farmhouse, acres of land he would never use, and two guest cottages. Adam was never quite sure how his brother came by so much money; he just called himself a consultant and changed the subject if you tried to ask him more, making a joke about not wanting to give away the secrets of his success. The success had come at a price, though, with two broken families already behind him. This would be the third of his wives, and she was young enough to breed more children whom Robert would leave behind.

After the accident the doctor gave Adam a textbook run-down of the expected symptoms of post-traumatic stress. Flashbacks and nightmares were common and might be vivid, certain smells might remind him of that night, and for a time he might be extra-sensitive to loud noises.

He had none of that; he had a void.

When Adam killed his parents it happened very slowly. They were chatting, his mother recounting, room-by-room, the designer décor of his brother's house. Every now and again his dad would interject with who he had met, what he had eaten and what he had drunk. Adam was rather amused by his bladdered dad; he didn't remember ever seeing him like that. As Adam applied the brakes and tried to steer, the car waltzed the last dance of the evening.

His dad wasn't much of a drinker. A couple of whiskies every now and again on a special occasion and a pint or two when he and Adam's mum went for lunch in the pub on a Sunday. It was a ritual they had started when the boys left home. No point in cooking for two, his mum said. Whenever possible, Adam, Julia, Amy and the boys would join them. His parents had been good parents – solid. They made sure to give Adam and Robert what they needed and they had brought up their sons to believe they should not be limited by circumstance; if they worked hard they would get what they wanted from life. They were neither rich nor poor, just comfortable. Comfortable parents in a settled home in a loving marriage. In Adam this had instilled a sense of belonging, but Robert had felt suffocated by it and had needed to get away as soon as possible. He left home to go to university and never went back, telling Adam he wouldn't 'be back to this boring dump ever again'. Adam remembered the comment cutting into him, destroying what he valued. He was careful never to tell his parents, who he felt had always favoured Robert. Robert was the bright one, the ambitious one; they were so proud of him being the first in the family to go to university. That was something they would never have imagined when they were his age. Adam had been reluctant to leave for university, opting for somewhere close enough to home that he could be back in a couple of hours if he needed to be. Robert had gone to

London, attracted to the biggest city and brightest lights he could think of. He hadn't cared about the extra financial stress it put on his parents to help support him. Visits home had always been a celebration because they were so rare. Robert would make an appearance at key events – Easter, summer, birthdays and Christmas – but never just because he missed his family. When he did arrive he was always the centre of attention, full of himself and what he had achieved. Showering his parents with gifts and then borrowing a couple of hundred quid before he left. Adam went home all the time to start with, needing security in an insecure world, unsure of his abilities and often uncomfortable in a world of drinking, partying and sex. As expected, though, he eventually got the hang of student life, but he still popped home for the day or the weekend more often than most. His parents were his source of comfort, and he wasn't yet ready to leave them behind.

It was 11.47 a.m. before Adam felt ready to try to leave the car park again, exhausted but finally more composed. He needed to get home. By the time he was out of the space his fingers hurt with the tension of gripping the steering wheel.

When the void had left Adam, even the sight of the car made him feel sick. A deep churning in the pit of his stomach, a gnawing reminder of what he had done. The smells of that night haunted him. The stench of cow shit, the strange metallic odour of blood, fuel and that pervasive smell like spent gunshot cartridges that had come from the airbag.

He hadn't managed to drive at all in that first year. He had tried, but oh, how he had failed. He had sat in the car numerous times, hearing the nervous thrumming of his fingers on the steering wheel, willing himself to start the engine. In the end circumstances, and Julia's leaving, had forced him to drive, but even now he didn't trust himself. He drove to the supermarket, he drove into town and he occasionally picked the kids up from school, but they got the bus most of the time as the stress was too much for him.

Nobody blamed Adam for the accident. The police didn't blame Adam, the coroner didn't blame Adam, Julia didn't blame Adam. He had been travelling at a sensible speed, he hadn't been drinking, and he hadn't been distracted. Yes, they had all been talking, but Adam had only been half-listening, concentrating hard as the patches of freezing fog came and went. The car stereo had been playing in the background, his lights were on, it was late but he wasn't tired. Then he had hit black ice on a slight bend in the road. He had steered one way and the car had gone in the opposite direction, sliding out of control. The car hit the telegraph pole at the perfect speed and angle to obliterate his parents and leave Adam and Julia more or less intact. The true facts were that the telegraph pole had obliterated his father; the front passenger seat, which had been forced back into the rear of the car, and his mother's refusal to wear a seatbelt because she hadn't wanted to dislodge the sequins on her dress, had obliterated her.

Even Robert had ceased to blame Adam. Nobody blamed Adam – except Adam. The shadows blamed Adam; they chewed at his mind, punching holes in his alibi, making him believe that he had wanted them dead, that there was something sinister about him, that he was jealous of how proud they were of his wanker of a brother and how their death would end his financial problems. That was when

Adam had locked himself away with the curtains drawn against the dawning of each day.

Adam arrived home and went about trying to catch up on some of the usual Thursday-morning chores. With the beds stripped and the washing on, it was time for lunch. He didn't feel hungry but it was one o'clock so it was time for lunch. On Thursdays lunch was beans on toast.

Julia had been promoted at about the same time Adam had been signed off on long-term sick leave, and then had resigned from his job. Moving hadn't seemed a good idea at the time; they'd thought it might be too stressful, and the kids were settled in school. Julia's relocation was supposed to be short-term. The house was also in the process of being extended, which was stressful enough without having to look for a new place to live. They had both had good jobs and worked hard to create what they had. Materialism... Julia liked expensive. She called it 'quality'. Adam called it a waste of money. Like the leather sofas he slid down while watching the vast TV surrounded by pointless yet tasteful objects.

Julia had been talking about trying to find another job, or getting a transfer back to the local office. She made big hints that if Adam could just get part-time work then this would give her greater flexibility when looking for a new job, as her salary could be lower. She missed them, he knew that, but sometimes he felt that having her there all the time would be too hard. She was intense, demanding, and there was no way he would be able to escape to his study for hours at a time and stare into space with music blasting out. The noise helped to empty his mind when it filled with intense horror. There were times when the smell of the blood and cow shit seemed to fill his nostrils from memory. Living in the middle of the fucking countryside, surrounded by the stuff leaking from the arses of the cows in the fields next to the garden didn't help.

His mum's desire to go on a world cruise was the reason Adam broke his brother's nose. Adam also created a fluttering storm of paper as he emptied large cardboard boxes of important documents all over the driveway. Julia managed to calm Adam down and Robert's wife took him to hospital. Adam retreated to his bedroom, for seven days, clutching a wax-crayoned picture of a fire engine.

Guilt consumed him and anger overwhelmed. Robert had just happened to be in the way. His parents had only been retired for a couple of years when they died. They had saved hard for their retirement and had intended to make the most of the last of their years together. Adam had wiped that out. All the luxuries they had denied themselves during their lifetimes seemed so pointless.

Adam didn't leave his room for a week, and he didn't leave his bed except to use the toilet in the en-suite. The stench became so bad in the end that Julia was forced to sleep in the spare room. The smell of ketones filled the room from exhaled breath, from a body pleading for food and fluids. Julia managed to get him to drink, sometimes, but he refused to eat. After ten days he was taken by ambulance to the psychiatric ward at the local hospital. He always felt that the initial sectioning had been over the top, but Julia had said his manner towards himself and others was far more destructive than he remembered. He tried to trust her on this but suspected that at the time she had just wanted him out of the way.

Robert had kept his distance since that day. Adam knew his brother had kept in touch with Julia; she had once let it slip, telling him that after the investigation into the crash and the inquest Robert had stopped blaming him. Adam didn't derive any comfort from the lack of blame. He found it easier to believe that, deep down, Robert hated him; it was better than facing him and dealing with a sibling who had also lost both his parents on the same night.

Following the initial seventy-two-hour sectioning, Adam was deemed to be not of sufficient threat to himself or others to be held under a mandatory section for any longer. However, he did agree to remain in hospital as a voluntary in-patient. He was released to a separate ward, which felt less ominous: that first ward, with the doors that locked, had been scary even for him, but the self-slashers and the shouters weren't as obvious here. Adam was a big bloke but, weakened from dehydration, lack of food and paranoia from lack of sleep, he had felt vulnerable. He had said as much to the doctor who came to talk to him and the doctor had concluded that Adam's desire to die had been short-lived. He stayed in the psychiatric wing of the local hospital for ten more days before being released. The follow-up care was patchy at best. The cognitive behavioural therapy (CBT) he just didn't understand. How on earth could talking about the fact that he had killed his parents in a car crash change his behaviour? He was driving; it was his fault. What else was there to say? *Focus on the now*, they told him. Focus on what? Apathy, guilt, hating himself? The therapist, a young girl with the kindest eyes Adam had ever seen, said there was a lot to say, but he didn't want to say it so he didn't keep his appointments. Julia found the letter, which had failed to catch fire, when she was cleaning out the wood-burner, and was furious. The letter listed the appointments he had missed and urged him to make future ones; he didn't. Adam had to concede that the drugs did work, but the talking made him feel worse. The medication helped to numb the pain, and the wonderful little white pill he took at night helped him on his way to five hours of dreamless sleep before a resentful awakening.

At 6.15 p.m. Adam realised he had wasted most of the day lost in thought. It was time to cook dinner and check the kids were doing their homework.

Eight o'clock and he logged on to Facebook; still no reply from Rachel. He had given up now. She didn't even remember him.

At 10 p.m. Adam found himself messaging a woman he once worked with in a rather inappropriate manner. He had been doing this far too often. He found he had a gift for making women feel better about themselves and he had about three of them on the go. He flirted, they flirted, but they were all tucked away on the internet, so there was no harm in it, was there? It helped to fill his long days and part of his dark, introspective, restless nights.

Adam hadn't gone on to Facebook with the intention of picking up women, he had just been bored one day, and some woman he had a vague memory of posted a comment and he sent her a private message. It was addictive and had, like most addictions, got a little out of hand – or in his case often *in* hand. A former work colleague with whom he'd had a one-night stand, before Julia, even sent him a picture of herself topless on the beach. She looked damn good for her age, he had to admit. For a while they engaged in a sexually heated exchange, and she made it very clear that she would rekindle things if he wanted to. She had been divorced for a couple of years and with no one else on the scene she was lonely. He did the virtual flirting and hadn't minded having a moment of casual self-gratification over her photo, but he had never been unfaithful to Julia and didn't intend to be. When she sent him a full-frontal nude selfie of her touching herself and suggested that he might want to send her a revealing picture back, he found himself explaining that he didn't think his erect penis in his hand was a suitable photo opportunity. He then blocked her on Facebook and sighed a big sigh of relief. This dangerous game he was playing was just a game to him, and if Julia found out he didn't want to think about the consequences.

Adam and Julia had sex. Once upon a time they had had great sex. That was one thing they didn't advertise in the medical world: they told you the drugs would help, but what they didn't tell you was the side effects. They left you to read those for yourself if you could be bothered. Sex, he had to admit, hadn't been high on his list of priorities for a long time, but Julia had felt that it would be good for them as a couple to at least try to be 'intimate', as she put it. When he couldn't get it up, he wasn't that surprised, but then, when he managed and still couldn't come, he resorted to the internet, the first port of call for overzealous hypochondriacs. Sexual dysfunction – the drugs that healed his head broke his cock.

Sexual dysfunction did not seem an appropriate consequence of the death of his parents, but then again sex was pleasure and he no longer deserved pleasure. All those years of missing out had now left him obsessed with sex. Sex was escapism, and sexual fantasy even more so. Over the last few months he had weaned himself off the drugs and his libido had returned with a vengeance. It all left him feeling drained and confused.

He knew he was going too far. Since the last incident he felt keeping it within the married set was less dangerous, they had as much to lose as he did. On one occasion he had been sitting at the table while Julia read the news on her iPad, Adam on his, both having coffee. She made remarks about the news; he muttered replies while at the same time typing what he would like to do with his tongue to a pretty redhead he had known from university. Sex that night with Julia had gone up a notch, and she'd seemed to appreciate his return to form.

On Friday at 7 a.m. Adam hauled himself out of bed as usual, still almost drugged with sleep even though he no longer took the sleeping tablets. The boys could see to themselves but 7 a.m. was time to get up. Friday was 'declutter and make sure everything was in its place' day. Then at 3.30 he had to drive to the boys' school to pick them up. Four days a week they took the bus, but Fridays was after-school sports – cricket or rugby, depending on the season.

At 4.30 p.m. they arrived home and Adam began the ritualistic de-manning of the house. An all-male household inevitably became a bit messy, and they made the most of it during the week, until Julia came home on a Friday night, finding fault with everything. This week he must remember to delve down in the sofa cushions and place all the remote controls in the basket. This time he would be more careful which cushions went on which sofa and in which order. Plumping and collecting them from the floor was not enough. What was the point of colour co-ordination if the colours were not co-ordinated? Oh, the joy of being a kept man.

When he was done he logged on to Facebook. He thought about Rachel and what might have been. There had been one party, when they were both drunk, when they might have got together if Rachel's boyfriend hadn't turned up. The party had been at Matt's house, an all-night affair with too much cheap alcohol and nothing to eat but toast and crisps. Rachel's boyfriend had been working and Adam's girlfriend had been unwell. On their own they spent the evening together, scrunched up on one corner of the sofa talking, endless talking. They were comfortable, cuddled up and relaxed in their inebriation, Rachel's head resting on Adam's chest, his left arm resting on her hip while with his right hand he played with the ends of her hair. Every now and then he would tilt his chin down and kiss the top of her head, taking a moment to linger and sniff her hair.

The casserole for dinner that evening went in the oven at 5.30 p.m. as it always did. Then if Julia was stuck in traffic he could just turn the oven off and it would stay warm until she arrived home.

Adam returned to Facebook to shut it down but there she was ... Rachel! She had confirmed him as a friend. He was shocked – he had given up by now.

Rachel, though ... He looked at her page. She looked thinner in her photos – a bit gaunt, but she still had that hair and her daughter had it too. That made him smile: a daughter, a carbon copy of Rachel, who would also be breaking hearts in a few years. Rachel's eyes looked a little hollow and even from her photo she looked as though life had given her a big knock. He wondered what it was. What had knocked her down to the extent that he could see it in a photo?

He noted that Rachel had also commented on a photo Julia had shared to his timeline earlier in the week. A

Saturday football game in the park, somewhere Adam felt comfortable, so they went there sometimes at the weekends. He was standing with the boys and Amy was there in the background, retrieving the ball. He had to admit they all looked great – a happy, functional family.

'Still looking good, Adam,' was all she posted, but it was reason enough for him to send her a message.

The next morning Adam was delighted to see a little '1' above the message symbol on his Facebook page. Contact with Rachel after all these years... He smiled. This was a good day.

Julia

Julia sat in her Solid Black Golf 1.6 TDI SE, shifting her numbing suit-clad behind across the black cloth upholstery. Traffic: the bane of her Friday night existence and her Monday morning dread. She liked her car, but she liked it more when it was parked on the gravel drive at home. Once the traffic cleared and she could put her foot down, she could tolerate her homeward journey. Stationary traffic made her boil.

The car was a perfect accessory for Julia. The Golf matched her style, and her suits and shoes looked good when she leant against it, but she still resented the driving. Black and understated it might be, but you could tell by the heavy thunk of the door as you slammed it that it was not cheap. Julia didn't do cheap. She had bought it new last year, when she had been sure her job was still secure and probate had paid off the hefty mortgage. Adam had messed about with the money for so long it had annoyed her. Her old car had been just that – old – and she had started to feel embarrassed by it. She had spent a long time before she even had the money, planning which car she would buy. It had to look and feel right. She'd thought about an Audi or BMW but they seemed so obvious, and, while a 4x4 had been tempting, owing to the lanes they lived down, the commute to and from Scotland made the cost of fuel prohibitive.

Julia resented the eight or nine hours she spent in travelling every week. Those precious hours of her life that were lost because Adam wouldn't move. It wasn't even as if going home was something she looked forward to; she endured it. If it wasn't for the kids she wouldn't even bother. She sighed – that wasn't true, but it was how she felt when she faced the drive home. The move to the Edinburgh office had been supposed to be for a year, but working in human resources in banking had not been a fun thing to do over the last few years. She was good at her job, very good, and had survived the general cull, but she had been responsible for the redundancies of close colleagues, those who were now regretting that extra sick day or the fact that they had asked for one too many personal days to look after family members. The selection process had been ruthless: points did not make prizes, they made a career in tatters. Most had not borne a grudge and settlements had been fair, but it was not something that sat well with her. A few had let her know what they thought of her 'uptight ass' as they made a detour past her office for the final time.

Since Adam had fallen apart, keeping her job had been the priority. Despite the difficulties she hadn't asked for extra personal days, rarely took all her annual leave and had not had a day off sick for three years. All of their debt and most of their huge mortgage had been paid off once probate was settled, but life was still expensive. Well, theirs was, anyway. Even though Julia was at the top of her game, her salary still wasn't vast. Her personal relocation package had been a massive help, and probate had paid for her studio flat in the city, though not even the tiny space she called home during the week had been cheap. It was a good investment. The relocation package had covered her rent and all her expenses for the first two years, with the expectation that by then she would have bought a house in the area, but, as Adam wouldn't leave his house, buying a studio had been the obvious solution.

The studio flat was in the city centre, with all the noises and smells of humanity doing what it did to survive, all crammed into one claustrophobic space. In the city Julia missed the size of the sky, the vastness that opened up each Friday as she drove homeward, no longer blocked by the endless towering architecture that shaded light from the streets and the constant glow that took the romance from the skies. She loved living in the countryside, being woken by the birds in the morning, the snorts of the lumbering cows moving about in the field not far below their bedroom window. Most of all she loved the variety of the smells: dewy grass that soaked her trainers on an early-morning run and the scent of honeysuckle in the light breeze of a warm summer evening. Cities smelt of cooked food and the rot of rubbish that littered behind the endless takeaways, restaurants and pubs. Most of all Julia missed the life she used to have. She missed the Adam who used to be her husband.

When she missed the past too much, she also drank too much. Sitting in her flat or in a bar until a bottle of red wine was empty, and regretting it as she sweated it out on the treadmill the following morning.

The drunken times were the times she wallowed in self-pity. She had hoped to have a much closer relationship with the boys than she had with Amy, but absence was just that, and nobody felt any fonder of anybody. Amy was five years older than Tom and for the first two years of Amy's life Julia had felt more like her big sister than her mum.

Her parents had just muscled in and taken over. She knew she should be grateful, because without their support her career would have been delayed by years. When Julia had plucked up enough courage to tell them of the pregnancy they hadn't reacted as she had expected; they had remained calm, almost kind. Their attitude had changed, though, when she had confessed that she knew nothing more than the first name of the father. The thought of their well-educated, well-mannered, untouchable daughter lying back and fucking a stranger for pleasure was too much for them to bear. She had tried to find Amy's father, before she told her parents, to let him know, but it seemed that he was nothing more than a gatecrasher at a party and nobody knew who he was. Julia had asked everyone if they knew him, but no one had any idea. There was a photo of him taken by her friend, just him standing in the background on his own, a bottle of Grolsch in his hand. He didn't look like Amy. Julia was rather horrified in her light-of-day realisation that he was not the dreamy stranger she had envisaged. He looked, she hated to say, a little common. The fact that he hadn't been talking to anyone at the party made her think he might not even have been a student, just a chancer who had heard the music, realised it was a student house, opened the door and walked in. Opening that door had impacted on Julia's life in a way she could never forget, and in a way he would never know. Julia hadn't made a mistake before but, when she did, she did it well.

Once Amy was born and her parents took over, Julia had done her best to forget her mistake. She hadn't fought to maintain her rights as Amy's mother. She focused on her career, but never planned her life with Amy; part of her hoped her parents would become so attached they would just keep her and bring her up as if she were their child, not their grandchild. She carried on living at home because that was the one way she could retain her freedom.

When Julia had met Adam, Amy had been two years old, and Julia still hadn't had any bond with her child. Julia liked Adam, and she didn't want him to dump her the moment he found out she had a child, as others had. He was very funny, easy to be with. He was also tall and well-built; the sheer size of him engulfed Julia and made her feel secure. With Adam you didn't have to pretend to be anyone. When Julia had admitted she had a child, she expected their brief relationship to be over, but he just asked her name and how old she was. He didn't ask questions and he didn't judge her or run a mile like most other blokes. When he said he would call the next day, he did. After a month of them seeing each other, he met Amy. Julia was astonished by how well the two just got along; it was a far more natural relationship than she had ever had with her own daughter. This was the point where Julia realised that, when she left home, Amy came with her. Adam was Julia's chance for a normal, happy future. She wasn't letting go of him.

Somehow – Julia was never quite sure how – she kept hold of Adam, and, even though he never proposed, she made sure they married. A late-night discussion on whether or not they should spend the rest of their lives together led to Julia planning the wedding and Adam just being swept along in the momentum. Amy was three by then. They were happy for a long time. Then too many kids and too much debt had soured their relationship. It hadn't been beyond repair until Adam had been broken by the accident. Now it was a relationship that went through the motions; like Friday-night sex, they did it because they felt they ought to.

Julia sometimes felt that it was her fault; maybe she should have given being a mum more of a go. She liked being married and she liked the idea of being a mother. There had been a brief time, when Tom and Alex were still young, where she had been at home for a couple of months between jobs, sitting out her notice period in the last months of spring on 'garden leave'.

One morning stood out among all the others: walking from the car to the local primary school, holding both the boys by the hand. Tom had been in Year One and Alex at the attached pre-school. The sun had been low yet strong, the morning already glorious and warm, their shadows clear on the pavement in front of them. Julia had stopped for a moment; her shadow seemed tall in the middle, despite her actual dimensions, and the two small boys by her side each with a hand in hers. It was beautiful. A monochromatic silhouette of motherhood. It made her sad and happy at the same time. She missed so much of their childhood but at the same time she was so driven to succeed, she seemed unable to stop herself. She loved her kids, she told herself she did, but she just didn't love being with them all the time.

Now Julia sat in her car on the long drive from Edinburgh to the village many miles outside York, which was home for two days, then back to her kitten-swingable apartment for five more days alone. She watched the windscreen wipers as they swished away the mizzle, leaving her a clear view of the row of glowing red tail-lights in front. It was a September afternoon, but the cloud was so low that it already held the dimming light of early dusk. The gloom of the afternoon matched her mood.

Julia shifted her leg from the accelerator, wishing she had changed out of her work heels into the flats she kept for driving. She had been late leaving and wanted to get home: the anxiety it caused Adam if she was late could ruin the weekend, sending him shuffling off to the study to hide. Julia liked the height her heels gave her; she also liked the way they made her walk. What she lacked in height she made up for in presence. She glanced at herself in the rear-view mirror. She looked tired but, she conceded, still rather attractive for a woman in her forties. She worked hard at it. The glossy, sharp dark brown bob that swung just above her shoulders didn't come cheap. Nor did the facials, the tooth-whitening and the gym membership. Her work suits were snug on her tiny frame, skirts sitting just above her knee or trousers that skimmed her hips and then fitted down her legs teamed with well-tailored jackets and, of course, heels. Flawless make-up and sleek hair. Nobody except Adam saw Julia without her make-up. She looked every inch the corporate part she played. Her days were long, and when she left the office early on a Friday for the four-hour drive home she was already worn-out and weary.

Julia was up every morning at 5.45 a.m. then straight to the gym. Back to her flat by seven, where she whizzed up a protein shake for breakfast. Then shower, dress for work and pick up a black coffee from the little Italian coffee shop that conveniently sat on the corner. There she waited in the queue to be served by the gorgeous but very young barista, who knew her well and always had her order ready by the time she reached him, before heading up the stairs to her office on the fourth floor. She was always at her desk before 8 a.m. Leaving before seven was rare, unless she had a hair appointment or other treatment booked. Lunch was always a salad at her desk that her assistant, Linda, picked up for her on the way back from her lunch break. Dinner was a work social or a solo affair in her flat. When the isolation of the flat became too much she would resort to dinner in a bar, but she was always in bed by 11 p.m. She did this so that she could leave at 3 p.m. on a Friday and arrive after 10 a.m. on a Monday. The flexible working hours had been agreed as part of the move. The move that meant she was as lonely in Edinburgh as she was in her cottage just outside York.

Julia changed gear and hung on to the clutch as she edged forward in the traffic and thought of home. Adam and Julia had bought the run-down cottage, which sat in a tiny hamlet, just outside a wonderful old market town, nestled at the edge of the Howardian Hills. It was a beautiful yet impractical place to live. It had been her dream to make a family home. Julia had imagined parties and suppers in her dream kitchen. The real kitchen was as cold in atmosphere as the stone floor that her heels clicked across on a Friday night, where she hugged a solitary figure hunched over the range cooker, preparing a dinner that they had little appetite to eat.

Family life wasn't what Julia had imagined. She preferred her fantasy of hardworking weeks and carefree, happy week-ends, barbecues in the garden and long sunny evenings sipping wine with friends while the kids played together. Curling up in front of the fire, in the depths of a dark Yorkshire winter, to watch a family movie with blissfully rosy-cheeked children and mugs of steaming hot chocolate, was in Julia's fantasy, along with children who went to bed the first time they were told and remembered to take off their muddy shoes before running through the house. The reality of family life with young children was very different: mountains of washing, endlessly tripping over toys, squabbling, screaming and the constant demands. Family time at home had been enough to push her, the most motivated and organised person she knew, to the limit. Julia preferred the idea of the family to the reality.

If Adam hadn't fallen apart, life would have been easier now. The kids were independent – still demanding but in a different way. Julia and Adam could have spent time together. They could have started to have time alone, something they had never done because Amy had been there from the start. Adam had been an amazing father to Amy, and even when Julia had told Amy the truth about her biological father she hadn't been fazed. Adam was her dad. She had been closer to Adam as a child than she had been to Julia, and had really suffered when Adam fell apart. It was then that she had finally turned to Julia. Amy deeply resented Adam's becoming unreachable. As a child she had always curled up on his lap, hooking her left arm behind his head and playing with his curly hair. The boys had been just as close to him. Tom had coped well after the accident, showing an immense amount of maturity, although his schoolwork had suffered a little. Alex was like Julia: he had a hot temper and found it hard to hide his disappointment at his father's inability to cope.

Julia would have moved them all to Edinburgh when she was promoted, where the surrounding countryside was equally beautiful, but even though the cottage had been Julia's project Adam clung to it, not wanting to let go of his security. Did Adam ever consider what her week was like? No, he just sat there waiting for her and refusing to get on with his life. The run-down cottage they had bought a couple of years before the accident had been transformed into a wonderful spacious home in which they just existed. Amy hadn't even wanted to come back after she finished university.

Amy lived and worked in Manchester as a trainee interior designer. She had been fascinated by the house renovation and couldn't get enough of fabric swatches and colour charts, often preferring to go shopping with Julia for tiles, curtains or soft furnishings than going out partying with her friends. Julia had loved the time they had spent together planning the décor for the cottage. They had seemed finally to find a bond, and as adults they were now close. Amy worked for a firm of architects who specialised in the refurbishment of pubs and hotels. She loved her job and like her mum was very career-driven, hoping to set up her own company in a few years, once she had gained a reputation for excelling at her trade.

Julia was often told how lucky she was to live in the amazing city of Edinburgh, but she saw very little of it. She tried to take most of her holidays around New Year and in August, when the tourists were at their gaggling worst. Traffic became unbearable then, and the journey home impossible. The traffic this Friday afternoon was bad enough, still with the tail end of the tourists losing their way and holding up those bound for home. The cars in front eased forward a few hundred metres and Julia shifted her car into second gear, before grinding to an almost bumper-touching halt once again. She shifted her shoulders up and down; they ached from the week of hunched-up anxiety at her desk and sitting through endless meetings. Adam used to massage her back...before. Lately, work had lost its appeal. Maybe it was time to look for a new career.

Driving with a hangover was not helping Julia's mood, either. She had spent last night drinking with her boss, Jim; he was somewhere way up the chain of command. A few years older than Julia, he had been her mentor since she joined the company when the boys were small. He was a good man, kind and conscientious. To Julia he had become a good friend, and her promotion had been a few months after his and the main reason she was picked for the job at the Edinburgh head office. She knew that Adam, and at least half the office, thought there was something going on between them. They were wrong. In Jim Julia had simply found a solid friend and confidant. He had supported her through all the years of Adam falling apart.

Julia switched on a CD, jabbing at the control button, then changing to the stem controls on the steering wheel. The local radio station had been sending waves of crackling interference through her iPod, rendering listening unpleasant. The CD felt wrong; she jabbed at the buttons again, changing the track then sighing and switching to the radio. The DJ's whiny singsong voice on the radio annoyed her, so she rummaged around in her side pocket for another CD. This was better: some girl power compilation Amy had given her as a joke one Mother's Day, but Julia rather liked it. The traffic stopped again, tail-lights and brake lights lighting up like tasteless fairy lights. She hit the off button and sat in silence. Leaning forward, she banged her Botoxed forehead on the steering wheel. The car in front inched forward then surged about twenty metres, catching Julia unawares; she made her gearbox graunch and the car kangaroo as she let the clutch out too fast. Stalling, she felt like leaving it stalled. She was tempted to get out of the car, stride off as fast as her four-inch heels would allow her and head to the nearest airport. Instead she would continue her monotonous trip, bitch at Adam for the way the house looked, drink too much wine, eat dinner and have meaningless sex just because that was what they did on a Friday night. Same old fucking routine; they couldn't break the routine. Christ, if they did, that messed up Adam's mind and he would throw one hell of a wobble and back to square one they would go.

Julia banged her head one more time before starting the car and moving forward to the accompaniment of more pissed-off people sounding their car horns. She raised a middle finger at the fat-faced bitch in the car behind just for the hell of it. Maybe she would take offence and they could fight it out right here in the middle carriageway. That would give the homeward-bound commuters something to talk about over their Friday night takeaway!

Julia thought picking up a takeaway would be a pleasant change, but Adam didn't do change. He did the same things at the same time. He ate the same meals on the same days. At 7 a.m. he got up – heaven forbid he might just want to cuddle up or have a quickie before the boys got out of bed. The boys didn't wake until late, they could have a relaxed morning just the two of them, but no, at seven he had to get out of bed, shower and be dressed and downstairs for 7.20. By 7.30 a.m. he had to have coffee and breakfast. At least the rest of them didn't have to join him in his routine insanity.

How did you go from marrying this nice, chilled-out guy to living with a complete weirdo? The first year after the accident she had understood; she wasn't that much of an insensitive bitch. The second year, yes, she could cope with that. But this New Year it would be four years. She found herself wanting to scream at him, 'It was an accident, a fucking accident!' It wouldn't help, though, she knew that. If he had just taken the support offered then maybe…and now he had weaned himself off the drugs and the obsessive behaviour was getting worse all the time.

Thank God for Jim, she thought, pressing her hand down hard on the centre of the steering wheel, wishing the car horn were armed so she could open fire on the twat who had just decided to force his way in front of her. He shrugged, his hands held out to either side – no point holding the steering wheel when the traffic was this slow. Then he blew her a kiss in his rear-view mirror and Julia laughed.

Julia looked at the other drivers around her. All stuck in their wheeled metal boxes, trying to be somewhere. The fat-faced bitch behind her looked sad. Julia wondered if she went home on her own and ate a meal for two just because she had no one to share it with. The guy in the car in front, who had blown her a kiss, was watching her in his mirror; she tried not to look back but even in the dim light he had lovely eyes. Julia looked away, and smiled at the family who were singing along to whatever music they were playing. They looked too happy, so she watched the young man to her left as he texted away on his phone. She looked back to the kissing man with the lovely eyes, who was still watching her, and as he caught her eye he pointed to the next sign for the services and mouthed the word 'coffee' into his mirror. Julia shook her head but smiled all the same, flattered by the attention.

The traffic started to move. Julia shifted the gear to fifth and put her foot down for ten minutes before grinding to another inexplicable halt. Shifting back to first and rolling slowly forward, she banged her head back on the headrest and let out a long, groaning sigh. She switched to Radio 4 but found the talking irritating today; she was too late for the afternoon play. Now it was the programme with the obituaries – last thing she needed, more death. Four years of nothing but death. Life was for the living and all that crap. 'It's not a rehearsal, Adam!' she shouted at the windscreen. At the same time wondering what he would write in her obituary – just the word 'bitch'? She heard him mutter it enough.

Julia's mind wandered back and forth, through past and present. This was her ritual on every Friday night journey. She tried to make sense of it all, yet her thoughts were random and inconclusive. She shifted her thoughts, from the kids, to Adam, to her lack of sex life and then to plans for Christmas. She made sense of nothing. She put the CD back on and tried to sing along but then her mind jumped again and for a moment she regretted the decision not to go for coffee with Lovely Eyes. She lost herself in wistful thoughts of a handsome single man, who gave her the night of her life and begged her to stay with him forever. With her luck, though, he would turn out to be a serial adulterer with herpes, a three-inch dick and a problem with premature ejaculation.

Julia wondered if she should just prove everyone right and get down to business with Jim. Adam thought she was shagging him all week anyway. More wishful thinking? She cackled to herself. No, Jim would be wrong; it would ruin the friendship she relied on to keep her going. He was her friend, not her lover. She valued that above all else. Change that dynamic and she would be lost. Anyway, Jim had a very happy marriage and a great family. She went there for dinner and left feeling lonelier than ever. His wife, Kath, was great, and Jim was too old for her anyway.

The traffic flowed. Julia calmed and shifted her body into a relaxed driving position. She was proud of her body; content with the way she looked. She had to work at it, though; it made her seem uptight, always having the low-calorie lunches and dinners, often skipping meals and living on her nerves and black coffee. Too much coffee also meant constant tooth-whitening, which made her teeth sensitive. At least sensitive teeth put her off her food. She thought about lunch with Jim today. He was such easy company. It was her Friday moaning session but today they had both been moaning: too much to drink the night before meant heads that weren't functioning the day after. She shared her dread about going home to Adam and how it was tempered by her desire to see the kids.

She should call Amy, see if she was avoiding coming home this weekend. Her daughter answered after three rings.

'Hi, honey, how are you?' Julia asked.

'Fine, Mum, I'm just leaving work. I'm meeting some friends and no, I can't this weekend,' Amy pre-empted her mum's question.

'Hangover on Saturday, then. Couldn't you just come up for Sunday? Gran and Grandad are coming. Bring the new boyfriend.' Julia laughed, hiding the hurt.

'Yeah, right, bring him home to the nutty family, with the officially insane dad, great idea...and Gran and Grandad – you're not really selling this idea, Mum. Think I'd better get him thoroughly hooked before I risk that one!'

'Amy! It's not that bad. Your dad can't help it. You had fun last time you came up, didn't you?' Julia asked.

'I guess it wasn't so bad, but I'm not ready to lose this boyfriend; I really like this one. I brought Tim up too soon and he dumped me three weeks later!'

'Tim dumped you because he found you texting that bloke you met in the pub, not because your dad is loopy.'

'I know, but I really like Mike, so I'm not risking it yet. I don't want Dad getting all wound up because we haven't had coffee at ten and lunch at one! And, before you say it again, I know he can't help it and yes, he is better than he used to be. But he might be better if he stopped just sitting around fretting and went back to work. It's nearly four years, Mum, and it's not fair on you. Sorry, none of my business.' Amy sounded annoyed.

'I know, sweetheart, but you know, he has finally updated his LinkedIn profile and he called some old work colleagues about references. I think he may be starting to get better.'

'Yeah, right, Mum, course he is. I believe you believe that. I have to go. I'll call you at home on Sunday. Take care on the way home and don't forget to stop for a coffee. Promise, OK?'

'OK, I will, I promise. Have a good night, sweetie. Speak soon.' Julia hung up.

She indicated, moved into the inside lane and pulled in at Washington Services as she always did. Hunting for space near the entrance, she spotted a family strapping the last of their kids into a large people-carrier, and pulled over, indicating. Impatiently tapping her fingers on the wheel as the reversing lights came on, she started to edge forward, wanting to make sure she didn't miss her space. 'Come on,' she sighed impatiently, edging very slowly on the clutch. 'What the fuck is taking so long?' She sighed again and released the clutch just as the car started to reverse, meaning she had to hit the brakes hard, and by the time the people-carrier reversed out it could barely get past Julia's car as she tried to squeeze into the space almost before they had left. She parked at a slight angle.

Gathering up her bag and holding her trench coat over her head to keep her hair dry, she splashed her heels over the wet tarmac. It was dark and cloudy, the rain now heavy. She felt the wet splashes on her tights and sighed. Maybe they should just move south and away from the rain! Julia stopped off at the loo and headed for Costa. Checking her watch, she realised that she wasn't making bad time despite the traffic. If she was late she had coffee to go. Today, she was on time so she could drink it from a cup at a table. Fifteen minutes out of the traffic would be a welcome break...despite the fact she was in a Moto services she smiled at her joke. The smile soon faded and was replaced by more sighing, along with a series of eye-rolls as the old man in front became confused by the array of coffee choices on offer. In the end he ordered a tea and a slice of lemon cake. Julia just hoped she didn't turn into something like that as she got older. She was quite sure she wouldn't.

She settled in a corner with her large Americano, the huge cup engulfing her face as she drank. Checking her phone for messages, she saw one from Adam, which made her give yet another sigh, knowing what it would say before she opened it. It would say the casserole was in the oven and could she call him if she was going to be late, see you later xx. It always said the same thing. She wondered how his world would crumble if he didn't send it. What was the consequence of a failure to stick to his routine? Julia crossed and uncrossed her legs, then crossed them again, agitated and unsettled by the thought of going home. She wondered, sometimes, if she should just have a weekend off and stay in Edinburgh. It was a great city and she never had a chance to explore it. Sometimes in the summer she walked into the city centre just because she was lonely. She would sit in a bar, have a couple of drinks and catch a taxi back to her flat. It wasn't unusual for her to have some male attention, but it was brief; she wasn't interested. She always made that very clear: she was married. If they ever asked if she was happily married, she would just smile, not committing herself to an answer. Those who were lonely and not just trawling in the hope of sex would sometimes stay and chat. Julia liked this, and once or twice she thought she might give in and use one of these men just for a few hours. She hadn't so far. What would be the point? That could just be messy.

Julia drained the last of her coffee, pausing for a moment before continuing the inevitability of her southbound journey and home.

The motorway was clear and the rain began to ease. Julia sat in the outside lane, coming up fast on the cars in front and flashing her lights at them until they moved over. She liked to drive fast, pushing the speed limits. She had been lucky so far, never having been stopped for speeding; traffic police were few and far between up here. The A68 was the worst, with a series of speed cameras, but she knew where they were. One hundred and sixty-one miles from Edinburgh she left the A1(M) and headed down the A61. This part of the journey drove her mad, twisting and turning, stopping and starting through the tail end of the rush-hour traffic, a series of mini-roundabouts that everyone drove over the middle of, impatient to beat the next person on to it and out at their exit. Julia sat on the bumper of the car in front, cursing them as they edged forward but failed to act, missing their chance. She shouted at them and pushed as close to their bumper as she could without touching, as if driving up their ass would turn them into the sort of driver she felt they should be.

'For fuck's sake, learn to drive!' she shouted to no one and everyone. 'Come on, come on. Fucking idiot!' She raised her hands skyward, almost hitting the roof and chipping a set of perfect painted nails. She rocked the car on the clutch and accelerator, holding on to the steering wheel with one hand, the other on the gearstick, ready, knuckles white on bony hands. All calm and reason had left her. Aware that she was losing it, she distracted herself by calling her mum and dad, making sure they were still coming to lunch on Sunday. They didn't answer.

Six miles of the winding, narrow lanes of the A170 led to home. Julia liked this part of the drive so long as she didn't get stuck behind some driver who was almost dead at the wheel. Hats and gloves, old people who hadn't figured out the controls for the heating! If the road was clear she could test the car, push it round the bends and then home.

Home! At least the boys would be glad to see her. Her arrival meant normality and freedom. She would take them places, drop them at friends' houses without all the hand-wringing anxiety. She knew it must be hard to be Adam, but what was the point of dwelling? In her job mental health issues were the one area she found difficult to understand, but sitting behind her desk she couldn't tell somebody with depression to pull themselves together without the threat of a claim for constructive dismissal landing on her desk. She had been to the seminars and done the training, but still she couldn't comprehend how someone could just give up and hide away. You had to face your problems head-on, challenge yourself and get on with life.

Adam had once been good for Julia – slowed down her stress, stopped her going off at the deep end. Now it was different: she felt as though she had a dependant middle-aged child. She had three kids, and she didn't need any more. Dismissing the needs of the depressed in the workplace was one thing, but living with it was different. She just didn't have the patience to deal with it any more.

She thought about arriving home. Before the accident Adam would have enveloped her in a huge hug and then kiss her as though he meant that kiss. Now she would almost peck him on the cheek, her lips floating above the stubble that he always promised he would shave off before she came home, so he felt her breath. Despite her stature she now felt bigger than him, his protector. It was a job she didn't want. She wanted normal. She wanted to go out to dinner, drink a bottle or two of wine together; she wanted to enjoy her life, not watch him wallow in his misery and succumb to his insane routines. It had been an accident, nobody blamed him; he could still care without it ruining all their lives.

Julia shuddered at the thought of that night. Glad that it had been dark, so she couldn't see the blood. Adam had been silent until he heard the sirens and then, almost as if they had been singing a song, he had joined in with a loud sobbing wail. Julia had felt embarrassed but the paramedic didn't seem at all perturbed and just smiled at her and said not to worry, it was just the shock. Adam rocked back and forth on the ground, so total was his distress, and the paramedic had to hold him with a firm hand while he gave him something to calm him down.

Adam had been concussed; the sliding car had caused him to shift in his seat and the airbag hadn't hit him straight on; the side of his head had been bruised and swollen. He had stayed in hospital overnight, but even when he left hospital he was given drugs that left him sedated. Julia had escaped with a fractured arm, not even a serious fracture, and minor cuts and bruises, not even enough for stitches. Yet Adam's parents... Julia tried hard, very hard, not to think of the last breath of Adam's mum. Sometimes, she would remember the enormity of the moment and she would feel vulnerable, but just as quickly she would dismiss it and get on with life.

Julia pulled on to the driveway, gravel scrunching under her tyres, driving round to the side of the house, where the York stone paved pathway led round to the back door. She loved the back door, a half glazed timber, painted stable door. Julia and Amy had spent hours poring over the Farrow & Ball paint charts and settled on a Purbeck Stone eggshell finish for all the exterior woodwork. They had tried to engage Adam in the process, but he just said white gloss would be fine. He didn't understand the importance of a quality finish. Julia spent hours liaising with the building firm and had to admit they were excellent. She had employed them after taking up several references and they had proved worth the extra money. The finish throughout the house was stunning. The architect had also done an amazing job, listening to everything she wanted for her home.

The cottage had been small when they started, but, by converting the stables at the rear and joining them to the main cottage, as well as adding an extra bedroom and en suite, they had made this an impressive home. Julia paused at the back door, taking a deep breath in. It was a shame she never got to show it to anyone, she thought as she took the last step towards the back door, pushing down the handle and stepping over the threshold on to the doormat before her heels clacked across the stone floor. The back porch led into the main kitchen/dining area; a high vaulted ceiling with skylights let the sun flood in and the moonlight cast shadows. Julia adored her kitchen.

'I'm home,' she called out as she opened the second door into the kitchen, wheeling her small suitcase behind her.

Adam turned round from the cooker and checked his watch before walking across to peck her cheek with terse lips. 'You're only four minutes late,' he said, half-smiling. 'Dinner will be ready in twenty minutes.' Despite his brusque manner he looked relieved. The evening was on schedule; he liked that.

'I'll just grab a quick shower, then, after a coffee. Did you open the wine?' Julia said the same thing at the same time every Friday. She sometimes worried that she was joining Adam in his obsessive behaviour. If the time was wrong, however, what she had to do was coax Adam from his study and talk to him and hold him. She had to spend time telling him it would all be OK and that she had called and spoken to the kids. She had to tell him there weren't any accidents, just heavy traffic; she hated it when she was late. Sometimes, Adam would just refuse to come out of his study for the whole weekend apart from to go to bed and to eat. On those weekends she would take the kids out. They would spend too much money, eat in too many restaurants and avoid the oppressive force that was Adam. She suspected the boys actually preferred the doom-and-gloom weekends to the tight schedule of the Saturday and Sundays when all was well in Adam's world.

'Yes, the wine is open and there's a fresh pot of coffee.' Adam said the same thing every Friday if the time was right, and in a moment he would walk across the kitchen in his black socks and pour the coffee into a white china mug and hand it to Julia. The coffee would be the right temperature and Julia would park herself at the large pine kitchen table for a few moments while she drank it. Then she would stand up, walk across the kitchen, place the cup in the dishwasher. Then she would tell Adam she would be just ten minutes. She would remove her heels and carry them upstairs along with her small suitcase; her handbag she would hang on a hook in the hall.

Once upstairs she would try to relax a little, take five minutes to unwind in the shower. Let the force of the water pummel her back. She would pin her hair up, but it would be damp and leave her perfect shiny bob wavy around her neck and face. She would dry herself, change into jeans and a T-shirt or jumper depending on the weather and return downstairs to find the boys in whichever hole they were hiding. It was a long time since they had rushed to the door to meet her.

If she was home on time Friday night dinner was OK, always some sort of casserole that Adam had made. He had become a good cook over the last few years. The wine and conversation would flow for an hour or so, then the boys would retreat to their digital corners and she and Adam would watch the television or a film from separate sofas until one of them had to admit they were tired. This admission meant bed and the inevitable Friday night fuck, a functional end to a frustrating week.

That particular Friday was not the same as usual. Everything up to the point of Julia yawning and saying she was tired was the same, but then, when she went to bed, Adam didn't follow. After waiting for half an hour, Julia went downstairs to check he was OK. She padded on bare feet into the lounge, where the television was still on. Adam was sitting on the sofa with his back to Julia as she approached. Standing behind him, she noted that he was on Facebook, and reading a private message. He realised she was there and flipped the cover over the screen before she could see any more.

'You OK?' Julia asked.

'Yes, sorry, be up in a minute, just catching up with an old friend.' He laughed.

'Not breaking out of the routine, are you, Adam?' Julia replied.

Adam didn't reply, just gave her an awkward smile, turned off the TV and followed her upstairs.

On Saturday Adam was still smiling. Julia wondered if he was smoking dope or whether she should check the house for opiates. The smiling unnerved her. She smiled all week. She laughed all week. If Amy came up or she escaped with the boys she would smile and laugh. At home, though, she was quiet, guarded, never sure what would set Adam off. If he thought she was laughing at him, the room would darken, doors would slam and expensive items were often smashed. All of this was followed by the deep gloom and then, before she left, would come the remorse. Adam and Julia together were a toxic mix of angry resentment.

By Saturday afternoon Julia noted that Adam was constantly checking his iPad. That was it, she thought. Some fantasy he was having on Facebook again. He thought she was stupid. He had left himself logged in more than once. The first time she had just glanced, not meaning to read the messages, but she'd been drawn in by the flirty and sometimes graphic language. There were several women's names in his inbox that he was sending regular messages to. For a while Julia guessed his password. What she read was amusing and reminded her of the old Adam, when he was fun to be with. It all seemed rather harmless and she had not felt threatened; after all, most of them lived miles away, and Adam was hardly likely to invite them into this sanctuary. The thought of him driving off to have an illicit affair was farcical. She imagined him checking into a hotel then panicking that he wouldn't be home for his Thursday lunch of ham and tomato sandwiches on wholemeal bread, or having to stop mid-coitus as it was time for coffee.

Every three months Adam would change his password and Julia had run out of guesses, so she could no longer check to see what he was up to. If it made him smile, maybe it was still a good thing? It might be nice if he could just make the effort to smile for her, though. He looked as though he was trying sometimes, but then his lips would get caught on his teeth and it would turn into a sort of snarl.

On Saturday evening Julia made the long round trip to get supplies for Sunday lunch with her parents. On occasions like this Adam and Julia worked well together, often sharing the cooking. Adam understood the dynamic of her relationship with her parents. They had never talked about it, they had never needed to, and even in his deepest times of gloom he would be there in the background when they visited. A reassuring presence in a turmoil of emotion. They were the only people who could leave Julia spinning on her head and not knowing in which direction to fall. Adam knew she could unravel in an instant and he would reach out and touch her, just to let her know he was there. She couldn't do that for him, she didn't know how; she always said too much and did too little.

When she got back, laden with bags, Julia found Adam and the boys in the lounge together, watching a movie and laughing. Adam was laughing. She sat next to him and he pulled her towards him. She laid her head on her chest. It was a good place to be, a place she felt at home, even now, after all that had happened. She stayed there for a long time, Adam's arm holding her to him, before she remembered the bag of frozen food and dashed off. She was sad to end the moment.

On Sunday morning Julia woke up with that 'wrecked ship' feeling. Her mouth was dry, as if she had woken face-down on a sandy beach, and her back was hot as if the sun was baking down on it. In reality she had a slight hangover from finishing off a bottle of wine while she was unpacking the shopping, and Adam had for some unknown reason shifted across worlds into her half of the bed and was hugging her. She disentangled herself and went to get a glass of water. She stood in the doorway, just watching Adam sprawled across the bed. It was a good feeling, waking up with him like that. When they had first been a couple they had always slept wrapped around each other. Sweaty in the summer; snug in the winter. Julia wanted that back. She wanted to come home at night, she wanted her husband fixed – she wanted her family back together. She decided she would start pushing harder for Jim to confirm her position in the Leeds branch and if that didn't work out she would start looking for a job elsewhere. She just needed to convince Adam it was time to go back to work; if he could earn an income, then it would make her own options less limited.

Ten a.m. and Julia was showered and changed into a 'nice dress', the boys were tidy, and even Adam had agreed to wear a plain black T-shirt with his jeans. The table was laid and the beef was in the oven. Julia paced. Parental lunches were not happy occasions. The expectation of the event was far worse than the event itself. Now all she had to do was convince Adam to make Yorkshire puddings to go with the beef.

Julia found Adam in his study. He was on Facebook again; she had a quick glimpse before he switched screens. She would have to find a way to work out his password so she could see what he was up to.

'Adam, is there any chance you could whip up some of your Yorkshire puddings for lunch? You know mine are rubbish...'

Adam stood up, wrapped his arms around Julia, then bent down and kissed the top of her head. 'No problem,' he said, and walked off towards the kitchen.

Julia had to lean against the door-frame. Coaxing and cajoling were the usual order of things, and she wondered if he was on new medication. She wondered if she should just ask him. Perhaps she would get a chance to have a root round later and see what she could find. She didn't have time now. Her parents were arriving soon and she still had to make an apple pie for pudding.

Julia heard the scrunch of car tyres on gravel, which made her stomach churn. It was 11.30 a.m. She was convinced that her dad pulled over in the lay-by further up the lane so he could arrive at precisely the appointed time. He was anal enough to do it. Julia glanced out of the window – her father was nowhere to be seen. And her mother marched into the house; normally she would knock and wait.

'Mum?' Julia asked what was wrong without uttering another word.

'Darling, give me the biggest glass of wine you've got,' her mother replied.

'Red or white?'

'Wine, Julia; the colour is irrelevant.'

Julia did as she was told and cast a sideways glance at a startled-looking Adam. Returning with the large glass of red wine, she waited until her mother had gulped down half. They all stood there in awkward silence. Adam approached.

'Why don't you sit down, Sue? Are you OK, and where is Richard?' Adam asked the questions Julia couldn't voice. They both watched as Sue downed the rest of the glass before handing it to Julia for a refill. Not daring to argue, Julia refilled the glass and they stood in silence again, waiting for her mother to speak. Sue sat at the table for several minutes, taking big sips of the second full glass.

The boys appeared at the doorway, sensing something was wrong. 'What's up with Grandma?' Tom said in his best stage whisper. Adam and Julia turned to the boys, both shrugging.

'I'll tell you what's up with Grandma,' Sue slurred. Her back to the boys, she turned to face them all, her face flushed. 'Grandpa is fucking some woman at his creative writing class. Apparently they have been "sexting"; I saw it on his phone. I didn't even know he knew how to send a text! I read them all and trust me, none of them were creative. Then again, Richard never was.'

The boys started to giggle in an uncontrollable teenage way. Adam ushered them out of the room. A drunk, swearing grandmother was not a positive role model for impressionable teenage boys! He tried to hide a smile, while Julia looked horrified. Sue carried on drinking and nobody knew what to do.

Helping Adam to get her very drunk mother to bed was not how Julia had expected Sunday lunch to pan out. She had expected the usual polite, somewhat tense conversation, compliments about the food, and the usual backstabbing session about Adam while they cleared the table and loaded the dishwasher together.

Julia watched her mum for a while as she drifted off to sleep; she took off her shoes and placed two pillows behind her to stop her rolling on to her back. As tempting as the thought was, she thought it best to prevent her mother from choking to death on her own vomit. She placed a bowl by the side of the bed, although she doubted her mum would need it, and a large glass of water and two paracetamol on the bedside table for when she woke up.

It was a strange feeling, seeing this self-pedestalising paragon of virtue start to crumble. Julia's parents were not quite what they seemed. Her father was off having an affair and her mother could down a bottle of wine in less than twenty minutes – although, from the effect it had on her, Julia suspected that her mother generally exercised restraint where the consumption of alcohol was concerned.

Julia returned to the kitchen, where Adam was finishing making lunch.

'Well, that's a bit of a turn-up,' he said as she walked into the room.

'Which bit?' Julia asked. 'The fact that my mother swears and drinks and has an unsatisfactory sex life, or the fact that my dad is doing some other woman?'

'Both, really.' Adam laughed, 'Do you think she'll want lunch when she wakes up? Or a nice greasy fry-up?'

Adam was leaning against the range cooker and just for a moment he looked like his old self, laughing, teasing her and standing up at his full height despite the leaning: he wasn't hunched over and his forehead wasn't screwed up in anxiety.

'What do I do now?' Julia asked, walking across the room and sliding into his big arms. For once she felt out of her depth and needed his support.

'You need to talk to your dad,' Adam said.

'I know, I do.' Julia looked up at him, tilting her head back and giving him her most appealing look. 'Couldn't you do it? You know, a sort of man-to-man thing. He might be less embarrassed to talk to you.'

'No chance,' said Adam. 'The one advantage of being an orphan is that I don't have to deal with wayward parents.'

Julia watched as a moment of pain flashed through his eyes. He smiled at her, kissed her head and spun her round to face the direction of her bag, where he knew her phone was.

'I think I'll use the landline in the study – this could take a while,' Julia said, changing direction and heading off with a pensive but determined look on her face.

'Do you want me to bring you a glass of wine?' Adam shouted after her.

'Strange thing: after seeing my mother drunk, I've rather gone off the idea of drinking! Coffee would be nice, though, please,' Julia shouted back as she disappeared round the corner. A moment later she reappeared. 'Adam, you don't think Dad is really having an affair, do you?'

'Jules, there's only one way to find out. Ask him.'

'Yes, I know.' Julia walked off round the corner again. It was years since Adam had called her Jules, and it felt strange. She also had butterflies in her stomach. How on earth did you ring your dad up and say his wife had passed out in the spare bedroom and ask him if he was having an affair with some woman he had been sexting?

She sat down at the desk she shared with Adam. His iPad and laptop were both sitting there. She was tempted to have a quick look at his Facebook page and emails to see what had changed his mood. She should get on with the task of calling her dad, but anything to stall. She chose his laptop. He was logged off Facebook. She flicked to the side of the screen, where his notifications were. He hadn't logged off from these. There the brief beginning of a message from a name she was not familiar with. A woman's name.

Julia dialled her father, trying to concentrate. She had to find a way on to Adam's Facebook page – she needed to read his messages to know what was going on.

'Hello.' It was her dad's familiar voice. Now she heard him she couldn't quite believe what she was about to say.

'Dad, it's Julia '

'So is your mother there, then?' he interrupted, sounding anxious.

'Yes, she's—'

'Gone mad?' her dad finished the sentence for her.

'Passed out drunk, actually, but yes, she was hopping mad. Is it true?'

'Oh, for goodness' sake, Julia! Do *you* think it's true? Your mother is senile. I tried to explain it to her but she wouldn't listen, just jumped into my car and shot off down the road. I hope my car is in one piece...the speed she drove up the road!'

'Mum and car are both fine. So what's going on?'

'Why don't you ask your mother to explain?'

'I can't, Dad – she's sleeping off the excesses of a bottle of wine she downed less than twenty minutes after she arrived. She swore and then told me about the texts.' Julia stopped short of saying the sexts and mentioning the accusations.

'Yes, the texts happened, but not in the context you think. It was an exercise from my creative writing class!

We paired up to text each other suggestive texts, or "sexts" as I believe they are called. Damn difficult it is too. It's an exercise in communication and clarity of understanding and how a brief message, especially with a suggestive content, could be misinterpreted. We have also been talking about the role of sexually descriptive scenes in literature and commenting on modern-day society and the failure to communicate other than through virtual media such as text and the dreaded Facebook. Oh, you should include me on your friends list, by the way – I'm quite the modern father now, you know.'

'And did you explain this to Mum?' Julia asked.

'Yes, of course I did, Julia. If I were having an affair I would hardly have left my phone open on the side table for her to read, would I? But the stupid women didn't believe me. Julia, I'm seventy-two years old – why on earth would I want to be sexting a twenty-six-year-old woman who has three children under the age of seven? She can barely string a sentence together let alone have any hope of writing a book. Sorry, that was judgemental of me, but honestly, she's not the sharpest! She just happens to have read *Fifty Shades* and thinks there may be some money in this writing malarkey! Although as far as sexting goes she certainly knows what to say.' Julia's father laughed, then sighed. 'Talk some sense into your mother, will you, Julia? You're a sensible girl, and I cannot be bothered with all this drama.'

Julia stifled a laugh. Her dad had never been that fond of her as a child, so the thought of him taking up with an unintelligible woman under thirty with three young kids in tow was rather amusing. She found herself wanting to rush through to the kitchen to tell Adam. It was a long time since she had felt she wanted to tell Adam anything...and then her enthusiasm waned as she remembered the Facebook message.

'I'll talk to Mum when she wakes up,' Julia said. 'In the meantime, why don't you drive up? It's roast beef and apple pie for lunch, will that tempt you? Mum has drunk too much to drive home, too. You can both stay the night and drive home in the morning.'

'Thank you, Julia, but, as good as the lunch sounds, I will decline on this occasion, as a night off from your mother currently sounds far more tempting. If Adam is up to it, why don't you drive her car back later and drop her off? I understand if you want her out of the way, but equally, if you want her keep her overnight, don't stop yourselves.'

Julia was a little shocked; she had never heard her father talk like that about her mother before. She hoped Adam was up to the drive. She'd better check how much he had drunk or they would be stuck with her mum overnight. The drive together might be a handy time to talk about Facebook and who Adam was messaging. She wasn't sure how she could work it into the conversation, but they would be alone so she would try.

'I'll try to get Adam to drive her back later, Dad.'

'Yes, I thought you might. Never mind, it was worth a try. I'll see you later. Good luck with talking some sense into her.'

'See you later, Dad,' Julia said.

'Yes, later,' her father said, hanging up.

Julia stood for a moment with the phone still in her hand. First she would check her mum was OK, and then she would think about how on earth she was going to talk to her. Adam and his missed opportunity from the past would have to be dealt with later. Julia reached for the phone: she needed to speak to a friend; she needed to speak to Jim.

part two

---

lives intertwine

One

Rachel stared out of the window, watching as a lone magpie hopped about the garden. She drank cold water from a glass still warm from the dishwasher and decided her life was tepid.

Rachel believed in true love, destiny, second chances and soulmates. Most people who believed in these things found life a constant disappointment, but today Rachel smiled as a second magpie joined the first. The smile warmed her harsh expression. That smile was more than a moment of happiness contained in a small droplet of hope.

Adam – Friday 6 September, 17.43
Rachel!! OMG. How is life treating you??

Rachel – Friday 6 September, 20.22
Hello! Gosh, big question from someone I haven't heard from for years. Have you got a lot of spare time? I'll fill you in, lol. I'm OK, I suppose. What have you been up to for the errrrr last 20 or so years, then?

Rachel hit return and wished her message regaled a tale of a life most fascinating, but instead she hinted at the truth. She doubted he would reply anyway. People were a little put off by her these days. She put it down to the greasy hair, monotone voice and glazed expression. If Adam returned her message she would pretend her hair was clean, that her voice had inflection and her eyes shone with interest and enthusiasm. In a virtual world she could, after all, pretend to be anything or anyone.

Adam and Rachel had been the best of friends at college in their A-level years, having both opted out of sixth form. Neither had been very happy at school, and they left the local comprehensive to reinvent themselves on the pretext that sixth form didn't offer the choice of subjects they wanted. Adam had blended well enough with his peers in school but he had merged a little too well and ended up almost part of the magnolia walls. Rachel, on the other hand, had stood out as the geek with the bad dress sense, and would always be remembered for the unforgettable first summer of high school when her mum had refused to let her use deodorant. Her mother had said she was growing up too fast, so, when all the other girls had encased their small growing breasts in a bra, Rachel stood out in the changing room as the only one who still wore a vest.

Over the summer before starting college she had restyled herself and done her best to forget the horror of school; taking a summer job at a woodland café, she had saved hard. It was a busy tourist destination, the hours were long, and Rachel had taken on every shift she could. Two weeks before college started she had spent all her money on clothes, make-up and a good haircut. She entered that large brick building on the first day exuding a confidence she didn't feel.

Rachel had thought about Adam sometimes over the years; each time she broke up with the last 'this is the one' boyfriend she would wonder what had happened to him. They used to talk and they used to laugh; side-aching laughter about nothing in particular. Adam would have understood what she was going through now. She thought if she had been with him then she wouldn't be in a pit of despair, because he would have held out his hand and hauled her out. He wouldn't have kept going to the pub to eye up the barmaid the way David did. David came home smelling of beer. She was pretty sure the tissues on his study floor were there from cleaning himself up after a post-pub wank; either that or he had a perpetual cold that she hadn't noticed. As Rachel slammed the vacuum cleaner into the skirting boards she figured that if he was going to have regular wank fantasies then he could at least have the good manners to put the tissues in the bin. To think he had the cheek to have a go at her about the state of the house!

Rachel knew which pub David went to and what the Bar Tart looked like. Men were so obvious. Did he think she was stupid? The Bar Tart was all tits, hair, tight ass and flat stomach. Rachel was disappointed in David. He had dropped into the stereotypical behaviour of the over-forty male, desperate for one last chance to beat the call of the grave. Did he think sticking his tongue up the Bar Tart would equate to drinking from the Fountain of Youth?

If Rachel was honest, though, it was the flat stomach that caused her a disproportionate amount of anxiety. Rachel hated her stomach – pinging back after children had not happened! Stretch marks, saggy puckered skin and a huge lump of fat that just wouldn't go were her reality of having kids. So at first she had focused more on hating her stomach than on hating David. She tried to carve the word 'ugly' into the saggy flesh with an old discarded razor blade that she found at the back of the bathroom cupboard, but Jamie had been banging on the bathroom door. He became distressed before she had even got as far as the 'g'. So she gave up. Something else she couldn't even get right. She felt tired.

David was careless. He had left a promotional leaflet for a forthcoming fundraising pub quiz in his trouser pocket. While performing pre-wash pocket-emptying, Rachel had found the folded flyer and almost thrown it straight into the bin, but the smell of it had made her stop and unfold it. The smell of stale, hoppy spilt beer slotted in the missing piece of a puzzle she had pondered over. They were raising money and awareness for testicular cancer. While this seemed a worthwhile cause, Rachel didn't think David had developed a sudden thirst for both beer and knowledge. This was obviously the unexplained regular whereabouts of her husband, who no longer came home before eight. At first she had presumed it was something he had picked up on one of his lunchtime 'meetings', but the pub was closer to home than work. It was in the next town, not far away, and en route from the motorway – a convenient stop-off for a man avoiding a home and a wife falling to pieces. Rachel did consider whether avoiding her was enough motivation in itself to keep him going back to the pub, but in a moment of paranoia she decided to find out for herself. They said that women had a sixth sense about these things, but Rachel just thought it was bloody obvious.

She picked up Maisie from school, strapped both the kids into the car and drove to the Crown. She called David to make sure he was still driving and then all three of them headed into the pub. Rachel had a cover story; she had no idea why, but she thought it seemed strange to be walking into a pub in the late afternoon with two small children. The pretence was that Maisie was desperate for a wee.

Despite Maisie's considerable vocal protests Rachel made her way into the pub. She held Maisie by the hand and Jamie on her hip. Maisie continued to whinge. Dear God, she needed to teach that kid that sometimes she just needed to keep quiet. Discretion, Maisie! Rachel needn't have bothered with the loo pretence, however, because there, behind the bar, was the reason David was spending so much time here: it was the hair. Looking at that woman's hair was like taking a step back in time, to before Rachel had kids: thick, dark, glossy, wavy and very long. Rachel became conscious of her own mass of grease piled in a half-ponytail that was falling sideways off her head. As the barmaid made her way from behind the bar she got to see the whole picture: the tits, the body, and the smile that was sent in Rachel's direction. Rachel grabbed the kids and bolted for the door, banging into a chair with her hip as she let go of Maisie's hand and turned on her heels and headed back to the safety of the car.

'But Mum, you said I needed the loo, even though I don't!' Maisie yelled as she trotted after Rachel. Rachel grabbed her hand and dragged her out of the door. She didn't stop to find out if anyone was looking. She strapped the kids back in, climbed into the driver's seat and concentrated on breathing. In her anxiety to leave she put the car into reverse instead of first and backed into a post. The kids shouted out and Rachel drove at speed, not caring if she had done any damage. She calmed as she drove, and pushed all the feeling deep inside herself, and withdrew from David even more.

Adam – Saturday 7 September, 07.30
Funnily enough I have the time…so fill me in! I think
it might be a bit longer than twenty years though!!

Adam had logged on and off Facebook all day, checking
for a response. Julia had been annoying him, prowling
around and fretting about the house being clean and tidy
before her parents came over the next day. He hated the
monthly Sunday lunch with her family. The worst part was
Julia's anxiety: even after all she had achieved, she stressed
that she still wouldn't live up to their expectations. They
were overbearing but they weren't that bad. Adam tried
to keep out of their strange family dynamic, just offering
Julia what he hoped was a supportive smile or touch of the
hand. He didn't understand her, really: her parents had done
everything they could to take care of her after she had Amy.
Of course they had been disappointed, but they had done as
much as possible to help her through a difficult situation. He
was a fine one to talk, though – Julia had done everything
to support him and yet he resented her. Perhaps the fact that
she had had him committed made his resentment justified.
He didn't like to think what would have happened to him
if they hadn't seen reason and let him out. Julia had no idea
what that place was like. Bitch.

Adam spent all day planning his response to Rachel – if
she replied, of course. When she did reply he realised he had
waited twelve hours for just one short line. He wanted his
response to open doors to an ongoing conversation, yet he
couldn't find the words to express his happiness, because
it felt a little bit ridiculous. He had waited until Julia
headed out to the supermarket before typing his message,
but even though he had plenty of time he didn't manage

to type a single word that he had planned. He wanted to say so much more. He wanted to say that he hadn't just wondered what had happened to Rachel but over the years he had often thought about where she was and what she was doing.

Julia was very particular when it came to what she served her parents for lunch. There was no way she would just defrost a chicken and bung it in the oven and serve it up with a bottle of white that was already in the rack. No, there needed to be an expensive joint of meat, the vegetables had to be fresh and she would peruse the wines for quite some time before adding them to her trolley. She wouldn't be home for a couple of hours at least.

Adam – Saturday 7 September, 20.02
I hate to say this but I think we're getting closer to thirty years than twenty!! Time flies, I guess. Life has been OK, nothing momentous. I'm married, three kids, one of whom has already left home. I have two boys who are younger, still at school. Although not for much longer! I live in Yorkshire, which is beautiful, nice cottage that we've done up. Only it's not really a cottage any more. I don't know what else to say. How about you?

It was weird seeing your name, I have to say. I always wondered what happened to you. I bet you left a trail of broken hearts and married a man who worships you. I like to think you got the fairytale ending. You had some crap boyfriends at college, lol.

At 8.30 p.m. Adam checked his Facebook messages again. After waiting all day the last time, he wasn't really expecting a reply, but there it was. Maybe she had also been happy to hear from him. He wondered if she had ever considered *what if…?*

Rachel – Saturday 7 September, 20.22
Oh, dear God, you can't say that! How did we get this old? It's definitely twenty-something years, but promise me it's still less than thirty!! I love the north! I live southwest, not far from Bath, and I have to admit it's a great place to live, much nicer than where we grew up! Your Facebook page says you're in York. That must be fantastic place to live.

Wow, you have three grown-up kids, or almost? Mine are still really young. I took a while to settle down. I'm married, have two kids, a girl and a boy. They are my world. I don't work any more. How about you? What did you end up doing?

The speed of the response made Adam smile but, although he wanted to be happy that it sounded as though she had a good life, his hopes felt dashed. Asking what he had 'ended up doing' worried him. What should he say? Perhaps he should be honest and see what happened. He could just say, 'Rachel, I'm fucked up.' This was Rachel, after all; they used to be able to tell each other anything.

Thoughts of those carefree, idyllic days at college made warmth wash through his unsettled mind and it calmed him and made him smile. He was still smiling when he sat down to watch TV with the kids, and laughing by the time Julia came home. This sudden surge of happiness made him glad to see her. Having her tiny frame curl up on the sofa next to him was strange. They hadn't done that for so long. When she left to put the shopping away, one side of his body felt cold, and he felt a tinge of regret; most of the time he was glad to see the back of her. He also knew that while she put the shopping away she would start drinking, and when she drank she didn't hold back on what she thought of him. Tonight he was determined not to let her ruin his mood. If she started on him he would ignore her. It was a long time since he had felt any sort of happiness.

Adam was desperate to message Rachel back. He was aware that he was acting like a teenager but found it hard to stop himself. He was determined to send a reply that evening. When Julia went up to bed he snuck back into his study to fetch his iPad before sitting on the sofa with the TV still on. He read Rachel's short message five times, then sat there just looking at her Facebook page, going through her friends list, her photos, reading through her old posts. When Julia interrupted him he was about to start typing.

After having sex with Julia, Adam lay awake wondering what it would have been like to be with Rachel. He would reply in the morning – at least that way he wouldn't seem so needy.

Adam – Sunday 8 September, 10.15
I don't feel so old on a Sunday morning. How about you? How is your weekend going? I unfortunately have to suffer the influx of in-laws for a traditional Sunday lunch!

So what did I end up doing? Well, I was a lecturer for a long time at a further education college. Business studies, nothing very interesting. At the moment I'm between jobs but looking for a new one. So mostly I'm bored looking after the house and the kids.

*So you gave up work to look after the kids? How
did that work out? What did you do?*

*Near Bath – that sounds like a lovely place to
live. I don't actually live in York, I live sort of above
the Howardian Hills and at the bottom of the moors.
It's very beautiful but very cold in winter, and a bit
isolated as we don't even live in the village.*

Adam read his message back to himself. He was just
about to delete it and start again when Julia interrupted him.
Flummoxed for a moment, he hit Send without thinking. He
had wanted to make that message so much more interesting;
he had wanted to sound witty, intelligent, and interested in
Rachel. Instead he thought he sounded dull and miserable. It
was too late now, though: the message had gone.

Sunday morning and Rachel stared out of the window in
the kitchen. Four magpies clustered on the shed roof. If you
were inclined to believe the modern version of the magpie
rhyme it was four for a boy; this sudden cluster of magpies
nearby could be a message from Adam, except he wasn't a
boy any more, he was a man. If however this sudden corvid
chattering activity related to the old version of the rhyme,
then death was imminent. Rachel decided it was wrong to
live in the past. She would catch up with Adam then let him
go. This wasn't serendipity, this was social media, connecting
those who hadn't made the effort to stay in touch.

Rachel could hear the kids laughing as they played in the
garden. David was still in the shower. She could hear him
singing, a tuneless drone not even improved by the acoustics
of the bathroom. Rachel felt restless. She wanted to check
for a message but she had looked before she went to bed

and there had been no reply and it was 8.30 a.m., still too early for a Sunday morning. Adam didn't sound sad and lonely, as she was. Perhaps his wife wasn't banging the local hostelry host. She felt annoyed at herself. Three messages from someone she used to fancy over twenty years ago and she was behaving like a lovesick teenager. What was this, time travel – travelling back in your mind and wishing for what might have been – or was it just an unrealistic moment of hopeful escapism? He was simply an old friend. She shouldn't read any more into his contacting her than that. Misery, however, left the mind wide open to the escapism of fantasy, and reality was unattractive at the moment. This was mind travel, not time travel.

Reality was depression. Not the dark, encompassing depression where she hadn't cared; somehow this lesser depression was more difficult to deal with. Now she was aware of how she felt, how she looked and how she wasn't coping. Reality was a husband who never came home and being trapped in the house alone with two kids. Reality was staring at a screen watching other people live their lives while hers was on hold. She wouldn't check for a message yet; the thought that it might not be there...well, that thought was just too depressing. Hope floated, but sorrow filled your lungs with water.

David sang in the shower to delay going downstairs to Rachel and the kids. He thought singing might improve his mood. It would be nice to have a day together, and to laugh. He would like to go somewhere and do something, anything other than let the kids run riot and avoid watching Rachel stare. Perhaps he would suggest it. They could just go to the park, then into town to a pub for lunch. Maybe they should drive into Bath and go to that pizza place, the proper Italian one they used to go to all the time when Rachel was sane and they just had Maisie to dote on. It was a good place, warm, inviting and a bit chaotic; it was also noisy, so if Jamie kicked off nobody would notice so much. Then they could head off to the park. He'd suggest it. No, he wouldn't suggest it – he would say they were doing it. Rachel would be negative, come up with a thousand excuses. He knew what would happen: she would start to get ready and then it would all become too much for her and she would burst out crying and say she was too tired. She was always too tired. But he would get the kids ready himself, just somehow bundle them all into the car. He stopped singing, towelled himself down and dressed and rushed downstairs before he could lose the impulse.

'Rach, how about we go out for pizza and take the kids to the park in Bath? It's a sunny day.' He said this to Rachel's back as she leant over the kitchen worktop, staring out of the window. He could hear her soft voice as she sang to herself but couldn't quite make out the words. It sounded as though she was chanting a rhyme. For God's sake, was this a new symptom of insanity to add to the list?

'Yes, OK. I'll have a shower if you get the kids ready,' Rachel said, deciding this would be a good idea – being busy would stop her checking for a reply to her message every few minutes. Going out was a hassle, but today the hassle didn't seem to matter. Two magpies hopped across the shed roof.

'What, really? That's OK?' David stood, unsure what to do next.

'Yes – sort the kids out, then.' Rachel turned away, and then turned back and kissed David on the cheek. 'It will be good to get out of the house for a change.'

Rachel – Sunday 8 September, 15.59
What did I do? Nothing very exciting, mostly admin-type stuff. I liked advice work. I worked for the CAB for a long time. I enjoyed the interaction with people. Some of them I think I actually helped, lol. Giving up work was tougher than I thought it would be. I thought I would enjoy being home with the kids more…that sounds terrible… I mean, I do enjoy being with the kids, but it's the monotony of the daily crap that grinds me down. I have nothing to talk about except my kids or a life I used to lead.

Marriage and kids…what happened to me? It all left me feeling invisible. I spend my life cooking, cleaning, and staring at other people's lives on Facebook! They seem to live…I exist!!!!!

Rachel hit return before she could regret being so honest. She had drunk far too much wine at lunchtime. Going out had been OK, but numbing the obvious tension between her and David helped. He was being too nice, which meant he was feeling guilty. After two glasses of wine it was also amazing how much less she had cared about the way the kids behaved! The numbness was starting to wear off, though, leaving her headachy, irritable, lonely and sad.

After the excitement of the unexpected swearing, drunk mother-in-law, Adam didn't get the chance to check his messages until Monday morning. Sunday was rather a strange day. The thought of his father-in–law sexting had been quite interesting. He thought he rather liked the idea of a creative writing class himself, but that would mean committing himself to leaving the house.

Julia had spent most of the afternoon trying to calm her mother down after she had woken up. She had been reluctant to believe the real reason for the sexts. Adam had listened outside the door for a while – not that he needed to be upstairs, as Sue's high-pitched voice was audible to more than the local dogs. He was glad they had cows for neighbours; he was amazed by the vitriolic berating and foul language that spewed forth from Julia's mother.

Adam had been so distracted by the drama that driving Sue home later that day had turned into a complete non-event. Julia had driven her father's car, with her mother as passenger, and he'd followed behind. On the way back Julia drove, but he would have had no qualms about driving; he knew the way well enough and this caused him less anxiety. They even stopped off at a pub for a quick drink. Life seemed almost normal as Adam sat in the pub garden downing his second pint, half-listening to Julia as she related all that her mother had said. It was late when they got home. The boys had already made their way to bed and Julia and Adam went straight upstairs. Julia was tired; it had been an emotional day for her. Adam had found most of it rather amusing, but then they weren't his parents. Julia was asleep within minutes and Adam lay awake, wondering at the overwhelming sense of dissatisfaction in his life. Numb had been easier.

Adam – Monday 9 September, 10.15
Oh, you have an excellent point there…it makes us all lose our individuality…a very scary concept. Perhaps you should break free from your voyeuristic tendencies and just chat to me instead!

I feel very invisible at the moment. My OH works away all week, so it's a bit lonely and boring during the week, just the boys and me. Teenagers with homework and friends don't exactly make good company. I'm not sure I am completely invisible any more, though – at least you are messaging me.

What happened in the part of life where we lost touch and you got married? Did you marry a nice chap, Rachel?

Rachel – Monday 9 September, 10.42
It's a good feeling, being noticed.

I missed you when we lost touch. How on earth did we let that happen? Let's not let that happen again.

Adam was surprised by the speed of Rachel's reply. He also noted the avoidance of his question about her marriage. He might be wrong, but he thought this suggested all was not well after all. The words 'I missed you' made him smile. It made him feel warm and sad at the same time. Warm for the recognition that what they once had was something special, and sad for the years they had let slip away.

Despite not wanting to look too desperate, he found himself replying straight away.

Adam – Monday 9 September, 11.01
Then we must make sure we stay in touch! Tell me more about the in-between years??

Rachel – Monday 9 September, 22.45
You replied again, and all in the same day!

So what happened to my life? I drank a lot, I got married – that bit is obvious, lol – I partied a lot, I partied some more. Somewhere along the way I gained

an education and I worked…most of the time in the voluntary sector – 'terribly rewarding', which equates to crap pay. I think I told you that already. See? I'm so dull now I have to keep repeating myself. Then I stayed at home with the kids, who are amazing. I'm supposed to say that, aren't I? But actually they are strangely amazing. Despite this, though, my own personality has become very elusive; sometimes I think I catch sight of it in a mirror, but if I look back it's gone again. So the birth of the children is when the curse that was enacted on me by a man in robes in a church became complete and I became invisible. I no longer have a name; I'm now referred to as Mummy, or with one of my children's names followed by mum. I think my OH sometimes uses my actual name, but this is only when he's not using a derogatory term ☺
And you?

Rachel hit return without thinking and the message was sent. It was a bitter message. She thought Adam would read it, label it bile, bid her a polite 'well, we must keep in touch' and wait for an opportune moment to delete her from his friends list. David was working away or she wouldn't even be on Facebook this late at night. She should be trying to sleep but that was as elusive as always.

When Adam read the message in the morning, the photos of a thin, hollow-eyed Rachel smiling her empty smile made sense. Rachel wasn't happy.

Adam – Tuesday 10 September, 08.53
Oh…the marriage is also cursed, then!

Me? Well… I found myself staying at home to look after the kids. Not while they were young – I kind of wish it had been then; I think I missed the best bits. It wasn't part of the plan, but yes, the kids are wonderful, but they are getting older and now I'm trying to do other things. Kids kind of end the drinking and partying, though, don't they, lol? It makes being married difficult when the kids are small, no time to be together. Then they grow up and you forget what you used to talk about and can't figure out why you are still together.

I suppose your family still live at home, then? Funny how we both moved away, me further north and you south. No help nearby makes it more difficult. We don't live that far away from Julia's parents, but too far away for them to do school pick-ups, so it was often childminders, which I've always felt guilty about. Too many hours in nursery when they were small, as well! So enjoy being home with them, Rachel. I have worked, but that has always had to fit round the kids' holidays – Julia didn't seem to mind them being at the childminders but I did – so that stopped me having what you would call an excellent or rewarding career! I should have just taken the plunge and done that photography degree like I wanted to instead of doing what my big brother did just because I wasn't sure what I wanted to do.

Life just went wrong about four years ago, Rach.

We both sound a bit sad and fed up, don't we, lol? Although I'm not sure lol is appropriate here.

This time of day the house is very empty… I watch the boys as they walk down the lane to where the school bus pulls in. It's just a double gateway one of the farmers put in, but it doubles as the school bus stop. We don't have neighbours nearby (there are houses in the distance), so they board the bus alone. It's a wonderful view; sometimes it's hard to drag myself away. We are on higher ground and the fields in front drop down to a small river and just beyond the nearest village. I can see the church steeple. Very pretty, and terribly middle-class!

Rachel read the message at about 11 a.m. while she was having a cup of coffee but today she didn't reply. The comment about her marriage also being cursed stung so much that it stopped her reading the rest of the message – she scanned but didn't absorb the content. If she had read those last two or three paragraphs, and thought about the boy she used to know, she would have understood that Adam was reaching out to her. Calling her Rach, the familiarity, despite the long break in their friendship. A friendship that shouldn't have ended when it did or it would have become so much more. Adam had always been far too easygoing to let life's going wrong keep him down for almost four years. If Rachel had been more perceptive on that day, then she would have realised that the 'wrong' was very wrong.

Today, though, Rachel just drifted. She picked up Jamie from pre-school, she rolled Play-Doh and cleaned sticky fingers. She folded washing, and she floated near the top of an almighty abyss of soul-sucking misery that threatened to drag her down at any moment. So Rachel thought about her cursed marriage and Rachel didn't think about Adam.

On Tuesday evening, when David still hadn't come home long after the kids had gone to bed, Rachel logged on for her daily dose of voyeurism. She read the message from Adam again and this time she read each word. She still didn't reply, not knowing quite what to say. She was lost in her pretence of sleep when David decided to join her in bed. This was unusual; a quick glance at her bedside clock made her realise he had spent too much time with the barmaid. She hoped she wasn't overdoing the deep-sleep acting as he pulled her towards him. What she actually wanted was to stiffen, move away from him. She knew why he had joined her in bed. Guilt.

By lunchtime the next day Adam thought that Rachel had lost interest already, but Rachel had been lost in thoughts about a husband who had decided to come to bed and whisper that he loved her. He thought he might have gone insane as he checked Facebook for the fifth time that day. He had been working on his CV, and that was depressing enough, but the lack of reply from Rachel might just send him over the edge.

Rachel – Wednesday 11 September, 13.45
What went wrong four years ago, Adam?

Adam – Wednesday 11 September, 13.55
I thought you weren't going to reply! It's daft – I haven't had any contact with you for so many years, and yet I felt sad when I thought you had gone away already.
Four years ago my parents died in a car crash.

Rachel – Wednesday 11 September, 14.20
Adam, I am so sorry. I don't know what to say. I can't believe your parents are gone, and they must have

been so young – well, younger than mine. I lost my
mum a few years back; my dad is alive but not really
with us any more. It's hard enough losing them, but
together – that must have been so tough. I'm guessing
you didn't cope very well and that explains the
unexpected being at home? How are you doing now?
It's OK to say. I will understand. I have to get ready to
pick up Mais now but I will be back later if you want
to message me.

Rachel was trying hard to be clean, tidy and on time these days. She cleaned up Jamie's hands and face then put on his shoes. She brushed her hair, tied it back in a neat ponytail and made sure there were no sticky food smudges on the front of her clothes. Jamie was out of his pushchair so the walk to school took a long time. Rachel regretted the times she had been so distracted that she had barely spoken to her son as she pushed him along at speed in front of her. Now they held hands, or he rode on her shoulders when his skinny little legs became tired. They pointed to the trees and they talked about colours. They counted how many steps there were between the gateways and they spotted the planes flying high in the sky. Sometimes, watching as the vapour trail disappeared, Rachel would wish she were sitting on that flight, going to where she didn't care; just going. Today she was OK. Jamie was smiling. She had slept a little. She was looking forward to picking up Maisie and listening to her as she chattered away about her day in the random way she always did. She had decided not to think about David any more. She focused on Adam, because he was two magpies and David was just one.

*

Adam wondered what time Rachel would get back from the school run. He also wondered what and how much he should tell her. Instinct told him not to rush. She might say that she understood, but he didn't want to frighten her away.

David, Wednesday 11 September, 17.05 (text message)
Hi, sorry, caught in a late meeting. Just leaving now but still have a two-hour drive... I'll try to be home to help bath the kids. x

David sent the message; he didn't know why. For months now he hadn't told Rachel where he was or what he was doing. He just knew it was time for a fresh start. He had been stupid. He needed to get back in touch with his family.

Rachel viewed the message and the kiss with suspicion. At the same time she was also disappointed it was not from Adam.

Rachel – Wednesday 11 September, 17.08 (text message)
OK

Julia walked back to her flat through the drizzle. September in the rain in Edinburgh felt like November further south. She was tired and it was late. She'd been in endless meetings, her mind was numb and her feet were damp. She wanted to go home. Not to an empty flat, but home. She wanted to feel needed and loved and she wanted to cuddle up next to Adam the way they used to before the accident. She should FaceTime the boys tonight when she got back to the flat, but she was aware they didn't miss her that much. She walked past a noisy bar; the smell of beer and the noise beckoned her in. She should go back to her flat, have a bath, a sandwich and get to bed. She had an early start...

She would message Adam later, tell him she had been held up.

Two glasses of wine later and she decided she should order some food. It was almost nine. The menu said they stopped serving food at nine. She ordered a tuna sandwich, no mayo, on wholemeal bread. She didn't want to eat but she needed something to soak up the third large glass of red wine that accompanied her order. She sipped the dark red liquid, letting it lie on her tongue for a moment before swallowing.

Her iPad was open on the table.

Julia – Wednesday 11 September, 21.01
Hi, darling...sorry, been caught up in meetings all day; the last one ran on so I'm just heading back to the flat now. Tell the boys I'll call tomorrow. Love you all.

Julia hit Send as the waiter dropped her sandwich in front of her. He was a pimply youth of no more than eighteen; she wanted to pull up his sagging trousers. The thought made her feel old. She took two bites out of the sandwich, downed her wine, paid her bill and left.

Back at the flat, she showered away the grime of the day. In her empty bed she reached for the vibrator that she kept in her bedside drawer. She brought herself to an efficient orgasm and fell asleep with the expensive silicone cock still in her hand.

She woke the next morning with a dry mouth and a feeling of empty loneliness. She stumbled from the bed, still half-asleep, heading for the bathroom, and sat on the loo for too long. This morning she couldn't seem to wake up: too much midweek wine. She splashed her face with cold water and shivered. Her head swum and she clutched the sides of the basin. She was cold and achy, her throat hurt, and her head felt as though it might split. She sank to the bathroom floor, feeling too weak to stand. The realisation that she was ill was quite a shock to Julia…she was never ill. She didn't have time to be ill. She tried to stand up by holding on to the side of the bath but she just couldn't make it so instead she crawled back to bed, pulled the covers over her head and cried.

She woke a few hours later drenched in sweat; she rolled over, knocking the abandoned vibrator to the floor, the bang making her jump. She reached for her phone…four missed calls and two messages. She noted with horror that it was lunchtime. She tried to listen to the messages but her brain was so fogged she couldn't understand what they said. She let the phone fall on to the bed. She was desperate for a drink but couldn't move, she was so cold, and she was asleep again in minutes.

It was 9 p.m. when she awoke and became aware of someone sitting on the bed next to her. She tried to sit up, but couldn't. She was scared but couldn't move. She tried to focus, but she couldn't make out who was on the bed. The voice was kind, though, and the soft accent familiar. She decided the person didn't mean her any harm and again she slept.

It was 2 a.m. when she heard the voices: a woman and a man. Opening her eyes, she saw Jim and a strange woman standing next to the bed.

'Julia, how are you feeling?' Jim smiled. 'This is Dr Neal. You gave us a bit of fright. Lucky you gave me that key.'

'I need a drink,' Julia rasped. Her head pounded, her body was wet with sweat, and she felt limp.

'I'll get you some water.' Jim left Julia's bedroom as the doctor began to speak to her.

'Hi, Julia, I just need to examine you if that's OK? I'm pretty sure you just have a bad case of the flu but I'd like to check you out.' The doctor had a soft Scottish accent and Julia felt she had no reason to object.

As the doctor listened to her chest, took her temperature and looked in her ears and down her throat, Julia tried to focus her thoughts. She needed to speak to Adam.

The doctor was satisfied that it was flu and all she needed was fluids, rest and paracetamol. She left, and Jim helped Julia sit up in bed.

'Are you OK?' He laid a hand on her arm and leant forward and brushed sweaty strands of hair from her face. 'I'll stay on the sofa for the rest of the night and then Kath will come by in the morning.'

'Thank you, Jim.' Julia didn't argue; she didn't have the strength, and she didn't want to be alone. She had never felt so ill in her life. 'I need to speak to Adam, he must be worried. Or at least send him a message.'

Jim passed Julia her phone. She checked her messages and texts. There was nothing from Adam. She was surprised how much that hurt. Tears slid down her face. She didn't say anything to Jim but from the look on his face it was obvious he understood. He held her hand as she cried, and when she stopped and lay back down he tucked her in and kissed her on the forehead. Neither of them said anything, and Julia slept once more.

Julia didn't go home that weekend; she was still too ill to drive. Jim and Kath looked after her. She hadn't even dared to hope that Adam would drive up. By the following Wednesday she started to feel a little better but was still too ill to return to work until the week after, and she spent a second weekend alone at the flat – Jim and Kath were away on holiday for a week, from the Saturday. She spoke to Adam on the phone every day, but somehow without the constant busyness her life felt very wrong.

Julia – Monday 23 September, 08.23
Hi, just thought I would let you know that I was back at work. It feels a bit weird. I've never been away from work this long before…apart from maternity leave of course and holiday, but then I'm always still in touch. Jim has been great keeping on top of my work as much as possible and Kath was amazing…but you know all this because I told you all this on the phone.

I know it's tough for you, Adam, but I wish you could have made the effort to drive up with the boys. I didn't say that bit on the phone because I didn't want to start an argument but I felt hurt and very alone.

Adam – Monday 23 September, 08.45
Glad you're back at work. I'll see you at the weekend.

Julia – Monday 23 September, 08.50
Is that it? And how come you replied so quickly?

Adam – Monday 23 September, 08.55
I've gone mobile. I know I let you down. I'm sorry. Can we talk about it at the weekend? It seems wrong to do it like this. You've had enough to deal with. I'm glad you're better.

Julia stewed on the message for a few minutes, made herself a coffee, and decided not to reply. She was too angry.

Two

It was two weeks since David had cocked up – or in fact *not* – with Emma. He felt as though he was hanging on a knife-edge. That any moment he could slip on to the blade and the truth would bleed out. He thought he might be better off coming up with an analogy that involved shit, because that seemed more appropriate; if Rachel found out, he would be up to his neck in it.

Sexual dysfunction was not his worry, though; Rachel and the kids were his worry. No! David was lying to himself, he knew that: sexual dysfunction was high on his list right now. He was so frustrated but so worried about failure he hadn't even tried wanking, and he didn't dare approach Rachel. It was all eating away at him, yet at the same time he also had a desire to go back to Emma, apologise and try again. He was conflicted, trapped between lust and loyalty. Or maybe just because it felt like unfinished business…if the truth came out…well, he might as well be hung for a full-on shag as for a moment of penetration.

David pulled into the car park of an office on an industrial estate. Another day with another meeting. It was just more of the same old crap. He rested his forehead on the steering wheel. He was early. He should call his mum, but he couldn't face it just now. His dad was worse, and David was going to visit at the weekend, without Rachel and the kids.

He was going with his brother and sister, to try to convince his mother that it was time to put his dad in a home. His mother was a strong woman but she was exhausted. That was enough to deal with at the moment, without his failure to fuck up with Emma.

As he got out of his car and headed towards the door of the grim grey building in front of him, his own phone, not his work phone, vibrated in his pocket.

Emma – Tuesday 24 September, 14.03 (text message)
Hi…I thought I would see you in the pub. I don't know what happened the other day…but don't worry about it…just come back in for a drink xx.

His first thought upon reading the text was 'fuck'! His second thought was to text Rachel.

David – Tuesday 24 September, 14.07 (text message)
I might be a bit late, last-minute meeting after this one. I'll let you what time later. Hope you are all OK? Love you xx.

He slipped his phone back in his pocket. Work first; then think about Emma later.

Rachel now had Facebook Messenger on her mobile; it was much easier than logging on to her laptop, and a certain amount of privacy could be obtained in the bathroom or in between the doors of her wardrobe when David was home. The kids were too young to notice. Messages flowed back and forth all day between her and Adam. Subjects came and went, and every now and then there was an emotional insight into each other's lives. It was early days, but somehow the process seemed to heal them a little. Maybe it was distraction, or the first signs of flirtation, but neither Rachel nor Adam dreaded quite so much the blaring sound of the morning alarm.

Yesterday, they had begun to reminisce, the start of a dangerous pastime that led them down the path of *what if* and *what could have been.*

Adam – Wednesday 25 September, 06.02
Do you remember that party? The one where you fell asleep on me? Matt had to wake you up because that awful boyfriend of yours arrived. Then I had to sleep on the sofa while you went off and shagged him. I sort of...well, kind of...let's be honest...I wanted that to be me.

Rachel – Wednesday 25 September, 07.49
Really?? OMG, I didn't know that! I'm a bit flustered now, lol. Oh, that was so long ago...life was still filled with hope...and all those other clichés.
　　And FYI I never shagged him, as you so subtly put it...in fact I didn't shag anyone until I got to uni!!
　　What happened to Matt? Did you stay in touch?
　　I wish I'd known...you might have been my first! Oh, dear, I shouldn't have said that. Now the question is, do I send the message or not? Oh, fuck it...

Adam – Wednesday 25 September, 10.02
Christ, Rach!!!!! You wait until I'm in my forties and hundreds of miles away to tell me that. Good God, now I'll never finish my CV! I have a job to apply

for!! Now I will just spend the day mooning about thinking about what might have been. Come (bad choice of word there, Adam) to think of it, we were only seventeen – the memories would have lasted longer than the event, lol. Really, though? Why did you never say?

And Matt is very happy, settled, an accountant would you believe; he can still mosh like a demon though. He's happily married this time – number three! With this wife he has three kids, none with the others, and is still madly in love with her after sixteen years. I used to see him a fair bit. Marriages, kids and life get in the way of distant friends, though. You have reminded me and I must get in touch with him again, see if he wants to meet up, maybe go and see a band, like we used to…today, when I've finished my CV…and finished considering our body parts colliding!

In fact I have to stop thinking about your body parts or I will never get on!! Job application deadline tomorrow…keep up the mantra…job application deadline tomorrow.

I'll message you tonight xx

Adam tried very hard to focus on his CV, and he did a reasonable job, but it took a lot longer than it should have done as he paused for one too many cups of coffee in the garden and spent just a little too much time smiling. It was a wonderful autumn day, with just a slight chill in the air as he breathed in deep. Coffee mug empty, he padded back across the lawn, his feet bare, and returned to his desk, not even noticing the cows.

*

After dropping Jamie off at pre-school, Rachel drove into town. She had an appointment to have her hair cut and coloured. This was a big step for her. She had done nothing for herself since having Jamie and, as he was now three, this was a little ridiculous.

The hairdresser held Rachel's hair at arm's length, as if small animals might emerge and bite at her scissors. Two hours later, though, and with at least four inches of spilt ends removed, there was a mass of glorious loose curls. There was not a single grey hair showing, and soft highlights framed her face. Even with no make-up and dark shadows under her eyes, Rachel already looked about five years younger.

'You have great hair,' the hairdresser said as Rachel paid her somewhat hefty bill, 'but you need to look after it a bit more. Come back in about two months and I will trim the ends and touch up your roots. It looks amazing.'

'I think I'll do that.' Rachel smiled and handed the young woman a five-pound tip.

'Mummy, put your hair back,' Jamie said as Rachel put him in the car after pre-school. He was tired, hungry and starting to get a little cranky. He objected to his mummy looking different.

'Don't you think Mummy's hair is pretty?'

'No!' he said, as he sucked his lip and sulked. Rachel smiled and kissed his head.

Back at home, with Jamie content, eating his sandwiches and watching TV, Rachel made coffee for herself and read Adam's message. Her cheeks flushed as she read it. She was surprised by his response. She liked it. It made her feel wanted. It also made her wonder if he would still want her now. The thought awakened something close to desire.

Desire wasn't a feeling she'd had in quite some time and it was a little unsettling. Rachel watched as two magpies once again landed on the shed roof. They seemed to have set up home.

Rachel – Wednesday 25 September, 13.22
Oh, wow, you are still in touch with Matt! I'm glad he's happy. But wife number three!! At least he found the right person in the end.

Why did I never say? Oh, you know…we were friends, and because I didn't know you fancied me…you were obsessed with whatever her name was. She was so pretty and I was just me. And despite my part-time party persona I wasn't that secure – but you know that, because I used to tell you everything. Home life looked great from the outside, but on the inside it wasn't the best place to be.

Sex might have ruined our friendship. I just wish we hadn't lost all these years.

Anyway, I hope you have finished the CV by now and please don't think too hard (lol) about my body parts, as most of them aren't quite where they used to be!!!!!!! :/

What job are you applying for?

When lunch was finished Rachel pottered round the garden, playing ball with Jamie and tidying up. She mowed the lawn, and Jamie followed behind for a while with his blue plastic lawnmower until he became bored with funny walks and follow-the-leader and went to investigate some old flowerpots. Rachel smiled as she watched his fascination with the woodlice he found under them. It was hard to think back even just a few months…life had felt so pointless, everything so difficult.

Adam finished his covering letter and checked through his CV once more. He attached both to the email and hit Send. He wanted that job.

The boys would be wandering up the lane soon, hungry, and disgruntled about homework. When he walked through to the lounge and stood in the window and stretched out his hunched-up back he could see them in the distance. He rocked his neck from side to side; he had spent far too long sitting at his desk today. Still, it was done now, and he just had to wait. He just had five minutes to dash off a message to Matt and to see if Rachel had replied. If she had, he would read it, but not send a reply until that evening. It was hard to resist: he wanted to send a message straight back. His days felt better filled with messages from Rachel. Today though he had a mass of things to do!

Adam didn't resist in the end. The self-deprecation in Rachel's message meant he had to reply. He waited until the boys were settled with their homework.

Adam – Wednesday 25 September, 16.41
I always thought you were lovely just being you. And despite your recommendation not to think too hard about your body parts I have now trawled all your Facebook photos and decided I would still be very happy thinking hard (lol indeed, you child) about all of them.

You told me once that home and parents weren't all that they should have been. I was lucky except for my brother, I suppose. My parents were good solid folk, who always supported me even though I never came to much, and without them I just seem to have lost direction. Did you get on better with your parents when you were older?

And the job...it would be the perfect job for me. It's working for the local council in a business development capacity. Heading up a team assisting small businesses as they set up. It's full-time, the pay is crap and initially it's only for twelve months but I haven't worked for four years so I can't be too picky. So, despite thinking of what might have been with you, I have put my heart and soul into my application and I do have some contacts...so fingers crossed.

And strange how I ended up messaging you before tonight...it seems I was missing you. ☺

Rachel – Wednesday 25 September, 17.04
Oh, dear, you trawled my Facebook photos! I must remember to put the good ones on in future!!! And despite you calling me a child I can very much assure you that I am now a woman ;) And thank you for saying I was lovely as me. I never felt lovely then and I certainly don't feel lovely now. I shall make sure I look at all your photos now!

I was devastated when Mum died. All those years of fighting with them seemed so stupid and such a waste of time. They had high expectations that I never lived up to, and Dad was always so disappointed in me. Mum was softer: she defended me, but then, when she and Dad argued about it, I got the blame. It was really screwed up! They should *never have stayed married, but then I guess they were trapped...a bit like I am now (not sure I should have said that...following body part admissions). I guess the distance of living apart from them allowed me to see how unhappy they were at times, but then at other times they seemed so together, still in love. But that doesn't excuse screwing up your kids in the process. I missed Mum, though, when she was gone. I suppose we had found our peace and our place with each other before she died.*

How did you cope with losing both your parents at once? How did the accident happen?

The job sounds perfect – I hope you get it. When would the interview be?

And strange how I replied straight away too...maybe I missed you as well.

David was home by six o'clock in time for dinner with the kids for a change.

'Rach, your hair!' was the first thing he said before even saying hello to Maisie and Jamie. The kids crowded in on him and he hugged them and tickled each of them before they drifted away back to the TV.

'Yeah, I just thought it needed a trim,' Rachel replied nonchalantly. She served up the food on to plates. 'Turn the TV off, kids, dinner is ready.'

'It looks great.' David moved forward to kiss her on the cheek as he always did when he arrived home, but this time the kiss was on her lips, and he ran his fingers through her hair at the same time.

'Thanks,' Rachel replied, and carried on preparing dinner. Part of her liked the fact that the way she looked had an impact on David, but the other part wanted to tell him to go and fuck the barmaid.

Julia was tired. She left the office early, picked up a take-away pizza on the way home. She left the pizza on the side in the kitchenette while she ran a bath. She soaked, immersed in bubbles, until she wrinkled. Towelling herself down and rubbing moisturiser into her skin, she thought she should call Adam. She decided there was little point. She could cope with him depressed and insane...but uninterested? This was a whole new feeling for her. She had been ill and he hadn't even made the effort to come up on the train. She understood how hard driving was for him, especially if he didn't know the roads, but there were other ways to get here. It wouldn't have been so bad if at least he had been concerned.

Julia felt alone and vulnerable; she had never felt like this before. She curled up on the sofa with a blanket and a romantic comedy and stuffed the whole pizza into her face before she could even think about counting the calories. She woke up two hours later feeling stiff and bloated. She crawled into bed, where she made a pillow man in the space next to her and fell asleep, crying on his feather shoulder.

Adam made burgers and chips for himself and the kids. He liked their company at this time of the day. They all covered their food in ketchup, ate without pausing and talked with their mouths full. He thought he should encourage them to talk to their mother but tonight he couldn't be bothered. She would be home at the weekend and none of them had missed her. He had missed the sex, he had to admit; the anti-depressants had taken away both desire and function, but everything was working just fine now and he no longer felt so guilty about pleasure.

Tomorrow he must spend less time messaging Rachel and more time getting on top of the housework. First thing in the morning he would start on the washing. Then later mow the lawn. He hated doing the lawn...but outside had been pleasant today.

He smiled to himself as he loaded the dishwasher with two days' worth of discarded dishes. He thought of a young Rachel...then thought to himself he had better think of that later.

The questions she had asked were ones he had been dreading. They were picking away at his mind. How did the accident happen? And how had he coped? He wasn't sure how to reply. He could keep up the flirting and not answer at all, or he could be honest. He could just see her face though as she read what he had to say. *Hi, Rachel, well, it happened like this: I was driving the car, I lost control on the ice, slammed into a telegraph pole which broke in half. The impact was on the passenger side so when the pole broke and landed on the car it killed my dad because it mashed a great big hole in his head. Which was lucky because part of it also splintered and severed a major artery at the top of his leg, so if his brain hadn't been turned to mush he would have bled to death anyway. Whichever way you look at it, he was fucked. My mum then died from internal injuries because the front seat ended up in her lap and because the stupid woman hadn't wanted to wear her seatbelt – she'd thought it might wreck her dress. She didn't want it snagging on the sequins! How did I cope? Well, it's like this: I didn't. I retreated into a very dark place and then I beat the shit out of my twat of a brother. Oh, and then for good measure*

I was then committed by my bitch of a wife. If I leave the house now I'm prone to panic attacks, and I've developed a ridiculous number of obsessive and ritualistic behaviours. If I don't do these things I think that the rest of my family will die in another car crash. I drive now, just about, on set routes that I know; I drive because I live in the middle of fucking nowhere so walking isn't an option!!! Happy days ☺

He realised this was the first time he had admitted to himself that he was angry with anyone other than himself. He'd better just stick to the flirting.

Adam – Wednesday 25 September, 21.54
I'm sorry I didn't get chance to message you back. I'll write properly tomorrow.
   Goodnight x

This bought him some time while he thought about how to answer. He didn't sleep for long and wandered the house in the early hours. He sat in silence in the dark, drinking hot sweet tea and trying to piece his mind back together. He didn't want to feel broken any more.

When David slid into bed next to her Rachel shoved her phone under her pillow. She had just read Adam's message and noted the kiss. She smiled as she dozed off to sleep, and slid her hand under the pillow so that she could touch her phone.

David sat in the supermarket car park. On the passenger seat a pre-packed ham salad sandwich, packet of crisps and muffin warmed in the sun, uneaten. David tapped out the beat of the music on the bottom of the steering wheel and held a cup of sugar-laden takeaway coffee in his other hand. The coffee was going cold and he had yet to take a sip. He was lost in thought.

Rachel had looked so good last night, but when he had slid into bed next to her she had turned away, and he'd retreated to sleep in his study. He rarely tried to make love to his wife these days, but when he did she let him. Last night, though, as he slid his hand along her hip and up under her pyjama top, she had shrugged him away. This was new – Rachel never said no. When he touched her normally she was like a grateful dog, happy to be stroked, and he had often felt guilty that he didn't go near her more often, but the tension between them made him want to stay away and his sexual dysfunction had made him wary of approaching anyone.

He still didn't know what to do about Emma, either. He thought he also should ring his mum but he couldn't face that. He'd text Emma first.

David – Thursday 26 September, 13.42 (text message)
Hi, I'm sorry about the other day. I have been avoiding you out of complete embarrassment. I've never done anything like that before and I think I just got overwhelmed with guilt. I'm so sorry. Xx

He still wanted Emma. Despite everything he had thought that night as he mulled it all over. He wanted to make things right with Rachel, but thoughts of Emma were stirring him up. His guilt and fear were stopping him, but he wanted to leave that door open, so he thought it better to be humble rather than defensive.

He was surprised when a reply pinged straight back. He'd thought she would ignore him, or at least make him suffer for a few days.

Emma – Thursday 26 September, 13.46 (text message)
Hey, babe, don't worry about it. It happens. Don't be embarrassed, come into the pub when you can. It would be good to see you again.

David smiled with relief as he read her text. She was still an option. Maybe he would call into the pub next week. There was something to be said for a no-strings-attached fling with a woman like Emma. It could relieve a lot of tension. Then he could settle to sorting things with Rachel.

Next, David called his mum. Miriam was fine – but she always said she was fine. He munched his way through his lunch; he bit into the muffin and then thought better of it. He popped his rubbish into the bin. Catching sight of his reflection in a car window, he thought perhaps he should renew his gym membership. With his mood mollified, he drove to his next meeting, car stereo blaring and a tuneless noise leaving his mouth as he sang along.

The weekend came too soon. He wasn't looking forward to meeting with his siblings at his parents' house. Dad's health had been poor but steady, and under control for so long. Now the decline was rapid, and in the last couple of weeks his mum had lost weight, her face pinched with exhaustion.

They were meeting at noon on Saturday. He laughed at the thought: 'meeting at noon'. He supposed, though, this *was* a duel to the death. Death for his dad was pretty imminent and they would have to all come up with some convincing weaponry. His mother, who could no longer cope, would stay with the man she had spent a lifetime with, nursing him until the end even if it killed her. The way she had looked last time David saw her, he thought that death might just take her first.

Between the siblings they had set up the pretence of a family get-together. It was supposed to be a long-overdue celebration of his dad's eightieth birthday, which had gone unmarked as he had had a brief admission to hospital. They told Miriam that they wanted to keep it as just them, as a big party was getting too much for Dad. His mother had been reluctant, but had agreed when they'd said they would all take some food. David was to pick up cake from the supermarket on the way. The others would bring home-made dishes. David didn't have time to cook anything, and there was little point asking Rachel to do anything. Chances were she would make toast!

The siblings had discussed their line of attack by group emails. He knew that his sister Sarah felt a little put upon. She was the closest, living a few miles away, and her children were grown-up. David also knew she was kind and tried not to complain. Mark felt guilty that he only went once a fortnight, and had tried to go every week, but he was busy at work and his family life was suffering. David just felt pathetic in comparison – most of his support was by phone – but he had noticed how much Rachel had improved and he felt able to tell the others he could do more at weekends. Their main aim was to get their stubborn mother to allow carers to come every day, to deal with Dad's personal care needs, to stop her having to lift him to wash him. The strategy was that they would start by suggesting their father needed to go into a nursing home and then negotiate back from there.

Their mother was shrewd, though, and she knew they had planned this and was ready for them.

'But Mum, you're exhausted, you can't go on like this,' David said for everybody, running his hand through his hair as he became more agitated. Miriam was not budging an inch.

They sat in the garden, as the weather was still so warm. Lunch was laid out on the table but no one was eating. His mother was stubborn, and negotiations had broken down before they had even started.

'When I married your father I took my vows very seriously. I will look after him; it's what we both agreed to do.' Miriam stuck out her jaw and set it. 'I will not have a stream of uncaring strangers charging through the house, when we can manage just fine on our own, thank you very much.'

David glanced at Sarah as she stood up and walked across the garden, standing with her back to them all. Their mother's refusal to have any help would put most stress on her, as she was the only one who had the time.

They sat in silence for a while, listening to the birds and the distant hum of traffic along with the laboured breathing of their dad, William.

'Miriam, love, we need help. The children are right and you know it.' William paused for a while until his breathing was steady again. 'You are completely exhausted, and I would like to die at home. If you keel over from exhaustion I'm stuffed on that one.'

Nobody else spoke for a while. It was rare for his dad to speak out, and everyone was waiting to see Miriam's reaction.

'All right,' she said with an uncharacteristic quiet. She leaned across and squeezed her husband's hand. He held on to it for a while then smiled at her and they let go. David became aware that his mother looked as if she might cry, and his dad knew well enough she wouldn't want any of them to see this. She regained her composure.

'Sort it out, then,' Miriam said. 'This lunch is going to waste. Come on, eat up.' The subject was closed.

They chatted for a bit, and Sarah cleared the plates from their first course while David cut the cake.

'Shop-bought,' Miriam said. 'That wife of yours still can't cook, then, David?'

They all smiled at each other, and David's father coughed as he suppressed a laugh. They would cope.

David felt deflated as he drove away from his parents' house. He was relieved his mother had caved in, it took the pressure off all of them, but he had expected more of a fight, and the absence of it meant his parents had all but given up. He was well on the way to losing them. He swallowed hard, and drove home to his family.

Three

Adam warned Rachel that Julia would be home that weekend. He wasn't quite sure why he had felt the need to do that, except by way of explanation that he might not be free to send quite so many messages. He thought he shouldn't send *any* messages as his behaviour – *their* behaviour – seemed to be becoming a little obsessive, and if he was truthful he was still avoiding the big questions.

Julia arrived on Friday night, to be greeted by a calm Adam, two standoffish children and a huge home-made pizza.

'No casserole, Adam?' was all she managed to say after a polite yet frosty kiss on his cheek. Her heels clicked across the kitchen to the hallway, where she removed them before taking her bag upstairs, not even stopping for coffee. She had expected a warmer reception and had prepared to be cool, even distant, to demonstrate to Adam her disappointment in his failure to care. Yet her behaviour had gone unnoticed by all of them. She felt as though she had invaded the pack and was being cast aside before she had even attempted any form of integration. Pizza, though – the pizza was the biggest shock of all. Friday night dinner was a casserole! With a casserole Adam could play it safe: nothing could go wrong. If Julia was late then he could turn down the oven. The pizza had just been taken out of the oven before she arrived. It seemed he no longer cared whether or not she was on time for dinner.

Well, fuck them all, she thought, stripping off her clothes and climbing into the shower; they can wait.

They didn't wait, and when Julia made her way downstairs thirty minutes later she could already hear happy banter and the sound of clanking crockery coming from the kitchen. She paused outside the door, because the sound was good. Gone was the normal tension and the speed-eating to escape from Adam and his pedantic fussing. Now the boys sounded relaxed and happy, and Julia felt as if she was an outsider.

She hid her feelings as she opened the door and made her way into the bright room.

'Were you lot hungry, then?' Her customary glass of red wine sat on the table in her space at the opposite end to Adam.

'Mum, you took so long!' Alex groaned.

'Sorry, love, the boys were starving and the pizza was getting cold. Sit down – yours is in the top oven. It should still be warm.' Adam pushed his chair back and went to get Julia's pizza while she helped herself to salad.

Julia sat smiling at the boys, but they didn't respond, so she sipped her wine before speaking.

'So, boys…what have you been up to?'

'Usual crap, Mum, how about you?' Alex said, his mouth still stuffed with pizza crust.

'Are you better now? You look really awful,' Tom said, not caring to spare his mother's feelings despite being aware of her vanity.

Julia knew that despite the recent diet of 'can't be arsed' takeaways she still looked very thin and pale. Although she was small, she didn't usually look insubstantial, but for the last couple of weeks she'd felt she needed to be labelled with 'fragile' stickers.

Dinner finished and the dishes cleared away, they all flopped on the sofa. They watched some pointless TV for a while then the boys drifted away to play on the Xbox and Adam and Julia were left alone. On Friday nights, her first night home, Julia would usually talk at Adam, but tonight she was too tired.

'I'm going to bed – are you coming?' she asked.

'You go up – I'll be up in a minute. I forgot to put the dishwasher on and I left some clothes in the tumble dryer. I won't be long,' he said.

The stairs felt steep as Julia plodded up them. She wasn't used to feeling like this. 'Just the flu' seemed such an understatement. She slipped into bed naked; the cotton sheets smelled of fresh air and fabric conditioner. She waited for Adam, trying not to fall asleep. After waiting half an hour, she slipped on a robe and padded back downstairs, her bare feet almost silent on the cold stone floor. The light shone through the laundry room door, which was ajar, and from where Julia stood she could see Adam in profile, typing away on his phone, a slight smile frozen on his lips. It was enough of a smile to make his eyes crinkle at the corners. The harsh light made him look his age, and Julia could see the streaks of grey through his curly hair. Julia turned away and left him unaware of her presence. She wondered what sad and desperate woman he was engaged in a world of fantasy with now. This time, when she returned to bed, she was wearing her pyjamas. She snapped off the bedside light and fell into an exhausted sleep.

When Julia awoke she was aware that Adam was still in bed next to her. She glanced at the clock, surprised: it was already gone eight. Adam was not following his usual obsessional morning routine: getting-up time had passed.

He rolled towards her. 'You were asleep already last night when I came up. I've missed you,' he said, pulling her towards him and kissing her neck as he slid his hand under her pyjama top, running his thumb around her nipple. 'These are mightily unsexy pyjamas.'

'I was cold,' Julia muttered, trying hard not to become aroused by him. Despite her efforts she felt her hips betray her: they rose up to meet his hand as he slid it across her in a clumsy effort to try to relieve her of her pyjama bottoms. In the end she helped him, kicking the bottoms out of the bed and raising up her arms as he took the top off over her head. Naked skin touching naked skin after two weeks of absence felt so good – and just a little less functional than usual.

Rachel stared out of the window. The kids were watching TV and David had already left for lunch at his parents' house. She was happy not to have to go; she wasn't fond of her in-laws at all. They were uptight. She used to laugh with her mum about them… Rachel shut down the thought. She didn't like to think of her mother. She should, but she couldn't, not since the day she had looked through the photos on her laptop.

Instead she thought of Adam. Last night his message had been a little more than flirtatious, and in the daylight with the kids around any response in the same manner seemed wrong. Maybe she had become a bit frigid. It was the lack of sex. On the rare occasion she had sex with David it was a gratifying fuck. She missed making love to him. Adam had left her feeling like that last night. Unable to sleep, she had touched herself in the way she wanted someone else to touch her, sliding her hands over her own body and making herself come. At least she slept after that.

She thought she would respond to Adam, tease him a little.

Rachel – Saturday 28 September, 10.51
Good morning. And how many women are you currently flirting outrageously with on the internet? You seem well versed in the art of virtual seduction. I can honestly say that your message left me a little wanting…

Adam read the message when he went to fetch coffee. Julia was still in bed and it was well past 11 a.m. He had heard the boys get up about half an hour ago. It was a strange but nice feeling, to be lying next to Julia, cuddled up and dozing in post-coital satisfaction. Saturday mornings hadn't been like this since before the accident.

He felt a little uncomfortable when he read Rachel's message. For a start it was true he was 'well versed in the art of virtual seduction' as she put it. He also felt confused this morning. Making love to Julia on a Saturday morning was like old times. He knew he shouldn't have sent that message to Rachel, but it had seemed amusing when he was standing in the laundry room and he had been annoyed at Julia. He didn't even know why he was annoyed at her; she had every right to be furious with him. She had been ill and he hadn't even tried to go up to Edinburgh and look after her. Her fallibility had floored him: he hadn't known how to respond, so he had made like a hedgehog and curled into a ball, prickles out.

Adam made the coffee and went back to bed. He would calm things down with Rachel later.

By four that afternoon David had returned and Rachel had checked her phone for a reply from Adam about twenty times.

'I didn't think talking to your parents would take quite this long,' she snapped the moment David came through the door. 'What did you do, stop at the pub on the way home?'

David paused for a moment, not sure if Rachel knew something or was just snarling her usual vitriol at him.

'Rach, it was a big thing for Mum and for Dad to admit they needed more help. You know that. There was a lot to sort out, but at least Mum agreed, so it was worth it. You could help more.'

'I'm sorry! I have two young kids and you are never here – exactly when am I going to get time to trail over to your parents' house in between school and pre-school runs? They don't live down the road, do they?'

'Well, you could cook stuff and I could take it over and put it in the freezer. At least it would be something.'

'If you want anything cooking for your parents, I suggest you cook it yourself,' Rachel shouted as she stormed out of the kitchen, stomped upstairs and slammed the bedroom door. She was fuming, and she noted how he had just done his best to make her angry and avoid the pub comment.

She hadn't been so angry that she had forgotten to pick up her phone on the way out of the kitchen, though. The message symbol was at the bottom of the screen and, as no one else ever sent her a Facebook message, it had to be Adam.

Adam – Saturday 28 September, 16.01
Lol! Yes, I have a string of wanton women all round the
country waiting anxiously for me to log on to Facebook
so that I can Hot Chat them into submission and help
relieve them of their frustrations. I'm sorry, I shouldn't
have said those things last night, but...anyway, too
much wine with dinner. I lost my inhibitions.

Are you OK today? Julia has been here all day.
She's been quite friendly – not what I'm used to, lol!

Hot Chat? Rachel was aware of the term but wasn't
even that sure anyone did it; she'd need to Google it later.
What was clear was that Adam regretted the content of his
message from last night. Rachel felt hurt and confused and
yet slightly relieved. Flirting a little was one thing, but he had
been quite explicit last night. She was also confused about
his relationship with his wife. He had intimated a while ago
that they hadn't got on that well since he left work. Maybe
he was trying to let her know that a reconciliation was on
the cards. She wanted to cry...

This was ridiculous. She wouldn't reply today.

Rachel Googled Hot Chat. She was shocked to find
a whole industry out there. Chat rooms, video rooms, all
with tempting pictures of plastic-looking woman with the
fakest, firmest cleavages you were likely to find. If that was
the sort of thing Adam was looking for, he could forget it.
How dysfunctional was that? She would stop messaging him
today. For good. She meant it.

Rachel – Sunday 29 September, 00.01
So where do I rank, then, in this list of wanton
women? And perhaps you had better describe exactly

how you help to relieve them of their frustrations. Do you just talk about it, or is there a gradual build-up to doing them in person and then when you're bored with them you move on to the next. Am I the next?

What's up with your wife, then – is she not enough for you?

Rachel was pissed off. Adam, she decided, wouldn't reply. God, sometimes she wanted to slap herself. She was an idiot. Strung along because a man said the words she wanted to hear. She couldn't sleep, and crept downstairs to see if David was still awake. Light shone from under his study door. She wanted to go to him and curl up next to him, her head on his shoulder and his arm round her. She wanted his familiar smell; she wanted to feel safe in his arms.

Then she remembered the pub and snatched back her hand from where it hovered over the door handle. She wondered if Hot Chat was what he did with the Bar Tart, in between fucking her. She hated men. She made herself a cup of tea, adding sugar, and went back to bed.

At 3 a.m. her phone buzzed.

Adam – Sunday 29 September, 03.00
WTF, Rach? I was joking. The flirting – OK, the explicit description of what I would have liked to do with you when we were younger…I just got a bit carried away. My wife, as you put it, is away all week, and our relationship has not been all that great since the accident. I think I told you that. I don't, however, engage in online flirtations or meet up with women for sex. I chat to you because you are you. Not because I think I might get laid! Goodnight! Actually, good morning!!

Adam wasn't sure what he was so annoyed about. The fact that he was lying to Rachel was bothering him. He was telling the truth about not meeting women for sex. He also thought it curious that he never felt guilty about how all this would make Julia feel. Well, he did think about it, but it didn't bother him enough to stop. Then again, he was pretty sure Julia was having an affair with her boss anyway. 'Oh, he was so supportive' – how many times had she said that?

Adam went back up to Julia at 4 a.m. She didn't stir as he eased back the covers. He cuddled up to her back; she smelt warm and sort of floral. He liked her smell. He liked the way her tiny frame tucked into his, her feet going just past his knees when she lay next to him. He felt like her protector like this, but when she was awake Julia didn't need a protector. He felt that she didn't want or need him; he thought she was there out of a sense of duty towards him and the kids. He knew she saw him as a pathetic waste of time. He found Rachel's vulnerability attractive. He hoped that he hadn't messed that up as well. He regretted sending the angry response. He should have laughed it off. He doubted he would hear from her again.

David heard Rachel as she paused outside his study. He also heard the kettle boil. He had been about to text Emma when Rachel came downstairs and now he was frozen in fear and guilt. He put his phone down on the bed. Resting his head back against the wall, he sighed: what the fuck was wrong with him? He had enough on his plate without screwing around and screwing everything up. He listened as Rachel passed his door, her footsteps slower this time, holding a mug of hot herbal tea and trying not to spill it. Sometimes she did this in the night, filling a large mug with a stinky brew of camomile that she hoped would help her sleep. David wanted her to stop at his door, to open it. He wanted her to sit with him while she drank her tea, and talk. They used to talk all the time, and smile, and hug, and laugh. Sometimes they used to lie in silence, just holding each other. Warm bodies hooked round each other, legs intertwined. Just breathing each other's breath and just being.

David couldn't sleep. He thought about Maisie. He'd never liked the name but it suited her. Then James, who became Jamie. At first the rhyming names had been a bit of a joke. When James was born they had made it clear to each other that he would be James, not Jamie. Maisie had different ideas, though, and her new baby brother had become Jamie before he had even left the hospital. Despite the difficulty of the first few years, the siblings had developed a bond. It was almost as if the bond lost between David and Rachel had transferred to the kids. They were a little team, the two of them, their closeness growing stronger by the day. Next year they would both be at school.

Time, however, had not flown as most parents said it did. It had been a painful, slow drag, sometimes feeling as if they were travelling backwards or just hooked into a never-ending loop.

David smiled to himself at the memory of when they had brought Maisie home. Rachel had read all the books. She had been confident she knew what she was doing. They'd bought all the gear. They had the kit, they had the baby, and they had the instruction manuals. Then they sat in the car park like two startled rabbits. They drove home at ten miles under the speed limit. Every approaching car or junction was a tragic accident waiting to happen. At home they were prepared, or so they thought. For two months, despite Rachel filling the freezer with healthy meals for two, they lived on takeaways. Rachel seemed to be able to hoover up her meal, most of his and an entire packet of chocolate biscuits and still lose weight. Every time he looked at her she was chewing. He found it amusing, as she had always worried about her weight. After four months of no sleep they were in a routine. Rachel's cud-chewing returned to normal eating as Maisie got into a feeding pattern, although she still managed to pack away a fair few biscuits. Naps and full nights of sleep meant the house was tidy again, clean clothes appeared in David's wardrobe once more, and they were settled. They had been happy, very happy. Motherhood had suited Rachel; she had admitted to enjoying being at home, and everything with Maisie was new. David couldn't wait to get home at night.

When Rachel became pregnant with Jamie he had expected more of the same. In the end, though, it felt as if there was more crap outside the nappies than in them.

Still unable to sleep, David crept upstairs and slid into the bed next to Rachel. She stirred and laid her head on his shoulder. In the morning she let him make love to her. Neither of them said anything. David wanted to cry. The next night they slept alone again.

Rachel thought about last night – David sliding into bed next to her and making love. When she woke in the morning she had closed her eyes to block him out. She didn't want to make love to him any more. It was nice to be touched, to have her skin stroked, for him to kiss her, to kiss her breasts, to slide his tongue down her body and kiss the ripples of stretch marks on her stomach. He had made her come because he knew how her body worked, and she had arched into the climax from his touch despite herself, despite her anger. He felt familiar, but that was all. She didn't want to cling to him afterwards. She didn't want to lay her head on his chest in satiated pleasure. The sex was pleasant but it felt functional. She knew he had betrayed her. The way he was acting was enough to give it away. The way he was avoiding her. She didn't need him to tell her. No massive life-changing confrontation was required. She had loved David, but never felt his equal; she had clung to him as if he could leave her any minute, but now she no longer cared if he did.

Rachel – Sunday 29 September, 09.30
But what if I wanted you to? To flirt with me? To meet up with me? We do this, we do this so often now...we don't let a day pass, do we?

Adam – Sunday 29 September, 10.01
Oh, Rach, of course I'd like to meet you...and flirt with you...and hold your hand...and kiss you...and...

But we are married. We have kids. I don't want to live on regret, but not being with you when I was younger...that is regret. We can't go back though...can we?

Rachel – Sunday 29 September, 10.20
You'd hold my hand...and kiss me?

We may be married but we aren't happily married. So what would it matter?

There is stuff I haven't told you – stuff about me, stuff about my marriage. You are a lifeline to me...you keep me sane. The way you kept me sane for those two years we were at college. As for regret, I regret it too – so let's not regret it again? Life's short and all that.

Adam – Sunday 29 September, 10.30
Rach, we live hundreds of miles apart. We don't have jobs. We have a lot to lose!

But life is short, so...oh, I have no idea what I'm saying. I thought of you so many times over the years. Just tell me stuff, let's get to know each other again. Just tell me things and I'll tell you things. Life hasn't been so great for a while now and you...well, you make it better...so I don't want to ruin that. OK?

Rachel – Sunday 29 September, 10.38
Well, that was the most non-committal reply ever. We HAVE been telling each other things!

OK...I'll tell you stuff, then, but then I must go and play with the kids. I have consigned them to the wonders of CBeebies. Screen time should be encouraged; it keeps them quiet. David is as usual in his study; I believe he is texting the Bar Tart that he is or has been fucking. And I drive a knackered old Citroën.

Adam – Sunday 29 September, 10.43
Well, that is telling me stuff. I don't know what to say. You said not happily married but I didn't realise it was that bad. It also makes me wonder when you found out? I'm not some sort of revenge, am I? Lol. Oh, no, I suppose I contacted you first, so silly thing to say.

And a strange thing to tell me about your car after that, but OK – I drive a very nice dark blue almost-new Volvo!! Julia has a swish black Golf. I got the sensible car for ferrying the kids around!

Rachel – Sunday 29 September, 13.51
He hasn't told me, I just know. I found a leaflet about the pub. He doesn't come home. He hasn't for a long time. I wanted to see for myself. She has my hair...well, the hair I had when I was younger. She looks a bit like me, only hard, as though she has had a tough life, and she's thin and toned...not like me, lol! I needed help – I've really struggled since Mum died and Jamie was born. He didn't sleep for years...I was exhausted and David just didn't come home any more. He sleeps in his study now. When I walked into that pub with the kids I just saw her and knew. Then a couple of times he just came up to bed. Never said anything, he just held me...guilt, I suppose.

The saddest thing, though, is that I don't care. He doesn't know that I already know.

And no, you have nothing to do with revenge. You just turned up one day, but you obviously thought that or you would have deleted that sentence from your message!

Adam – Sunday 29 September, 14.10
You don't know for sure, then...you just suspect. But if you no longer share a bedroom then I guess all has not been well for a long time?

OK, I'm not revenge. Sorry, it just crossed my mind... we flirt – well, I flirt, lol, and you do too sometimes ;)

Julia is not the sort of woman I should have married. She is cold, hard and ambitious. I think I irritate her. I suffered from depression after Mum and Dad died. So she got a job in Edinburgh and left me to it.

Adam knew that wasn't quite the truth of things but if he was honest to himself that was how it felt. He tried to spend the rest of the day not messaging Rachel and not thinking about kissing her.

That night he made love to Julia again.

'What, again?' she said. He covered her mouth with his to silence her. She would be so much nicer if she just didn't talk. He tried to remember the sound of Rachel's voice as he pushed himself into Julia. He kept his eyes closed and tried not to imagine fucking Rachel.

Four

Julia wondered what was going on. Adam was acting out of character. Well, out of order, if she was honest. In just two weeks of her not coming home he had changed. She tried to think positive thoughts. Maybe he was just getting better. Maybe he had even sought out that counselling. The extra sex was a definite bonus; she wasn't complaining about that. The only thing she'd had between her legs for the last couple of weeks had been silicone. Oh, my God – an embarrassing thought suddenly occurred to her: before she was ill she had fallen asleep without putting her vibrator away. She didn't remember it being on the bed or finding it on the floor when she was well enough to tidy up her bedroom. That could mean only one thing: Jim had put it away in her bedside drawer. Now she was distracted from thinking about what was going on with Adam. How the hell was she going to face Jim on Monday, knowing he had picked up her vibrator?

'Christ,' she groaned, flushing pink even though she was alone in the kitchen.

She made coffee for herself and Adam. The boys were in town, hanging out with mates. Adam was holed up in his study, working on a job application. That was positive. She didn't want to disturb him. She wanted him to get a job so she could come home. There was a position opening up in a couple of months but it would mean a pay cut. Leeds was still a big commute, but at least she would be home at night. If she were home, things would get better.

Julia also needed to call her parents and set up lunch for next weekend. She hadn't been able to face it this week. The flu had stopped her in her tracks and she was still suffering from an overwhelming exhaustion such as she had never experienced before. She had talked to her GP on the phone but she had told her not to worry, it was normal. She just said to eat a healthy diet, keep the exercise light and get plenty of rest, and it could take a few months before she was feeling herself again.

She had spoken to her mum and dad on the phone while she had been ill. Sue had even offered to drive up to look after her. More than her bloody husband had. She gathered things were still a little frosty between her parents. Her mum was so stubborn and her dad so pig-headed. Julia decided just to leave them to it. Lunch, however, still needed to be arranged, and she had decided to book a table at a pub. It would limit the time they all had to spend together.

On Monday morning Julia overslept. It made her cranky and flustered and she drove too fast. As the camera flashed she braked hard but too late. Fuck it, she thought, just over the limit. Her licence had been clean until this point. Now she would have to be more careful.

She had been thinking about whether she should say something to Jim. They were due to meet after work to talk about how to get her back to the Leeds office. She had decided she should just ignore it, but then she wasn't sure if just saying 'thank you for putting away my sex toy' might be the better way to go. She'd just see what happened.

As she drove, she became more obsessed with the thought of Jim picking up her vibrator. She was dreading the moment when she had to face him. She decided the flu had affected her brain; she would normally be able to laugh that sort of thing off. She thought it was because she really cared about Jim's opinion of her. She occasionally fantasised about him but he was far more important to her than sexual gratification. He was her good friend, mentor and confidant.

She groaned aloud as she approached the parking area for her flat. She was late, very late. She left her weekend bag in the car, grabbed her heels and tried to jog her way to the office. Her first meeting was at eleven; she had ten minutes.

Jim was waiting in her office when she arrived, glowing and still in flat shoes.

'Are you OK?' he asked. 'It's not like you to be late. Here, coffee. I'll fill you in on the meeting as we walk, all right?' At work Jim was her boss and he behaved as such. In the pub later he would behave like her closest friend.

Julia slipped on her heels, flushing red from both heat and embarrassment. She walked, sipping the warm black coffee as she went. They took the lift, and as the doors closed Julia felt she had to get it over with.

'Jim, when I was ill…I just wanted to thank you. And I wanted to thank you for your discretion on another matter…that you must have put away before the doctor arrived…' Julia's face burned.

'It was no trouble!' Jim smiled, then looked at her and started to laugh. 'I don't think I've ever seen you flustered before.'

Julia laughed too, with relief. She felt like an idiot. She was so embarrassed she wanted the lift floor to open and let her free fall away, but she was glad she had said it. In the end they were unable to control their laughter, and all through the meeting had to avoid eye contact as the slightest smile threatened to set them off again.

Adam stared out of the window, watching the boys as they went down the lane to wait for the bus. He was waiting for the post, or an email, he wasn't sure which; he was waiting to find out whether or not he had an interview for the job. He seemed destined to watch and wait. He doubted it would be today but he had little else to do but wait, or send messages to Rachel.

Yesterday had been strange. After Saturday, things had changed. On Sunday morning, Rachel had made her first real admission that all was not well. As the day went on she had told him more. She'd told him things about the state of her mental health that worried him, really worried him...yet at the same time, if he had been able to get in a car and rescue her, he would have. He laughed at his 'knight in shining armour' moment. He wasn't in a position to rescue anyone.

Adam let out an elongated breath as he moved away from the window. He could clean, or he could send a message to Rachel. Rachel it was, then. On this Monday morning it dawned on him that the distraction of Rachel had put a stop to his obsessive timekeeping: morning coffee was sometimes late, and last week he had swapped around what he had for lunch. For a moment he panicked. When he hadn't noticed his altered routines he had been fine, but now he realised that his safeguarding had gone, it left him feeling like a small child who had had its sucky blanket taken away. It was a good thing, he was aware of that, but the idea of taking it to the next level and pushing himself further was terrifying. Message Rachel now, he told himself. He needed the distraction.

He went to his study, but Rachel had beaten him to it.

Rachel – Monday 30 September, 05.20
I wake up so often in the night but it's the mornings that are the hardest. When I've slept for a few hours I forget I'm alone. Groggy with sleep, I reach out, but all my hand finds is the space of cold sheets, not the warmth of another person. Sometimes I just want David to sleep upstairs to be near me...because I'm lonely...but then I think about what he's done and I just want to shout at him to get out. I don't, of course. I can't...I'm trapped here...

I need to start thinking about getting a job, I really do, but it all seems so hard and I feel so tired all the time. Remember how we used to talk about the fact that we were doing the wrong courses at college? A-levels in Sensible Studies, we used to call them. You wanted to be a photographer, and I wanted to be a writer or an interior designer. That seemed so much more glamorous. Funny, I ended up all worthy and you ended up teaching the next generation of boredom-seekers. Now I don't know what I want really. I just drift from day to day, surviving with little aim. We all need an aim, don't you think?

Anyhow, enough of my early-morning ramble on. When do you hear about the job? I forgot to ask, or I think I asked when the interviews were being held but you didn't say.

Adam – Monday 30 September, 09.06
I understand the lonely, Rach...Mum and Dad were so solid, and even though I am supposed to be all grown

up I feel as if somebody uprooted my foundation and left me floundering. I keep looking for an escape but there isn't one…it happened and I have to deal with it. You, however, are the most wonderful distraction.

Looking for a job is a big thing and an important step for me and I think you are right…start looking at your options. Is your little boy at pre-school yet?

Thanks for reminding me I worked as a boredom-seeker. Off to dust off my camera or spend thousands on a new one. I wonder if that would make Julia cross, lol.

Are you OK? Your ramble was insightful. xx

Rachel – Monday 30 September, 09.30
It's the vicious bite of lonely that gets me every time. Life is OK, then it washes right through – not over, but through. I want to reach out to someone but there is no one to hold but the kids. With things so bad with David I miss full-size hugs. I miss a life, which makes the day-to-day grind matter so much. Does that make sense?

Yes, Jamie has settled into pre-school. Both the kids will be at school next year and that will feel strange…the last few years have taken so long, they've felt like another lifetime. I sound ungrateful, as though I don't love my kids, and I do, I really do. They are what keeps me trundling down the track. I just miss happy. I miss Mum. I really thought David was the person I would be with forever; I didn't expect it all to go so wrong. He has just shut down and shut me out when I need him the most. It's gone on so long that I no longer care…I'm not lonely for him, I'm just lonely.

Enough of me...I hope you get your job, but dust off that camera just in case. I really need to start looking at my options. I've thought about teaching or being a teaching assistant. Today I shall do something positive and find myself a course for next year – I think I'm too late for this year now, they will have already started. It's time to start taking control of life... my life, lol.

Telling you makes it feel better. xx

Adam – Monday 30 September, 09.45
Then keep telling me.

You have had a strange effect on me...my life used to be a little regimented; almost obsessive... it was the routine that got me through the day. I still do it to some extent but less so...it's freeing. You are a distraction, Rachel, but then you always were.

I may just go and find my camera and polish those lenses. Also I need to trawl the job websites...just in case, and before you distract me any further.

Rachel – Monday 30 September, 09.50
And how could I distract you, Adam, all these miles away from you?

Adam – Monday 30 September, 09.52
I think you know exactly how you could distract me, don't you?

Rachel – Monday 30 September, 09.53
Maybe I do...but right now I need to put the washing out.

Rachel bit her lip as she pegged out rows of small clothes. She looked at the basket; there never seemed to be much, but all the tiny colourful clothes took so long to hang out. She wondered if it might be interesting to describe to Adam what she would like to do to him if he were with her. She wondered if she would take things to the next level if he were closer. She smiled…who was she kidding? Of course she would.

She had never been unfaithful to anyone and had never considered herself the unfaithful type. She had looked at those websites that catered for affairs for married people. Discreet and almost guaranteed a fuck. Meaningless sex, though – she didn't think she could do it. It would eat her up with anxiety and fuel her already depressed state of mind, with all the insecurities that would go with it. After the message from Adam about the 'Hot Chat', she had also seen on some websites the suggestion of a harmless virtual affair. Was it harmless, though? Maybe if it was with a stranger, but with Adam? She let her thoughts drift as she continued to peg. Concluding nothing. It would be what it ended up being.

Rachel – Monday 30 September, 10.45
We could just meet up…see what happened, lol.

Adam read the message after realising he was late for coffee. He'd been busy trawling job sites; if he didn't get an interview for this job, he needed to keep applying for others. He read the message and panicked – another subject he didn't want to answer, but this one wasn't wrapped up with anything else.

He'd treat it like a joke.

Adam – Monday 30 September, 11.02
Well, that would be something, lol.
You've finished the highlight of your day, then?

Rachel – Monday 30 September, 11.31
It could be something.
What highlight?

At 12.55 Adam stopped cleaning the house. It was time for lunch. Monday was bacon sandwich day. He felt unsettled by Rachel today. The problem was, what she wanted was what he wanted too, but he just couldn't do it. She lived too far away. Later this week he planned to drive to a random somewhere. If he got the job he would have to drive. So he had to force himself to go out...he needed to push himself. He could tell Rachel all of this, he supposed, but how lame did it sound? He wouldn't delay the drive – he would go out now, drive into the village, then drive to a random destination on one of the road signs. Bacon sandwich first, though.

Forty minutes later, Adam sat at the strange junction, unsure where he was or which way he should turn. He regretted his impulsive decision – and the consumption of bacon even more. It sat undigested in his stomach and was threatening to exit. The car behind was growing impatient and had sounded its horn twice; in his rear-view mirror he could see a young woman shouting something at him.

He watched the traffic for a gap once more and turned left. Left was easier. He suspected that he should have gone right. After driving for another ten minutes he found a lay-by and pulled over. He wound down the window and let the sweat on his face dry; his hands had been slipping on the steering wheel and they were icy cold from gripping.

The lay-by was by woodland; leaves fluttered across the windscreen and Adam watched them. The desire to sleep was overwhelming but he had to get home; the boys would be back soon and he hadn't left a note. He should have used the GPS but he hadn't expected to go this far and be out for this long. He wasn't sure if he was lost or just afraid to look.

A deep inward breath and he started the car, turned it in the direction he had come from and did his best to retrace his journey until the surroundings became familiar.

The boys were sprawled on the sofa, screens in hand, by the time he got home. Without anyone to remind them to change out of uniforms or get on with homework, they hadn't bothered. Crumpled crisp packets and an empty biscuit tin sat on the coffee table between them.

'Nobody doing their homework, then?' Adam asked, making both boys jump.

'Jesus, Dad!' Tom replied.

'You came back, then? Tom thought you might have a secret woman stashed away somewhere and you had got her into bed. I just thought they had carted you off to the nut-house.' Alex laughed as Tom threw a cushion at him.

'That's enough, Alex – go and get on with your homework.' The words stung Adam. Alex had a sharp, derogatory side like his mother; at least Tom thought he was capable of something more interesting. Adam went to make himself a coffee and to reply to Rachel.

Adam – Monday 30 September, 17.10
The highlight of your day…putting the washing out, obviously!!

What else have you been up to today? I have been trawling for more jobs to apply to. Deleting junk emails, cleaning and mowing the lawn.
Oh, and thinking about you.

Adam felt he shouldn't lie to Rachel, it felt wrong – but he wasn't going to tell her the truth. That was the wonderful thing about a virtual relationship – you could hide what you didn't want the other person to know, and you could pretend to be what you wanted to be – but if he did that with Rachel he knew this would be as meaningless as all his other virtual flirtations. Adam was hopeful that he could face his fears; if he managed it, *then* he would be able to tell the truth. Maybe she was right. Perhaps this could be something.

David was bored. Work was tedious today. Rachel was doing his head in. His parents were, however, sorted, and doing OK with the extra help. It was amazing how everything had dropped into place.

He had finished work. His last meeting had been cancelled. He should go home and see if Rachel needed any help. He should go and play with the kids, if he could prise them away from Rachel long enough. He found it amazing how they adored her, when most of the time she seemed to just drift about. Perhaps she was different when he wasn't there. He thought about going to the pub. It was several days since the text to Emma. He'd made love to Rachel and despite his worries everything had worked. His emotions were in turmoil…that wasn't something he wanted to think about now. He should avoid the pub, but it was so tempting.

He drove towards the pub without thinking but pulled into the car park near to the kids' park instead. He watched the kids from a distance, staying in the car, hoping his voyeurism wouldn't be misunderstood by the mums and grandparents in the park. Everything felt wrong. He checked his phone, wanting to look as if he was doing something other than staring at the children playing. When Rachel had been at home with Maisie, years ago, it had been full of texts updating him on her day. They used to make him laugh. Rachel hadn't wanted him to miss anything. She hadn't expected him to reply. It was just that she used to get so excited that she had to tell him everything. Then, after her mum died and Jamie was born, there had been silence. Then there were the arguments and after those came the ranting voicemails and the endless demanding texts. Now there was the aching, empty silence.

The sex the other day had felt so right, yet everything about it was so wrong. It was a gentle and tender reminder of what they had once been together, but there had been no passion. He hadn't wanted to stay with her afterwards; he'd had no desire to lie with her, just stroking her hair. She had turned away from him as if she couldn't bear to even look at him.

He knew that she hated the fact that they didn't sleep in the same bed. She just didn't understand that he couldn't cope without sleep. She thrashed about the bed, crying out in her sleep; and that was when she did sleep. She woke throughout the night, getting up to go to the loo or disappearing to check on the kids. Sometimes she went downstairs, made a drink and came back to bed. She took the not sleeping with her so personally that he couldn't even do it at weekends because of the bitching that was directed at him. As a couple they felt done…finished. It couldn't ever be finished, though – they had the kids.

In the past month Rachel had become more herself, but she felt like a stranger. David had no idea what would happen next – he thought they should just drift for now. She didn't work and he didn't earn enough to leave, the kids were small, and she was too fragile, too unstable to live alone with them. He guessed they just had to stick with marriage for now. Emma was just escapism and at the moment he had to deal with his reality. He started the car and drove home.

Rachel smiled as she read Adam's last message and closed her laptop. She had just enough time to clean upstairs before David got home. She'd reply to Adam later, when the kids were in bed and David had retreated to his study. She liked it when he flirted with her.

A loud, impatient knock at the door interrupted her drifting and rather lustful thoughts. The gruff-looking man didn't smile, just thrust a large parcel at her and waited for her to sign. Rachel was delighted. New clothes – she would try them on now, then she could get them stashed away before David came home. She smiled at herself in the mirror.

Five

Rachel – Thursday 10 October, 21.42
You know what we should do…get together and go and see a band like the old days…even get Matt to come.

Adam – Thursday 10 October, 21.47
Where have you been all day??
  Aren't we a bit old to go out moshing?

Rachel – Thursday 10 October, 21.52
Busy catching up on all the house-crap I should have been doing but haven't because I spend too much time on Facebook messaging you, lol. Then David came home early and was hanging about playing with the kids and annoying me. He's doing that a lot lately. Obviously the Bar Tart doesn't want him any more.
  I haven't moshed for years so I have no idea…but are you ever too old to mosh???

Adam – Thursday 10 October, 21.55
Last time I went to see a band with Matt we stood at the back of the pit…so maybe we are, lol. Don't want to break a hip or anything.
  Are you OK about David?

Rachel – Thursday 10 October, 21.59
I don't think I'm old enough to break a hip and anyway aren't your forties now the new thirties or something? We could try??? Just need to find a band somewhere in the Midlands.

I don't care about David any more, Adam. I'm OK.

Adam – Thursday 10 October, 22.30
I'll see who's playing!
Sleep well xx

Adam would look for a band and wonder if just maybe he could travel far enough to meet Rachel. He'd keep trying. Try to break the endless routines and the paralysis of fear.

Rachel had taken to falling asleep with her phone under her pillow. That way she didn't feel so alone. She fell into a dreamless sleep that night, and for once slept until morning.

Rachel – Friday 11 October, 09.51
I am in Costa!!! Alone. I have a large skinny hazelnut cappuccino and no children!!!!!! I have my phone for company and nothing to do but sit – oh, the bliss! Maisie is at school and Jamie at pre-school. I had forgotten what leaving the house alone is like. I can't think why I haven't done this before! I could zoom round the house like a madwoman, changing the beds and wielding the vacuum cleaner, or I could sit and just be!!!!! Sitting and just being seems to win out today and it means I also have time to chat to you – that is, if your little green dot appears, of course!

Well, as you're not online I shall have a meaningless ramble. Sometimes I feel as if I'm going out of my mind, the days seem so long. Sometimes they are lovely sunny days filled with the park and kids in a good mood and laughter. Other days are an endless monotony of juggling pointless household tasks with whining kids and cleaning up paint, wiping up mess, and the most exciting thing that will happen all day is a conversation at the school gate but even then the majority seem to have somewhere they need to be going: an after-school club or popping round to their mum's or their sister's. We sometimes have to rush off to clubs too, but mostly it is just the three of us heading home to nobody…

I should be cheerful today, I have head space – maybe that's the problem: too much time to think. The hum of conversation surrounds me but I am not part of it. The coffee is, however, good and very strong. The barista has done an excellent job and the foam is dense, the chocolate sitting now in a crisp layer as the foam gradually recedes – which means I should stop moaning to you and drink it, lol.

I enjoy the people-watching, though. The man in the corner absorbed in his paper. The guy up in the other corner typing away on his laptop. I used to see him all the time with his daughter. She must have gone to school now and I guess he works or always worked from home; he must have been a stay-at-home dad…should I ask him how he copes? The couple behind me are hilarious – they sound as though they've been married forever. So far they have had a five-minute conversation about receding gums and now *they've moved on to her hair colour. Although maybe the marriage is more alive than you first think, as he has just suggested she dye her hair red and has told her not to forget to match her collar and cuffs. I missed the last bit due to a screaming child but they've moved on to waxing!! I'm not sure now if they're talking about her collar or her cuffs. And now apparently somebody is a giver...I wish I were sitting closer!!!!!!!!!!!!*

Adam – Friday 11 October, 10.32
You've left the house!!!! How does that feel?
 I have news! Job interview next week.

Rachel – Friday 11 October, 10.33
Hello. It's almost like having you come out with me, lol. It's great – I have a paper and my second coffee.
 Adam, that's amazing news...which day?

Adam – Friday 11 October, 10.45
Next Wednesday. I'm terrified. I have so much preparation to do! I'll message you later. xx

Rachel – Friday 11 October, 10.47
Oh...good luck. I must go home and do stuff. I've been meaning to look up those teaching and teaching assistant courses. Yes, later xxxxxxx

Adam noted the flurry of kisses and smiled.

Rachel felt worried that Adam would move on with his life and leave her behind.

*

Julia felt back to her old self. Her energy levels were back up. She was sleeping well and her appetite was back. Work was going well and since the helpless laughter over the vibrator incident her friendship with Jim had reached a new level of intimacy. She told him things. She always had confided in him, but she had kept the more personal stuff back. Now the floodgates were no longer held in check, and over wine there was an outgushing of her emotions. She told Jim how hard it had been to cope with the accident and all that happened afterwards. She told him how her love for Adam had been betrayed by his online flirtations. She was hurt, angry and missed the boys. She wanted to go home before her marriage was over.

In turn Jim told her of his relocation to the Leeds office and how he would make sure she came with him. He was a kind and solid man. Julia concluded his wife was very lucky as they hugged a drunken goodbye. She made a note to pick up an extra coffee on the way into the office tomorrow – they would both need it.

Julia thought she should text Adam with the news. It was too late to call. It seemed pointless, though. She could see how often he was on Facebook; his little green dot appeared all the time. She wondered who it was this time. His social media dalliances were usually short-lived. This time, though, she was worried. She told herself it would be fine once she was home all the time; it was just because he was screwed up and spent too much time on his own.

Adam had meant to tell Julia about the job interview. The weekend had been more pleasant than usual, though, so he had decided not to: she would put too much pressure on him. She would want to check his CV and go through his presentation point by point as though he were a small child. In the end he decided that what she didn't know wouldn't hurt her, and it would make it easier for him, if he didn't get the job. The post-interview interrogation could be avoided and comments like 'if we work on it you could have a better outcome next time' could be left where they should be left – unspoken. Anyway, Rachel was more than enough emotional support.

The night before the interview he didn't sleep until 4 a.m. He woke with a headache and nervous turmoil in his stomach. The interview was at ten, which was good, he felt, as he had less time to dwell.

Before he left in the morning there were two messages. One from Julia reminding him to pick up her dry cleaning as she needed her black suit for an important meeting next week, and the other from Rachel.

Rachel – Wednesday 16 October, 06.59
Really, really GOOD LUCK today!!! Don't reply, don't be late. Focus and breathe… You will be amazing…or you will really suck, lol. Make sure your shoes are clean, double-knot your laces and don't forget your presentation xxx
Oh, and go to the loo before you go in ☺
Big hugs. Message me later xxxxxxxxxxxxxxxx xxxxxxxxx

He laughed when he read her message, and felt calm. He could do this.

Rachel worried about Adam all morning and tried to keep busy with housework but soon got bored. The kids were at school and pre-school. She put on the new fitted black tunic she had stashed in the wardrobe; with black leggings, boots, make-up and her hair framing her face, she didn't shrink from the mirror. She went to town to buy new mascara and drink coffee.

Adam – Wednesday 16 October, 13.10
It went well! I'm so relieved that it's over. They will let me know this week. All the interviews are today, so I suspect if I get it they will let me know tonight. There is only one round of interviews!! I don't think I could cope with any more. I feel mentally raped. I'm sure interviews have got much harder than they used to be.

Thank you for your message this morning, it made me laugh.

Rachel – Wednesday 16 October, 13.30
Thank goodness for that. I was worrying about you all morning!!!

Adam, you will still message me, won't you? I know you will be busy, but...

Adam – Wednesday 16 October, 13.32
Of course I will. (Assuming I even get it!) There is before-work, morning coffee break, lunch, afternoon coffee break and not forgetting loo breaks from all that coffee-drinking. You make life better, Rachel. Much better. Why would I want to lose that?

Rachel – Wednesday 16 October, 13.40
Well, just make sure you take all your breaks, then. No lunch at your desk...

Adam – Wednesday 16 October, 13.45
If I get it! I would have to go to a lot of meetings outside the office but I can have you online in the corner of my screen all day if you like ;)

David was home early again. When he walked through the door, he wasn't met by the vacant, wafting Rachel and mounds of mess. Instead he was greeted by his wife, looking the way she used to look, with happy, contented kids sitting at the kitchen table doing puzzles with their mum. He could smell food, a wonderful smell that seemed to be coming from the slow cooker. He also noticed that Rachel's phone was on the table next to her. He had noticed that her phone always seemed to be next to her.

Rachel – Wednesday 16 October, 16.55
David is home early again. It ruins my late-afternoon messaging, lol.

Adam – Wednesday 16 October, 17.25
They just called. I didn't get the job.
The good news is, though, that they offered me a different role and I accepted. I have a fucking job!!! How easy was that? I've been tearing myself up with fear and anxiety for months and the first job interview I have, I get offered a job. Not the job I was after, I admit. The pay is worse, in fact the pay is dire. But the good news is, this one is much more home-based. They were worried that I had been out of the loop too long to take on a managerial role. So now I am one of the underlings doing online 'business initiative support' at home. How cool is that?

Rachel – Wednesday 16 October, 20.10
That's fantastic! You should celebrate. Open a bottle of wine. I've got a cup of tea. I've gone to bed early…I said I felt ill. How about an online party for two?

Adam – Wednesday 16 October, 20.25
Were you waiting for me to be online, or were you chatting up various other potential lovers???
    An online party for two it is…I have a good bottle of shiraz. The kids are busy. So it's just you and me. Next you'll be telling me what you are wearing ;)

Rachel – Wednesday 16 October, 20.35
Of course I was waiting for you. I got rid of all the others last week ☺ Well, obviously I'm not wearing very much – I'm in bed.

Adam – Wednesday 16 October, 20.37
So when you say not very much…do you wear knickers in bed?

Rachel – Wednesday 16 October, 20.38
Oh, no, I fling those straight off!
    So when you told me what you would do if you were in the room with me – you know, a few weeks ago when I got a bit cross with you because I thought I was just one of many? Well, I don't think I ever told you what I would do if you were in the room with me…

Adam – Wednesday 16 October, 20.40
I think, as you are in bed already, then now would be as good a time as any…

Rachel – Wednesday 16 October, 20.41
OK!...but if you ever post this in a public place with my name attached to it I will hunt you down and kill you.

If you were in the room right now I'd pull you towards me and kiss you until your lips were bruised, then while I was still kissing you I would slide my hands down beneath my crisp white cotton sheets and push my fingers deep inside myself, then I would take those ever so wet fingers and slide them across your very bruised lips and watch as you licked your lips and tasted me for the very first time.

Adam – Wednesday 16 October, 20.47
Christ, Rach! Taste you...that would be rather, err, interesting...

Rachel – Wednesday 16 October, 20.49
I'm dying of embarrassment now. See what you do to me!! I really shouldn't have said that. FFS, that was not what I meant to say...stupid Facebook – I can't take it back. Adam...oh, just forget I said it. It wasn't supposed to be err, interesting!!

Adam – Wednesday 16 October, 20.50
You've gone offline! Rach...come back, don't leave me hanging.

When David walked into the bedroom Rachel pretended to be asleep. She had shoved her phone under her pillow. She had expected more from Adam's response. She wondered if she was just having a one-sided fantasy about him. They flirted all the time; she wasn't so stupid that she could no longer identify flirting.

'You OK, Rach? I thought I heard you crying,' David said.

'Must have been in my sleep,' Rachel mumbled.

The urge to touch another adult person overwhelmed her. She reached up to kiss him and for a moment he kissed her back, but then the kiss seemed to drift away, lips parted and they said goodnight.

Adam was furious at himself. Why hadn't he said more? *Err, interesting*! What the fuck had made him type *err, interesting*? It was the shock…he hadn't expected Rachel to come out with something like that. Not that it was unwelcome – quite the opposite. The flirting had been going on for weeks, and if there was ever a chance that he would be unfaithful to Julia then Rachel was it. He had been prepared for the teasing banter to continue. If Rachel wanted to take things to the next level, though…really, was he going to be that stupid with her – reduce what she meant to him to Hot Chat and a good wank?

Adam, Wednesday 16 October, 21.20 (text message)
Hi, Julia. I tried to call you but no answer. Just wanted to let you know I have a job ☺ Call me if you get the chance. I will explain more.

Six

The house was empty and quiet. Everybody else was where they should be, and Rachel was staring out of the kitchen window, leaning on the kitchen worktops and sipping hot black coffee from a large white mug. She watched as a lone magpie hopped across the roof of the shed. Adam had sent her a message every day for the last four days. Today was the fifth day. Rachel had read them but not replied. She watched as another magpie joined the first and she hoped the two would be happy together. As two more magpies joined them, Rachel felt her throat constrict and her breathing and heart rate quicken. The magpies flew about, swooping down. More seemed to join them and as they flew about and moved out of sight she could no longer count them. Rachel just wanted to see two magpies on her shed roof…two for joy. If she couldn't count them, then she didn't know what they meant. Sorrow, joy, girl, boy, silver, gold, secrets never to be told… What if there were eight, eight for a kiss? Or was it eight for a wish and nine for a kiss? Didn't an old version of the rhyme have death or heaven in it somewhere?

Rachel panicked and ran outside, but was left with a distant blur of black and white and no way of knowing how many magpies had been there, as the slam of the back door frightened them away. She retreated inside and slid to the floor in the hallway, her back against the wall, and cried until nothing made sense any more. At 10.15 a.m. she blew her nose on the tissue that was up her sleeve and then went to find her phone. Life wasn't right without Adam.

Rachel – Monday 21 October, 10.20
Hi. I missed you.

Adam – Monday 21 October, 10.21
I've been sitting here waiting for my phone to ping at me. I gave you your own sound so I knew it would be you.
   I missed you too.
   What happened and are you OK?

Rachel – Monday 21 October, 10.22
You gave me my own sound? Lol.
   I felt like an idiot. I said the wrong thing. Then died of embarrassment.

Adam – Monday 21 October, 10.33
It wasn't the wrong thing, Rachel...I was just taken by surprise. When I've flirted with you online before, you've flirted back, but I'm the only one who has ever been graphic before. We chat on here all day, messages fly back and forth...obviously this is something more than friendship. But I worry that it's just regret about what we didn't do when we were younger. Then I think about it and the things we say to each other and I want to touch you. I want to hold you close to me. I know people do the whole sexting or Hot Chat thing, but do we really want to? It takes things to a whole new level, and it requires a lot of trust.

Rachel – Monday 21 October, 10.34
I trust you.

I know already I want to be with you. I lie alone in bed at night and think about being with you.

Adam – Monday 21 October, 10.37
OK, so if I made the drive to see you and I was alone in a room with you I'd drink the coffee and I'd sit with you and we would talk.

Rachel – Monday 21 October, 10.38
Lol, really – we'd talk?

OK...but something that worries me...I can't touch you, I can't be with you but if I tell you how I want to touch you, well, then I worry that it could all be a bit seedy. Couldn't we just meet up, take it from there?

Adam – Monday 21 October, 10.41
I've got so much on right now – the job and everything.

It doesn't have to be seedy, but the other night when I had too much to drink I just wanted to tell you how I felt, and that was wrong. If you have real feeling for someone, it's not seedy. Just think of it as fantasy.

Rachel – Monday 21 October, 10.42
I can't quite believe I'm having a Facebook chat about virtual sex while putting away the laundry...

Adam – Monday 21 October, 10.45
Oh, I don't know – depends if you're folding your underwear. Unless of course you wear big turquoise knickers. If you do, that could be a bit of a turn-off.

Rachel – Monday 21 October, 10.46
But big turquoise knickers are just so comfy. Doorbell!!

Adam – Monday 21 October, 11.48
Finally! Your little green dot has come back. I've been stalking Facebook for an hour.

Rachel – Monday 21 October, 11.49
Sorry, lol. I didn't know you were going to wait online for me. You do realise you now sound rather creepy!!

Adam – Monday 21 October, 11.51
OK, just crossing 'stalker fantasy' off my list – won't be playing that one out, then. I had stuff I wanted to tell you…but you distracted me with talk of big knickers.

Rachel – Monday 21 October, 11.52
What did you want to tell me?

Adam – Monday 21 October, 11.53
I wanted to tell you how I want to hold you close to me, to watch your eyes close as I kiss you, to breathe in the essence of you…I want to run my hand through your hair, to feel the softness of your cheeks as they brush against mine and to look into those beautiful eyes that I now only see in photographs. I want to let you know the hundreds of ways I want to touch your body and your soul. I want my lips to travel down your neck…

Rachel – Monday 21 October, 11.57
Oh, and how I want those lips to touch mine, to taste you, to find your tongue as it entwines with mine, to

feel your hot breath as you kiss my neck and hold me close. I want to hold your face cupped in both my hands and draw you to me…I want my hands to travel down your back and under your shirt, touching your skin and feeling the warmth of your body as it presses against mine…

Now go away, stop distracting me!

Adam – Monday 21 October, 12.02
You are a cruel and heartless woman – how can you leave me in this state? Actually I think I need to go and spend some time alone somewhere!

Rachel – Monday 21 October, 14.36
I shall say nothing more about all the places I would like my tongue to travel over your body, as I have the school run shortly. Actually, all that in one sentence sounds really wrong!

David has just texted me to say he has a meeting somewhere up north on Wednesday so he will be away. The kids are usually in bed by eight…

I'm just saying I will be alone in bed with my phone and I won't be interrupted…

Adam – Monday 21 October, 15.22
I can't think of a better way to spend Wednesday evening… Well, I can, but that would involve an awfully long drive xxxx

Rachel smiled to herself. This morning she had been in a pit of despair. Adam had made everything better.

*

Adam closed the cover over his phone and wondered what the hell he was doing. Somehow, though, he knew he couldn't stop himself.

When David arrived home he noticed Rachel's phone was on the kitchen worktop next to her. She was smiling, and singing to herself. She even turned round from the sink where she was peeling potatoes and kissed him on the mouth. She looked amazing: her eyes sparkled, her cheeks were flushed, and he liked the way the T-shirt she was wearing clung to her body.

Julia tried to call Adam to tell him her own good news. Her transfer request had been approved and thanks to Jim it was a sideways move, so she wouldn't have to face demotion. She would start in Leeds straight after the Christmas break. She called six times but nobody answered. She sent a text and left a message on his voicemail. Adam didn't take the kids out in the week; she wondered where they all were.

As a rare Monday night treat Adam took the boys out for pizza; he needed a break from messaging Rachel. It was becoming obsessive, he knew it was, but how did he stop? Those days with no contact had been terrible; without her constant distraction all his old obsessions had come back with a great big wallop. Life was better with Rachel in it, but he was worried she wanted more than he could offer.

No message from Adam on Tuesday morning made Rachel grumpy. She had sent a message the previous night and had woken up expecting one from Adam. That was what they did now. They had developed a pattern as they got to know each other's routine. Coffee time, mid-morning, they were often both online and would chat and flirt. Twenty or thirty messages a day between them wasn't unusual if they were reminiscing about college days. Then Rachel would be busy with the kids and cooking dinner and they would message each other again late into the night when they were both in bed alone. One or the other would end a message with a 'Goodnight' and then a response would be sent the following morning.

This morning there was no message, and last night he had gone offline early, without saying why. He had stopped messaging her, she just knew it. The implied suggestion of Wednesday night had frightened him away. She had thought this was something that was going somewhere, and he had just been flirting with an old friend. She was stupid and irrational. She told herself this repeatedly, but as she helped Jamie on with his coat she wanted to cry.

Rachel looked better these days, and sometimes she even smiled when she said hello to the other parents. Today it was raining and her hair was tied back in a severe ponytail to stop it frizzing in the wet. She had applied make-up, as she did every morning now. Even David had given her a compliment a few days ago. This morning he had ruined it, though, by commenting on her hair, asking her if she was working as a dominatrix. She had scowled at him and shepherded the kids out of the door.

Autumn had arrived with bluster. Rain stung their cold cheeks and yellowing leaves were swirled around as they were ripped from trees before they were ready to fall. The children were excitable, and Rachel had to laugh as Jamie jumped from puddle to puddle and chased after fluttering, floating leaves like a crazed puppy. The house felt warm and cosy as they tumbled through the door, fighting the force of the wind as it tried to snatch the handle away from Rachel's hand. With a damp Maisie deposited at school, Rachel and Jamie had half an hour together before pre-school. She changed his wet trousers for dry ones and made them both a cup of tea, Jamie's being more a cup of tepid discoloured milk. Rachel indulged them both with the addition of sugar and they cuddled on the sofa, chatting, until it was time to leave. It was hard to think back to a time when she had been so desperate she'd thought she had suffocated him. She blocked the memory and kissed him on top of his head.

Alone at home and still with no message from Adam, Rachel started looking at courses she wanted to do to get back to work. The PGCE seemed the obvious choice – become a teacher. Applications started at the end of the month. If it was such a good idea, though, she wondered why the thought of applying left her feeling about as enthusiastic as a long walk to the gallows. All day with other people's kids! The problem was she had no real career path to follow. She had drifted into jobs without aim or purpose. Maybe she should just start looking for an admin job. She definitely needed a focus other than mooning around thinking about Adam.

The Monday night pizza with the boys had gone well. Alex and Tom had been delighted by Adam's spontaneity. Driving in the dark had been something he wouldn't have done a month ago. He felt good. He felt his life had value for a change. He wanted to tell someone. He wanted to tell Rachel. He thought about taking a risk and explaining the whole sorry saga of the last four years. When he tried to log on, though, his internet connection had disappeared into the ether and the urge to tell her went with it. His connection to his virtual life was not restored until late Tuesday afternoon.

Adam – Tuesday 22 October, 16.22

Hello! So sorry, I have had no internet since last night! And my phone signal is too weak here to use Facebook. You don't get a high-speed connection in the middle of nowhere; apparently the cows don't use it or something. Sorry, talking rubbish, as usual. So where were we? Ah, yes, Wednesday…

So how was your day? Mine was spent shouting at people, telling them that they needed to get me back online pronto!!!

Other than that I have a start date for my job, which is 28 October. So now I am panicking!

Rachel – Tuesday 22 October, 16.35

It was a long day without you. I have done some soul-searching and decided a career in teaching is not for me. I've decided to look for an ordinary job. Jamie will start school next year and I need to do something, especially as David will probably run off with the Bar Tart soon.

Now I have to see to the kids. Later?

Adam – Tuesday 22 October, 16.39

Good for you! Later, yes. Go feed the kids. xx

Adam – Tuesday 22 October, 16.52

So you weren't cross with me for disappearing, then?

Rachel – Tuesday 22 October, 16.55

Distraught, yes. Cross, no. Later! xxxx

Seven

Julia sat at her desk, tapping her pen on a yellow Post-it note pad. She had been about to write something on it, but now she couldn't remember what. She was still thinking about the weekend. No sex. Not even on Friday night. Adam had been so warm and loving in the past few weeks, then all of a sudden this weekend he had been cold and distracted, checking his phone every hour. On her iPad she watched his little green dot appear on Facebook as she left herself logged in. Then it would disappear just as quickly.

This was different from the flirting he had done before. This was affecting his mood. Either that or she was overreacting and it was as he had said, that he was anxious about starting the job. She had tried to log on to his Facebook account as him, trying all his old passwords, but none of them had worked and she didn't want to lock him out and make him suspicious. Her phone rang and she was back, lost in the world of work.

David sat in a lay-by in his car. Rain was being swept off the bonnet by the driving wind and he watched the rivulets as they mapped their route across his windscreen. The intermittent wipers swooshed them away. He was up north and it was cold and wet. He was miserable.

Rachel – Wednesday 23 October, 21.59
Where are you?

Adam – Wednesday 23 October, 22.03
In my study, waiting for you. Large squashy leather sofa, earth tones throughout the room. There is, however, a lock on the door and the boys are in their rooms. They're extremely unlikely to disturb me again tonight. I told them I had to do some work for my new job.

Rachel – Wednesday 23 October, 22.06
The large squashy sofa sounds nice.

Adam – Wednesday 23 October, 22.07
Should I ask where you are? And perhaps what you are wearing, lol?

Rachel – Wednesday 23 October, 22.08
Sure, why not start with a cliché?!

I'm in bed, the door is locked; I have black lace pants on (does that sound a bit obvious, because actually they are cotton ones from the supermarket…I'm not sure I'm setting the scene here!) and a matching bra (obviously matching the fantasy lace, not the supermarket cotton…er, I don't think I'm very good at this!) but on top I still have a pair of jogging bottoms and a T-shirt. Very comfy before bed but I think I should take them off now, don't you?

That was about as un-Hot Chat as you get, wasn't it??

Adam – Wednesday 23 October, 22.10
Lol. Oh, I definitely think you should take them off…

So if you have taken them off, does that mean you just have on the black lacy underwear (I'm going with the lace-and-thong-type styling and ignoring other references) and apart from that you have naked flesh lying on crisp white cotton sheets??

Rachel – Wednesday 23 October, 22.11
I do indeed and of course I already told you the other day that I have crisp white cotton sheets! So what would you do if you were here in the room with me?

Adam – Wednesday 23 October, 22.13
Well, if you're lying on the bed it would seem rude not to join you. Perhaps I should lie next to you. Would you like me to kiss you? I presume you would, but instead of kissing your lips I'm going to lean over and kiss your neck, nuzzle into your ear (that doesn't sound quite right, but I'll go with it for now) so that you can feel the warmth of my breath. I'm lying on your right and my hand is on your shoulder, gently pulling you towards me; my left hand I have slid under your head…

Oh, dear, this really isn't going well. I'm starting to sound like somebody giving instructions in a game of Twister!! I shall try again.

I'm running my fingers through that wonderful long dark hair of yours. I brush my lips across your cheek and find your mouth. Your lips are already a little apart, moist where your tongue has touched them, wanting to be kissed. You taste of toothpaste and red wine. Have you been drinking?

Rachel – Wednesday 23 October, 22.18
The hair has a little help these days! I don't need to tell you that, lol. Just the one glass – I thought it might help to relax me.

Oh, I have licked my lips and I have waited for your kiss for so long. You taste of toothpaste and coffee...this is not a good time of night to be drinking coffee.

Adam – Wednesday 23 October, 22.19
I know, but I wanted to make sure I was very awake. I want to take my time touching your body. Where are your hands?

Rachel – Wednesday 23 October, 22.20
We are lying on our sides face to face...still kissing; now your tongue is touching mine, more passionate; your hand is still in my hair. Your right hand is on my hip, gently pulling me even closer into you, and you move it into the small of my back so you can pull me closer to you. I'm pushing my body into yours. My right hand is behind your head, pulling your mouth deeper into mine, and my left hand is travelling slowly up and down your back (this Twister thing is catching!).

Adam – Wednesday 23 October, 22.23
I have to pull away from you so I can unhook your bra and take off my T-shirt. We lie back down, your breasts soft against my chest. I have to touch them; your nipple hardens as my hand closes over it. I move my mouth down, kissing all the way, and run my

tongue around each nipple. Just run your fingers over where I would put my tongue and tell me how it feels.

Rachel – Wednesday 23 October, 22.24
It feels as if I really have your tongue there. If I close my eyes I can feel you. I'm lying back, wanting you to touch me everywhere, my body arching towards you as you kiss my breasts, looking down so I can watch you. I start to feel that I really want you inside me but I don't want to rush this moment; I've waited so long to touch your skin…to run my hands through your hair. But I'm impatient to feel you, so I begin to unbuckle your belt.

Adam – Wednesday 23 October, 22.27
Rachel, you have no idea how much I need you to unbuckle my belt right now! I want us both naked. We take off my jeans together, laughing as I struggle to undo the zip. Pants come off and I slide my hand between your legs just for a moment, wanting to feel how hot and wet you are inside. I need to touch you, just for a moment…

Rachel – Wednesday 23 October, 22.29
Oh…that moment felt so amazing, just teasing me for a second…now I want you so much. I hold back…kissing your chest, gently biting one of your nipples, a little too hard maybe as it makes you gasp. I run my tongue down your body…I want you in my mouth. I want to taste you. I want to feel you hard against my tongue. I slide my tongue from the base of your cock to the top, gently flicking my tongue across

the tip, before, painfully slowly, moving my tongue all the way back down. You push against me and I know you want me to take you in my mouth, but I'm going to make you wait.

Shit, one of the kids is crying. Stay there, I'll be back!

Adam – Wednesday 23 October, 22.51
You're not coming back, are you? Rachel, where have you gone???????? Off to crawl walls. Jesus, you have no idea how much I currently want to get in a car and drive for five hours to touch you!

Adam – Wednesday 23 October, 23.04
I'd just like to say I didn't wait for you any longer. I resorted to porn featuring the rear view of women with long dark brown hair :/

I guess it's goodnight, then!!!!!!!!!!!!!!!!

I hope everything is OK. I realise now I have been absorbed in my own frustrations and obviously something has gone badly wrong at your end. It also went badly wrong at my end but I'm not dwelling on that!! I shall shut up now. Hope you are OK xxxxxxx

Adam – Thursday 24 October, 06.55
Is everything OK? I'm now rather worried as I expected a little message symbol and a message telling me what was wrong last night. The fact that I can only get in touch with you like this is now rather frustrating!

Rachel – Thursday 24 October, 07.22
So sorry – Jamie was running a really high fever! I've been up half the night, got to get Maisie to school. Sorry...

*lol. Were you OK? Sorry again, I shouldn't laugh! I'm
just kind of imagining how I might have left you…*

Adam – Thursday 24 October, 07.31
Is he OK now, though? You must be shattered.
    *And don't worry about me…I mean, I just carried
the fantasy on by myself, lol.*

Rachel – Thursday 24 October, 11.59
*Yes, we were knackered; we both fell asleep on the sofa
this morning. The miracle of Calpol…he's better now,
bouncing around eating jam sandwiches, lol. As for
the rest…oh, OK, really? How did it end, then?*

Adam – Thursday 24 October, 12.20
The usual – ejaculation and a tissue!!!!!

Rachel – Thursday 24 October, 12.25
*Adam!! I can't believe you just said that! Lol, not
exactly what I meant but never mind!*
    *It wasn't quite what I expected to feel. When I
closed my eyes (except when typing obviously), and
touched my own body where I wanted you to touch
it…well, it felt more intimate than I had expected. I
was worried it would feel desperate, seedy even, but it
didn't. It made me think how much I wanted you to
really do those things, though. How much I want to
spend real time with you.*

Adam – Thursday 24 October, 12.31
*I know, Rach, it was the same for me. Next time we
should do it when the kids are out!!!!!!*

Just take things slowly. I need to start work, get my life back in order. We are OK like this, aren't we??

Rachel – Thursday 24 October, 12.33
For now, I guess. I'd better go and see to Jamie. Later?

Adam – Thursday 24 October, 12.33
Always later, lol xx

Rachel – Thursday 24 October, 12.33
xxxxxxx

David was home much earlier than expected on Thursday. When he walked in at lunchtime Rachel was in the kitchen, filling a blue plastic beaker with water for Jamie. Her laptop was open on the dresser. He glanced at it, not really meaning to pry, but noticed a message chain with someone called Adam and the last line ended with a row of kisses.

Rachel jumped, as she hadn't heard him come in. 'Hi, you made me jump,' she said as she leaned across and snapped the lid of her laptop shut.

Adam – Thursday 24 October, 20.22
You OK? I've been busy getting the house tidy for the weekend. Otherwise Julia will bitch about the fact that I haven't plumped the cushions on the sofa!
I have to go into the office (that sounds strange) to take in some paperwork and pick up bits and bobs for my home office. It all feels very real now.

Rachel – Thursday 24 October, 20.35
Then you will be too busy for me ☹

Is she a bitch, then, your wife? Why haven't you left her if she makes you so unhappy?

Adam – Thursday 24 October, 20.36
I will always have time for you...I told you that several times already ☺

It's not always been bad. In fact it was once pretty good. We always had kids around, though, right from the start, which was difficult. Since Mum and Dad died...well, I needed stability. She provides security, a home for me and the kids, and it was hard for her, I suppose, taking a job so far away. It was harder for me, though. I don't think she minds being away that much.

I'm rambling. I'd rather talk about last night...

Rachel – Thursday 24 October, 20.40
Do you think that's what it would be like if you were in a room with me? Do you think we should have talked first?

Adam – Thursday 24 October, 20.42
Rach, we talk all the time, many times a day...well, we don't actually talk, but we type, lol. We tell each other in great detail the circumstances of our daily lives. I even know how often you are late taking your daughter to school.

I suppose some time we should actually talk...that would be weird, to hear your voice after all these years.

I feel as though I'm part of your daily life without even being there, but yes, if I were in a room with you I would want to talk to you. The first thing I would want to do is to hold you, though, clothes on, to let all the years melt away. Rachel, you do understand how special you are to me, don't you? You understand that what I said to you last night...well, if circumstances were different, then that is how I would want us to be.

Rachel – Thursday 24 October, 20.43
Then make circumstances different.

Adam – Thursday 24 October, 20.44
If only life were that easy!!!! We just need time, don't we? Time to see where this goes.

Rachel – Thursday 24 October, 20.46
Yes, I guess. You do keep telling me that.

David came home early today. Which actually makes talking difficult. I was using my laptop to chat to you. It was open on the side...I think he saw the row of kisses. He left about ten minutes later. He said he had a text and had to go out. It was probably the Bar Tart beckoning him to her lair. He didn't say anything but it makes you wonder what our spouses would think if they read some of this!

Adam – Thursday 24 October, 20.50
We've never actually done anything, but I suppose it would look pretty bad. You need to be more careful, though. If he read this it could end everything. You really need to be careful for the sake of your kids.

Rachel – Thursday 24 October, 20.52
Cheers, thanks for the concern! I wasn't expecting a lecture about the security of my kids. I care about my kids!

Adam – Thursday 24 October, 20.53
Sorry. I know you care about your kids. I was just a bit shocked, that was all. I'm always really careful at the weekends.

You sound all feisty and angry…do you feel all hot and are your cheeks all flushed??

Rachel – Thursday 24 October, 20.55
Sod off!! Next you will be telling me we should have make-up sex.

Adam – Thursday 24 October, 20.56
I can think of much better ways you could bite at me…

Rachel – Thursday 24 October, 20.57
You can go watch brunette-headed porn being thrust at from behind and wank yourself silly. I'm going to bed early. I'm tired.

Adam – Thursday 24 October, 20.58
I'd much rather be holding your hair tightly as I thrust into you from behind.

You aren't really cross with me, are you?

Rachel – Thursday 24 October, 20.59
No, not very. Well, just a bit. Now it appears I'm hot and flushed for another reason! And now I think I may just have to go to bed early for lonely self-gratification!!!!

Goodnight xx

Adam – Thursday 24 October, 21.01
Well, make sure it's me you think of while you're doing
it. Goodnight xx

Rachel – Thursday 24 October, 21.02
Actually tonight I fancy someone a bit younger :P
xx

Adam smiled to himself as he plugged in his phone to charge. Julia would call soon. She would speak to him for a minute or so and then say goodnight to the boys.

He wasn't sure how he felt about the news that she would be home for good in the New Year. They would be a family again, and it would be nice to have her in bed with him every night, but she wasn't the easiest person to live with. And then there was this overwhelming desire for Rachel. She distracted him; she had stopped him obsessing about everything. She had allowed him to feel normal and stop thinking for ever and ever about the accident. Maybe that was it: just the fact that she didn't know let his guilt take time off and restored him to humanity.

But nothing could happen with Rachel, no matter how attracted they were to each other. Once he started work and Julia came home, he figured the intensity of the messages with Rachel would lessen. She would become bored with him; she would get a job and probably leave her awful husband. Or maybe he wasn't really that awful and she would realise that the grass wasn't necessarily greener further north – maybe Rachel was like him, just bored and lonely and looking for someone to play games with. That was a sobering thought indeed.

It would all work out fine in the end. He sighed. Shame, though – Rachel would remain a regret. Strange really how she had never quite understood how attractive she was.

Two days of Julia would have him thinking differently again and wondering how on earth he could leave her.

Rachel slept fitfully that night; the room felt hot and claustrophobic even though it was a big room with high ceilings. A light breeze swished the curtains back and forth. Rachel felt frustrated, alone in her big bed with her crisp white sheets, her duvet and deep, soft pillows. She hugged one pillow to her, but although it had substance it had no weight. For a while she leant her head on it as she might have laid her head on the shoulder of her lover. For a while she cried, although no one could hear her. She felt full of despair and loneliness.

She thought of Adam and imagined him touching her. She touched her own body where she wanted Adam's hands and mouth to be. She slid a finger across her lower lip with pressure, letting it drag across the flesh; halfway along she bit down on it, the slight sensation of pain leaving her more aroused. She crossed her hands and slid them down herself, uncrossing them as they travelled to her breasts. She could almost feel his lips on hers, their tongues entwining. If someone had asked, she would say she already knew what it felt like to have Adam kiss her neck, and hold her breasts. She would say she already knew what it felt like to have her nipples harden to the touch of his tongue. She wanted him so much to run his hands across her hips and pull her body towards his; to rain tiny kisses all over her skin. The desire to have him part her legs and push his fingers inside, to feel how wet she was, was overwhelming.

She wanted to whisper how much she liked what he was doing. She groaned to herself, as she thought of his finger encircling her clit. She was so deep into her imaginings now that they were his fingers playing with her, teasing her, not letting her come just yet.

As she slid her own fingers into herself she imagined Adam's hard cock pushing into her, that wonderful feeling of penetration. She let out a long, shuddering sigh of desire. She imagined him pushing himself deep inside her, bringing himself right out of her so each time he entered her his penis slid down her clit and then deep, deep inside her, with her hands pulling him in as far as she could, pubic bone grinding on pubic bone. As she slid her own fingers over her clitoris she imagined him withdrawing from her and trailing his tongue down the length of her body then using it to make her come before entering her again and fucking her hard, her hands restrained above her head, biting down on her breasts. Her own fingers worked now and with the help of her imagination she shuddered to orgasm three times before falling into a restless sleep.

Eight

Rachel – Tuesday 5 November, 21.56
Fireworks!!! I keep thinking they are going to wake the kids.

Adam – Tuesday 5 November, 21.57
I hardly said anything…surely there can't be fireworks yet??

Rachel – Tuesday 5 November, 21.58
Groan…sometimes you are tragic…the sparkly, bangy kind.

Adam – Tuesday 5 November, 21.59
Bless, very rural Yorkshire; there were some in the village earlier. I went down with the boys but all is now quiet. Want to talk fantasies??

Rachel – Tuesday 5 November, 22.01
How quaint! We're going at the weekend. I let the kids have a couple of sparklers in the garden earlier, then they sat in the window watching all the pretty colours before bathtime.
Fantasies. So we've been doing it straight for the last couple of weeks, then.

Adam – Tuesday 5 November, 22.02
Well, I'm not sure it was exactly straight, and if you can get into some of the positions you say you can, then you must still be pretty flexible, lol.

Rachel – Tuesday 5 November, 22.03
What, you mean flexible for someone of my age? Oh, sure, why not just sideline me for something younger and more attractive? Let me go to a commune where all the other pre-menopausal and undesirable woman over forty hang out!!

Adam – Tuesday 5 November, 22.05
Touch of the rattled cage there. What's up?

Rachel – Tuesday 5 November, 22.06
David's Bar Tart. I went back for another look. She is so much younger than me.
Just forget it…let's talk about fantasies, then, since fantasy is all I have.
Double penetration.

Adam – Tuesday 5 November, 22.08
OK!! Are we talking sex with the addition of toys or are we actually talking two partners?

Rachel – Tuesday 5 November, 22.09
Two blokes, obviously!!
What about you then…bit of a gasper???

Adam – Tuesday 5 November, 22.09
Gasper?

Rachel – Tuesday 5 November, 22.10
Auto-erotic asphyxia, of course!

Adam – Tuesday 5 November, 22.10
Have you been on Google again?

Rachel – Tuesday 5 November, 22.11
I get bored, what can I say?
    So share, then. Yours? Bloody bangers!

Adam – Tuesday 5 November, 22.12
I make no comment to the bangers, lol.
    Well, twins, obviously! Although I did think you might start with something romantic like a moonlit beach!

Rachel – Tuesday 5 November, 22.13
Blonde with big tits – of course! And never a beach. A woodland maybe, or a hay barn as long as you had a thick blanket – don't want to get distracted by spiky bits going up your ass.

Adam – Tuesday 5 November, 22.14
And there was me thinking you rather liked things up your ass.

Rachel – Tuesday 5 November, 22.15
Cock, Adam! Not spiky bits of dried grass.

Adam – Tuesday 5 November, 22.15
Rachel!!!!!!
    You're in a very funny mood tonight.

Rachel – Tuesday 5 November, 22.16
I'm pissed off and frustrated.

Adam – Tuesday 5 November, 22.17
Well, I'm here to help you with your frustrations ;)

Rachel – Tuesday 5 November, 22.18
No, Adam – you don't. We type all the things we would like to do to each other and we masturbate. Therefore technically I relieve my own frustrations!

Adam – Tuesday 5 November, 22.19
I can't get there and back in one night!

Rachel – Tuesday 5 November, 22.19
I don't think you ever want to.
    Goodnight x

Adam – Tuesday 5 November, 22.20
Rachel, don't say goodnight like this!

Rachel – Tuesday 5 November, 22.20
I've gone!!!!!!!!

Adam – Tuesday 5 November, 22.21
Talk to me in the morning, then????

David sat in the pub, stewing over his pint. Emma wasn't even at work; he wished he had checked – or then again in this mood maybe it was better that she wasn't working. Rachel, the new haircut, the clothes, the fact that she had been wearing make-up again...David wondered how thick he was. The way she had jumped when he walked in was a giveaway on its own. All that time she spent mooning over her computer. Her phone was like an umbilical cord.

He remembered an Adam. She'd talked about him. 'The one that got away' or something like that. That Adam had been from sixth-form college, though, years ago; surely she hadn't hooked up again with someone from so long ago? People did, though – he'd heard that story loads of times. He logged on to Facebook and went through her friends list. There he was, smug-looking bastard. He was married, kids, happy family profile picture – just showed what lies you could put on Facebook. His location was wrong – he lived in York. David concluded it couldn't be him, then. But there were no other friends called Adam. He was sure she had been on Facebook, so it had to be him.

David felt confused. Maybe he had just got the wrong end of the stick. Maybe the kisses were just because of something he had said. The clothes, the hair, the make-up – they could just be Rachel feeling better about herself; perhaps she was even trying to get his attention – he hadn't thought of that. Jamie slept better now and the house was tidier, the kids happier.

He struggled to resolve his feelings. He had thought his marriage was over and they were just there for the kids, but the way he was feeling could only be described as jealousy and fear. He was also enraged, just at the thought that anyone had touched his Rachel.

He left the pub and went home. What he should have done was help Rachel with dinner and the kids, but his indignation and anger got in the way. So instead he found every reason he could to bitch and shout at them all and then slammed himself shut in his study.

The next morning he left before anyone was up, without saying goodbye.

Rachel – Wednesday 6 November, 04.55
I have woken up with a horrible cold. My throat is sore, I am aching and my head is throbbing. I am also a snot factory!!!!

Adam – Wednesday 6 November, 07.22
Rachel, I'm sorry you don't feel well – but why have you acquired a batch of new Facebook friends that all seem to be mine? Have you been sending out friend requests to all my connections?

Rachel – Wednesday 6 November, 07.30
What amazes me is how many of them said yes, lol. I do know some of them! Also, you could only know that if you had been on my page. Why were you on my page?

Adam – Wednesday 6 November, 07.45
I was looking at your photos. I was thinking about what you said.

Rachel – Wednesday 6 November, 08.15
And what did you conclude? Shit, school…

Adam – Wednesday 6 November, 09.05
Were you late again?
I didn't conclude anything. I just think better while looking at your photos. Your kids are so young still. With David…you look happy. Are you lying to me?

Rachel – Wednesday 6 November, 09.20
No – skin of my teeth!!!

Of course I'm not lying to you. Why on earth would I do that? If I were happy, why would I be playing weird sex chat games with you?

Adam – Wednesday 6 November, 10.06
But in the photos you look up at him with a look of complete adoration. You rarely look straight at the camera. You look at him.

Rachel – Wednesday 6 November, 10.07
What about you? You seem rather practised at typing dirty!! How do I know you don't do this all the time? You could be perfectly happy, just bored and lonely during the week when Julia is away. I've seen her photos too, you know. She is beautiful, tiny and really thin. And nothing like me!

Adam – Wednesday 6 November, 10.09
Then why would I continue to send you messages all weekend? Surely if that were the case I would just tell you it wasn't possible at the weekend?

Julia is very pretty, but she's a bit of a poison dwarf and has a predisposition for causing pain. When I really needed her she let me down. She took the job away from home because she said we needed the extra money. I wasn't working, but we were just waiting for probate to be completed and Mum and Dad's house to be sold and then it wouldn't have mattered anyway. The money came through two months later. It's taken her three years to apply for a *transfer back to either the York or Leeds office. She is coming back in January to work in the Leeds branch. She could have gone to the York branch but that would have meant a demotion. Her 'boss' is moving to Leeds and apparently he wants her on his 'team'.*

Rachel – Wednesday 6 November, 11.04
But if she comes back, and with you working, that will be the end of us. Aren't you supposed to be working now?

Adam – Wednesday 6 November, 11.31
Coffee break. Things aren't very busy yet. I had a training course this morning but it was cancelled so I'm doing 'research', lol. It will get busy soon but I will still have coffee and lunch.

Did you actually read what I typed about her 'boss'?

Why would it be the end of us? I will still be working at home.

Rachel – Wednesday 6 November, 11.34
You think something is going on with her boss?

Adam – Wednesday 6 November, 11.37
I don't know, really, but she is very close to him.

Rachel – Wednesday 6 November, 11.39
We rarely chat like this any more. Maybe we need to do this as well as the other stuff. It makes it seem more real.

Adam – Wednesday 6 November, 11.42
I know…you're right, we should…we started to tell each other stuff then we kind of got into all the virtual sex. It's difficult (note how I stopped myself using the word 'hard' there) – I look at your photos and all those things I type to you are things I want to happen. Sometimes the desire is overwhelming.

Rachel – Wednesday 6 November, 11.45
Smooth talker. You always say the right things, lol.
    Now I have to hang the washing out and then it will be time for pre-school pick up.
    Later?

Adam – Wednesday 6 November, 11.48
Yes, later. You could carry on telling me your fantasies.
☺

Rachel – Wednesday 6 November, 11.49
What did I just say about talking?

Adam – Wednesday 6 November, 11.50
Yes, but surely sharing your innermost thoughts and secret desires gives me an insight into the real you? More than you would share with anyone else?

Rachel – Wednesday 6 November, 11.51
You're incorrigible!
    I kissed a girl once.

Adam – Wednesday 6 November, 11.51
Really???? (Did you like it, lol?)

Rachel tried hard to be cross with Adam but she knew deep down that things would go somewhere one day. She just had to be patient or maybe give him a little push in the right direction to speed things up a bit. Two magpies hopped, swooped down and settled high in the tree at the bottom of the windswept garden. Rachel pegged out washing and smiled to herself.

Adam tried to settle back to work. He felt swamped and overwhelmed by all the things he needed to know. The software he needed to download alone was giving him a headache. He felt better now things were back on track with Rachel, though. He did wonder why she had started connecting with his friends, but she was right, she did know some of them, as she'd said. He would also make things up with Julia at the weekend. Life would be better once she was home at night. He just had to hope she would stop irritating him so much once he got used to her again. Rachel was right, Julia was beautiful, but she was also cold and very ambitious. Rachel in comparison was a bit scatty and had a warmth you couldn't fake.

Adam decided to book a restaurant just for him and Julia on Saturday, and he would order a taxi so they could both relax. He would make it a celebration for starting his job and because she was coming home. She would enjoy it; she could dress up and wear some super-spiky heels. They hadn't been out alone for years.

He growled at the software. It would all come good in the end.

Adam – Wednesday 6 November, 20.22
So when you say kissed…are we talking tongues? And how long ago?

Rachel – Wednesday 6 November, 20.36
Thank you for asking about my cold. David is nowhere to be seen and the kids are settled in bed.

I had a very busy afternoon. I have been shopping and folding washing. Cleaning of course and cooking. The house is much tidier now the kids are at school and pre-school. All in all, not a bad day. How was yours?

Adam – Wednesday 6 November, 20.36
Sorry – how are you feeling? I will order you some Olbas Oil on Amazon, lol.

Rachel – Wednesday 6 November, 21.22
You have a lot of female friends on Facebook.

Adam – Wednesday 6 November, 21.33
I thought you perhaps felt really ill and had gone to bed early.

Rachel – Wednesday 6 November, 21.34
I have. I took my laptop. The phone is too small for looking at photos.

Adam – Wednesday 6 November, 21.35
You have a lot of female friends too. Did you kiss one of them?

Why are you looking at my friends again?

Rachel – Wednesday 6 November, 21.37
Just trying to get a picture of your life, lol. Where do you live? Your profile still says York but you said you don't live there.

Adam – Wednesday 6 November, 21.38
I don't suppose you live actually in Bath either? You said you live in a village. It would be a daft idea to put our exact location on Facebook, wouldn't it? I live in a hamlet just up the road from a village/small town. I told you that a long time ago. The postman finds me by the postcode.
    Did you find anything else of interest?

Rachel – Wednesday 6 November, 21.42
Not really.
    Yes, the girl I kissed is still a friend…we were drunk. It was a dare at uni and it may have gone a little too far, lol, but we are still friends.
    Goodnight xx

Rachel – Thursday 7 November, 06.30
I thought I had better say good morning before you got all busy with work. Have a good day ☺

At 8.30 a.m. Adam logged on to his computer ready to start work. The first flood of today's emails had started to come through. He wasn't enjoying the work. Despite how it had been described, the job was low-level admin work, at least one grade below the job he had been offered before his life crashed. It was part-time but seemed to take up many more hours, and the pay was appalling. Somehow the feeling that the job had been given to him out of pity was overwhelming. He had been into the office for training and he'd felt as though the other staff were treading on eggshells around him, being extra-nice, telling him not to worry; he felt like a patronised figure employed to make up the equal opportunities statistics. He knew despite everything that he would still have been capable of taking on the managerial role.

Still, it was a job. He was coping with the driving. He hadn't had a meltdown. Time on his hands had been his enemy, allowing the patterns of obsessive behaviour to develop and keep him a prisoner in his own mind. He knew he was a long way from being OK, but the ghosts that haunted him had started to slip away to a more secure place in his subconscious, where he could lock them down for long periods of time. When they emerged they did so with less ferocity, and he sometimes even found himself apologising. He started explaining to them – sometimes he even called them Mum and Dad – that he had done nothing wrong that night, it had been an accident. And he had begun to find peace of mind in forgiving himself. Sometimes he even thought he heard his parents telling him it wasn't his fault.

Rachel, on the other hand, was starting to worry him. All was well with her one minute, then she'd do something strange like the friends thing. Adam wondered about all the things she hadn't told him about her life. At first they had messaged about the way their lives had turned out, but he always had the feeling there was something she wasn't telling him. She had never explained why the marriage had gone so wrong. The death of her mother had affected her badly, he could sense that, but she said very little about it.

The explicit messaging was a mistake, he knew, and yet he couldn't stop himself. There had always been something about Rachel. Sometimes he wondered if he could do it – drive down, meet with her, spend the weekend with her and get her out of his system. He had thought about her so many times over the years and he wanted her more than he wanted his sanity. To touch her, taste her, to slide himself into her body… He shook off the thought and focused on the emails. To fuck Rachel could fuck up his whole life. Julia would be home by Christmas.

Rachel sat at the table eating dinner with David and the kids. She resented his invasion. The way his knife scraped on his plate irritated her. When he took a drink, the audible sound of his swallowing made her want to slap him. She had never before noticed how his jaw rotated as he chewed, and the tiny clacking sound made her simmer. She noticed a small fleck of dandruff just above his right ear and she got up to clear the table before looking at it made her boil over with rage. Maybe she had noticed all these things because the kids were quiet. She also noticed his smell, a mixture of the stale smell of his car and aftershave. He smelt stale.

Rachel banged yoghurt pots in front of the kids and wondered how she had ever let him near enough to her to create them. Their perfection was tainted by his input.

She had sent eleven messages to Adam today and had only had three replies. She'd predicted that this would happen. She wanted to see two magpies fly across the window as she stooped to load the dishwasher. She wondered where they were but it was a silly thought; it was already dark outside, a grim, wet darkness; even the thought of the illuminating sparkle of Christmas just weeks away was not enough to penetrate the depth of her mood. Rachel loved Christmas. By next Christmas, she decided, she would be happier. After all, there was more chance of snow in the north.

David looked at his wife, and even with the scowl on her face he realised how beautiful she was. He'd been wrong in so many ways. He hadn't known how to help her when she needed him. He had withdrawn; taking her to the doctor endless times hadn't been enough. She had needed him to hold her, to give her space to grieve and time to sleep. He had needed to man up and take charge, and all he had done was dither around hand-wringing in the background, hoping the medication would sort her out. The pill in the packet had done very little.

He noted how much time she spent on Facebook. He suspected that this Adam whose name he had seen was just one of many old friends she was reaching out to because she was lonely. Rachel wouldn't betray him, not the way he had betrayed her; she just wasn't like that. He would stay away from the pub too, and no more texting. He had been wrong the other night when he'd thought that making love to her had been the end. His emotions had been mixed up with a desire to escape the past. He wanted his life back. His kids were amazing now; Jamie slept and was a proper little boy. Maisie was a total prima donna but hilarious with it. Christmas was approaching; he'd make it special this year. Rachel loved Christmas.

Julia sat on the compact two-seater sofa in her studio flat. She felt content that her days here were numbered. They wouldn't sell it, they would let it out; it was central to the city so they might even hand it over to a holiday let company. Despite the housing market dip it had been a good investment. Her successor would be appointed by the beginning of next month; chances were it would be an in-house promotion, so her handover would be easy. Her finish date in the Edinburgh office was 20 December and a van would arrive on the morning of the 21st to transport all her personal belongings home. She then had annual leave left, which meant that she would start her new job at the Leeds branch on 6 January.

Christmas would be special this year, she would make sure of that. First task, however, was ridding Adam of his current online flirtation. She would contact the recipient direct, if necessary. Then they could all settle back to family life. Amy would start to come home more, she would get to know the boys again, and now Adam was much more stable she would get him back on track with his career. Yes, she decided, Christmas would be special this year.

Nine

Adam – Wednesday 27 November, 16.55
You're sulking.

Rachel – Wednesday 27 November, 17.02
I'm not sulking. I am trying to cook.

Adam – Wednesday 27 November, 17.03
You are sulking. I told you, I'll reply when I have time. The job got really busy. The hours I work go so quickly now. In the past week things have changed; it suddenly feels like a proper job. I need to apply myself. I make time for you at lunchtime…so don't sulk.

Rachel – Wednesday 27 November, 17.08
You promised there would be coffee breaks as well ☹. I just miss you so much. You get me through the day. When Julia gets back you will send even fewer messages, won't you? Have you thought any more about me driving up to meet you? I have a really good excuse: I made friends on Facebook with an old college friend who lives just north of Manchester…it's perfect. I could visit her for the day then you could arrive later on Saturday and we could both go home on Sunday. If not before Christmas, then maybe after?

Adam – Wednesday 27 November, 17.20
I thought you were looking for a job. Isn't that keeping you busy?

I don't know, Rachel. It may be easier once Julia is home. It would be better still if it were in the week – I could say I was going on a training course or something. Don't think about it now, let's have Christmas first.

Changing the subject completely, I know you got upset when we tried to chat about your mum the other day, but you know you can tell me anything, don't you; this isn't just about…well, you understand that, don't you?

Rachel felt better. Adam was at least thinking about meeting her. She wondered if she should open up to him and tell him just how bad the last few years had been. It might make them closer; or maybe it was better said once they were together.

Over the past few weeks, as Adam's sanity returned, he had had the feeling that Rachel wasn't quite right. Comments she made worried him. He was familiar with the signs! He knew he needed to be careful, though; it would be cold and callous just to cease communication. He knew that was what he should do but the thought of Rachel not being there every day to talk to…he just couldn't do it.

Adam – Tuesday 3 December, 05.55
Thank you for last night…I do wish David worked away more often, lol.

I woke up thinking about you. xx

Rachel – Tuesday 3 December, 06.59
It was my pleasure. I woke up several times thinking of you too, lol. He's not away again for a while. Perhaps just once now before Xmas. Looks like you might have to have some extended lunch breaks.

Adam smiled as he read the message from Rachel. The last few days she had seemed more normal – if having virtual sex could be described as normal. She had stopped saying strange things. She hadn't acquired any more of his Facebook friends. Sometimes he wondered if it was down to his interpretation or just that she dashed off a badly worded message because she was interrupted by the kids. He decided he should stop being paranoid.

She hadn't said any more about meeting up. He switched between wanting to, and knowing he couldn't or wouldn't meet up with her. She seemed to have accepted that maybe they would meet in the New Year. That was just fobbing her off, though. There was no way he could manage that distance from home yet. If he could go that far, the first thing he should do was take the kids on holiday. Julia usually took them, while he stayed at home.

The explicit descriptions of all the things Rachel would do to him when they did meet had him almost convinced that he should meet her just the once, though... Adam would see what it was like living with Julia in the New Year. He needed to think about what he wanted and stop all this switching back and forth. He needed some time out from everything, to get some perspective.

Keeping his mind this busy stopped him worrying which day he was supposed to have a ham and tomato sandwich for lunch, at least. When Julia returned, he was concerned that the stress of it all was going to send him spiralling off somewhere different. Rachel or Julia? He laughed…or maybe both. He took his coffee to his desk. It was still early but he needed to get started; he had a lot of work to do.

Rachel wondered what she would wear when she finally met Adam. She had started getting her hair trimmed and coloured every month; it was long and glossy, the way it used to be. She had her legs and her bikini line waxed; she did sit-ups until her stomach muscles burned in a vain hope that the stretched skin would somehow decide to shrink back to where it should be. She had facials when the kids were at school and pre-school; she had manicures and pedicures and bought new underwear online. The moment Adam couldn't bear to be without her a moment longer, she would be ready. She just had to be patient and keep him wanting her.

Adam – Thursday 12 December, 16.44
So how's the Christmas shopping coming along?

Rachel – Thursday 12 December, 16.49
Just two more clicks, then my credit card details and I do believe I'm done!!
    Except for you – what do you want? And where should I send it?

Adam – Thursday 12 December, 16.51
You know what I want…

Rachel – Thursday 12 December, 16.52
No, I am definitely not buying into your Santa fetish and I haven't got a webcam!!!!!!

Adam – Thursday 12 December, 16.54
Lol. I was thinking of something blacker and with more straps...and you have a MacBook, you told me that, and I know for a fact they have a webcam built in.

Rachel – Thursday 12 December, 19.54
I am not having a virtual Christmas wankfest by webcam!!! Not even if you beg, or dress up as a reindeer.

Adam – Thursday 12 December, 19.56
Will you make me beg?

Rachel – Thursday 12 December, 20.21
I suppose what you really want is me chained up, face down, ass in the air, while you instruct big bad elves to perform unspeakable sex acts on me.

Adam – Thursday 12 December, 20.24
Have you been watching Festive Fetish Porn again??

Rachel – Thursday 12 December, 20.27
Well, I need to keep my hand in ;)...keep up with the seasonal trends! I get bored filling in job applications and I've got nobody to talk to when you are at work ☹

David will be back soon...he is being weird and nice to me and the kids at the moment. He actually suggested we take them to see Santa together at the weekend and then go out for lunch as a family! Bar Tart has obviously dumped him. You may have real competition.

Adam didn't reply. He let the words sit in his mind. He decided there was nothing wrong with Rachel and it had indeed been his own paranoia working overtime. Making his mind tick, tick, tick, always expecting the worst. She was just unhappy and lonely. She had never said whether or not she still had a sexual relationship with her husband. He had presumed she didn't. He wondered if he was wrong and was surprised by how much it bothered him. In the last few weeks the Hot Chat had been hot. At the weekends sex with Julia now seemed…well, if he was honest, it was precise and efficient – but Julia *was* precise and efficient, and he hated the way only moments after they had finished she would, in her words, 'pop and take a quick shower'. Sometimes he thought she might suggest putting a towel under them to save marking the sheets: a sex coaster. With Rachel, Adam imagined tangled sheets and wild abandon. She would also have amazing post-sex hair, a halo of uncombed satisfaction, and her pale skin would flush a gratified pink. He smiled; Rachel was starting to get to him. Thoughts of how to be rid of her no longer plagued him. He had once again resumed his lengthening drives and he was gaining confidence. He found himself looking at hotels and imagining himself there with her.

Rachel didn't send another message when Adam didn't reply. She left him with the thought of her and David together. They hadn't been together at all, since that last time. He still slept in his study and she still sprawled across her king-size bed.

She had noted that Adam had ignored her question regarding his location when she asked; it had been bothering her ever since. The next day she spent time leaning against the kitchen worktop wondering about it: just how hard would it be to find him? She had a vague idea of his whereabouts from things he had told her. She knew he lived in a hamlet that was just outside a large village, nestled somewhere between the Howardian Hills and the North York Moors. York, she also knew, was his nearest major city. The house itself he had implied was large, and he'd said that it was in a rural situation on a hill overlooking a small river, with the steeple of a church in the distance. She also knew that there was a large gateway just down his lane, big enough to be used for the school bus; she remembered him telling her how he watched the boys as they walked down the lane. Google Maps seemed a good place to start. Rachel felt quite excited as she began her search.

The area was largely unpopulated. Rachel zoomed in and out of various locations, spending the whole morning looking at the terrain. Then there it was. She sat back from her laptop, shocked; in fact horrified for a moment that she had found it. Guilt surged through her; she had not expected to find him. She felt a little dirty, as though she needed a shower. She had invaded his privacy and not even expected to get this far, but it had been so easy. She sat for a while, staring at the screen. The knowledge was addictive and, unable to stop herself, she carried on. She needed to know more.

The Google images were quite blurry – when she zoomed in, she couldn't see enough – but what could she find? The location was right, she was sure, but she needed confirmation. The curve of the road into the gateway that looked more like a lay-by. The river, the church – they were all there, but the village seemed to be more of a small town and the house was much closer to it than she had anticipated, although it did stand alone and was surrounded by fields. She noted down the address and searched for the postcode. Pencil in hand, she scribbled it down. Where next? she thought, tapping the pencil, in a repetitive three-tap motion on the side of her laptop. Property websites! She was sure during one conversation he had said they had moved there a couple of years before his parents were killed, and had renovated the place.

There it was, pictures and all. Adam existed. She took a tour of the house but supposed it was nothing like that any more. Still, she imagined herself cosying up to Adam in front of the huge wood-burner in the lounge. She saw herself in the bath filled with bubbles and she imagined herself lying in that bed at night, but not alone. Imagining herself in Adam's bed was the best she could do for now. Rachel smiled, the guilt gone. Adam had given her all these clues so she could find him. He was playing a game with her; a very adult version of hide and seek.

It was a beautiful day. Cold and sharp, the strong sun making skeletal shadows of the trees. After pre-school Rachel took Jamie round town. They had no particular purpose and they went to the park. The big one, the colourful one in the centre of town; she remembered how difficult it used to be just to get there. She'd had no motivation to leave the house – all those irrational fears she had, the panic that would rise like choking bile in her throat. Now she walked along, bending to the side to hold Jamie's hand as they chatted away. They pointed to trees and they stood in amazement watching the birds that flew high above. As a military aeroplane flew low, Jamie jumped into her arms, afraid of the noise, and she held him tight, kissing the top of his head until the plane had passed by. For a moment she buried her nose in his hair, sniffing the fresh cold smell of it and wondering why it had all started so badly with him.

It was too cold to stay in the park for long despite the sun, so they retreated to a coffee shop for lunch. They shared a toastie and a chocolate cupcake and Rachel laughed and smiled as Jamie disappeared behind his hot chocolate mug and revealed himself not only with a chocolate moustache but a chocolate mono-brow to match. She cleaned him up with a wipe and then they wandered around the shopping centre, looking at all the Christmas decorations and lights in the shop windows. She would miss living here. Next Year would be very different. She presumed Adam would have to sell the house, so they could rent for a while. She was sure he wouldn't want to delay them being together. She would have to sell her house too. These things took time, she thought, but it would be worth it in the end. Wait, though – now Julia was at home, of course, it would be daft for his boys to move out of their home; Julia could just get a flat on her own, and maybe them all moving into his house would be a better solution. Rachel pondered these thoughts and concluded they had a lot of options. She and Adam had a lot to talk about when the time was right.

She smiled as she drove the car to school to pick up Maisie. Her daughter would be happy being picked up in the car; it was a real treat for her, as Rachel always made them walk. David wouldn't be home for hours; maybe she should just treat the kids a bit more and take them for huge strawberry milkshakes at the American-style diner by the new cinema. She didn't treat them enough, and she had a lot to make up for over the last few months. Being out of the house would also stop the temptation to message Adam. It wouldn't hurt him to be left with the thought of her and David together for a bit longer.

When Rachel arrived home she checked her phone. There were two messages from Adam, one from early afternoon and one about an hour ago. She was busy with the kids; she would reply later. Reading between the lines, she could tell that Adam was bothered by the thought of her and David.

Rachel – Friday 13 December, 20.45
Don't just hint at the subject, Adam, ask me.

Adam – Friday 13 December, 20.46
Well, do you?

Rachel – Friday 13 December, 20.47
Well, do I what? Or perhaps you should tell me. Do you still have sex with Julia?

Adam – Friday 13 December, 20.52
I asked you first!

Rachel noticed the evasive response. He was online and yet it took five minutes before he replied. She waited, already knowing that his discomfort meant that he did still have a sexual relationship with his wife. She was surprised at first, and then filled with anger; he had implied on several occasions that he no longer had sex with Julia. Colour flushed up her neck and her cheeks burned.

Rachel – Friday 13 December, 20.53
So you do!! You wank yourself silly all week over the things I tell you I would do to you and then you fuck your wife all weekend. Do you think of me while you are doing her?

Adam – Friday 13 December, 20.59
*I never said I didn't have sex with my wife. The two
things are very different.*

Rachel – Friday 13 December, 21.10
*YOU IMPLIED YOU DIDN'T HAVE SEX WITH HER
A LONG TIME AGO...AND WHAT, NOW I AM A
THING?!*

Adam – Friday 13 December, 21.12
Simmer down, Rachel, and don't shout at me.

Rachel – Friday 13 December, 21.14
*Go fuck yourself...oh, you do all week. So I
suppose tonight I am intruding on your real fucking
time...better get to it, Adam.*

Rachel fumed. She threw her pillow across the room and
it hit the wardrobe door with a loud thud. She cursed herself,
hoping it hadn't woken the kids.

Adam didn't reply. He didn't know what to do or what to
say. Telling an angry woman to simmer down was always
a mistake. He guessed sex was off the agenda with David,
which was why she was so upset with him. His thoughts
fluctuated between it being a good thing – he would never
hear from her again – and wondering what the hell was he
going to do without her.

Saturday dawned still cold, with bright, clear skies. The
frost sparkled hard on the shed roof and a robin perched
on the edge. Rachel thought how apt: the magpies were

nowhere to be seen. David had the kids out of bed, dressed and eating breakfast, by the time she staggered through the kitchen door still in her pyjamas and in search of a hot drink.

'Tea?' David said as he handed her a large white mug.

Rachel sipped, but the tea was tepid and sweet, more like something you would give to the kids. She poured it down the sink. She watched David, expecting confrontation; instead she saw him lock his jaw and look away. But Rachel wanted an argument and she wanted to vent. She looked at the kids eating cereal and decided to cool off in the shower.

'Don't forget we're going out,' David shouted after her.

'I'll be ready in twenty minutes,' she shouted back.

Despite the bad start to the morning, the day out with David and the kids was actually fun. Rachel kept her phone in her bag and didn't even look to see if there was a message from Adam until she was back home.

Adam – Saturday 14 December, 10.01
Rachel, I'm sorry. I thought about it overnight and I realised how awful that must have sounded. What I have with you is special, it's intimate; we use words to express how we feel about each other. With Julia it's just an efficient act of mutual gratification, done mostly out of habit.

I keep thinking about us being together one day. To spend a weekend with you would be wonderful, even if we only ever managed one weekend together in the whole of our lives.

I'm really sorry for upsetting you.

Rachel – Saturday 14 December, 16.22
I know what we have is intimate – and what do you mean, just one weekend ever??

Adam – Saturday 14 December, 17.45
I thought I'd upset you so much you were never going to speak to me again! Where have you been all day?

Rachel – Saturday 14 December, 17.48
Out with David and the kids…you know, family stuff. Seeing Santa.

Adam – Saturday 14 December, 17.52
Sounds very cosy.

Rachel – Saturday 14 December, 17.52
Actually we had a really good day.

That night after David had gone to bed Rachel went down to his study, and with the lights still on she made love to him. David was rather blown away by his wife that night but she didn't look at him or speak once. He thought he was being stupid, but somehow he felt as if she was using his body to make love to someone else.

Rachel – Sunday 15 December, 03.00
I can't stand the thought of you with somebody else, Adam, not physically, not emotionally.

Rachel – Sunday 15 December, 03.20
Why isn't Julia on your friends list on Facebook? I can't find her. Has she listed herself under her maiden name?

Rachel – Sunday 15 December, 04.06
I can't sleep. I can't cope with the thought of you lying there next to her and soon it will be night after night. I want to be with you, Adam. I really do…

Rachel – Sunday 15 December, 04.22
OK, just one weekend. Let's just arrange one weekend so I know I will be with you just once.

Adam – Sunday 15 December, 07.31
I know it's difficult, Rachel, but that's how it is. After Christmas…we'll talk about a weekend after Christmas. If it's any consolation at all, I had a blazing row with Julia when she came home on Friday and she seems to be spending the weekend in the spare room.

Rachel's comment left a slight chill creeping over Adam. Yet, he still didn't want to say goodbye. The alarm bells that had tinkled in the background before were now blaring in his ears at a decibel rate well exceeding safety guidelines. He knew he should block her from Facebook and forget about her. She wouldn't be able to contact him or Julia; he knew she had a vague idea of where he lived, but she was hundreds of miles away. He knew he should stop all this today and yet he didn't. Rachel aroused him in a way nobody else had ever done. In his dull life with his perfect-to-look at wife, she was the antithesis of Julia; she was warped and she excited him. The distraction of her had stopped his frenzied mind replaying the accident over and over. They didn't just Hot Chat any more now, they role-played virtual sex games. Rachel started it; changing the themes all the time, she would describe in detail where they were and what they were doing, and Adam liked to play along. The desire for her had given him back his confidence. She had noticed him and spent time with him in a way that was so much more intimate than anything he had ever shared with any other woman. How on earth did he just let that go?

Rachel didn't see the argument Adam had with Julia as consolation. Adam was hers...the only way forward was to get rid of Julia. It didn't take long to find the company she worked for on LinkedIn. Adam had told her lots of pieces of information and Rachel had an excellent memory; all she had to do was piece them together. She set up her own LinkedIn profile with a false name, using her Hotmail account just to be sure; she didn't want to reveal herself just yet. Now she had to decide whether or not to contact Julia or just threaten to. A threat would push Adam along a little.

Rachel – Monday 16 December, 03.03
I want you, Adam...I mean really want you. I imagine you touching me, not just when we are telling each other things on here but when I am alone. I fantasise about...oh, all sorts of things. Things we could do that you would probably find appalling...

Adam – Monday 16 December, 07.30
Lol... Oh, I doubt I would find it appalling. I really want you too...

Rachel – Monday 16 December, 08.01
I mean...I don't just want you for a weekend. I mean I want more of you...a relationship...an affair to start with...then we could see.

Adam – Monday 16 December, 08.05
But things work as they are for now, and I did say I would try and get away for a weekend...we'll talk about it then. Just see how that goes first??

Rachel – Monday 16 December, 08.10
I think you're lying to me, Adam...stringing me along because virtual sex is what you get off on!

Adam – Monday 16 December, 08.12
That is not true. I am not discussing this now – you will be late for the school run again. I'll talk to you later.

Rachel – Monday 16 December, 09.45
Children safely deposited in appropriate locations and on time but now of course you will be working!! Oh, you're there.

Adam – Monday 16 December, 09.46
I am working but yes, I'm here. I am not stringing you along. The fantasy time we share together...it works. Reality might be something entirely different. Reality is kids and arguments over damp towels. It's shouting about toothpaste lids left off and socks that don't get unfurled before they're thrown in the laundry basket. Reality with Julia hasn't always been wonderful and loving. She let me down when I needed her most. Her standard of living was more important to her than my welfare. With you, Rachel, I have the most amazing sexual fantasies that are not ruined by domesticity – and before you start railing at me about it just being about the sex, it is not. I have become slightly

obsessed with you, and if I'm honest always have been, and transferring that into reality could be the biggest mistake I ever make.

Rachel – Monday 16 December, 09.58
But I want reality, and I don't mind unfurling socks!

Adam – Monday 16 December, 09.59
Rachel, we live hundreds of miles away from each other. If you take into consideration traffic and loo stops it would take us over four hours each to meet in the middle, so it would be a very infrequent affair. How on earth would we get to know each other again? Do you not think the reality of reality would drive us insane? If we were closer, if it only took an hour or so to meet, then it would be more realistic. The fantasy we have works and, not only that, we chat all the time without all the crap that goes with it.

And can you imagine what would happen if we were caught? Think of the emotional and financial implications.

Rachel – Monday 16 December, 10.04
So this is about money!!!!! Financial security!!!!! What about taking a risk for something that might turn out to be the best thing that ever happened to us? You have a job. I could get a job…we would manage.

I guess I'm just not worth the effort!

Adam – Monday 16 December, 10.05
And in time the job may work out to be a better one, but not if I don't do it! Rachel, we only started talking

*to each other three months ago – just be patient. You
have to think about your kids as well.*

Rachel – Monday 16 December, 10.06
*Of course I think about my kids!!!!!! We could sort
things out and then I would come back for them.*

Adam – Monday 16 December, 10.08
*Stop! You're worrying me. You cannot leave your kids,
they mean the world to you. You tell me that all the
time.*

Rachel – Monday 16 December, 10.08
Whatever!!!!!!!!!!!!!!!

Ten

Rachel – Monday 16 December, 21.05
You were a very bad boy this morning and you really upset me. I'm pouting.

Adam – Monday 16 December, 21.06
I'm sorry. I presume I'm in for some serious punishment. Please will you forgive me?

Rachel – Monday 16 December, 21.08
I said you were a very bad boy...no, you are not forgiven.

Adam – Monday 16 December, 21.09
Am I forgiven if I ask what you are wearing?

Rachel – Monday 16 December, 21.10
Always with the cliché! I may not be wearing anything.

Adam – Monday 16 December, 21.11
Not even knickers?? So that means you are naked – and where am I?

Rachel – Monday 16 December, 21.12
Oh, my knickers are definitely elsewhere, lol.

You are in a rather sparse hotel room and you are tied to a wooden chair. You are also gagged and blindfolded because I have heard enough crap from you lately. I am in control. You will do as you are told.

Adam – Monday 16 December, 21.13
I really will do as I'm told.

Rachel – Monday 16 December, 21.15
I'm wearing boots with spiky heels. You know I'm near you; you can hear the click of my heels as I walk round you, you can smell my perfume. You are very vulnerable tied there but you want me, you can sense me close, you can feel my breath just above your cock; it's so hard, you want me so much. I touch it momentarily with my tongue, tasting the lubricant that is slowly oozing out. You are trying to thrust up towards my mouth but no…I'm not going to suck your cock, so stop. Now imagine me standing in front of you. You can't touch me. I'm going to stand here for thirty minutes while you think about what you've done. I may touch you occasionally, and I am standing close enough that you can feel my breath and the heat of my body…

Adam – Monday 16 December, 21.20
I'll do whatever it takes for you to forgive me… Please just tell me you will untie me or touch me… Tell me how you will touch me…please…

Rachel – Monday 16 December, 21.50
Now, if you promise to behave, I am going to untie you.

Adam – Monday 16 December, 21.52
Oh, I so promise that I will behave.

Rachel – Monday 16 December, 21.53
OK, so you can sit at my feet and watch, but no touching. Remove your own blindfold. Don't take off the gag – I don't want to hear you speak. Later I might let you beg. Now watch as I slowly make myself come. Do not touch me. You are only allowed to watch if you do exactly as you are told, otherwise…well…I suggest you do as you are told. Do you understand?

Adam – Monday 16 December, 21.56
I understand.

Rachel – Monday 16 December, 21.56
I know the best way to make myself come, so you can watch and learn as I gently slide my fingers inside myself and slide the moisture over my clit. You can just wait and watch until I am done.

I don't really want to make you suffer today – forgiveness is coming easily. Anyway I want you inside me…I want you in my mouth. You can get on the bed now. I'm going to sit astride you and work my tongue painfully slowly down your body. Do not touch me and stay very still or I will move away. I'm going to let you slide a little of that hard penis into my mouth now…just a little. I'm using my tongue and just occasionally my teeth, just so you know that I am in control. You are all wet and hard in my mouth, trying to push yourself right in. How far down my throat do you want to go?

Adam – Monday 16 December, 22.02
How far can you take me?????

Rachel – Monday 16 December, 22.03
Shame you will never know. I do believe room service has just knocked on the door and ruined your chances of coming in my mouth. You so shouldn't have been a bad boy.

Adam – Monday 16 December, 22.05
Actually I rather liked being a bad boy. Perhaps it's something we should explore a little more?? I have to admire your cruelty but you had better put your knickers back on if room service is here!

Rachel – Monday 16 December, 22.07
I can't, I've posted them.

Adam – Monday 16 December, 22.11
Posted them??? Lol, what's that, then – some sort of new internet venture...pre-worn undies for men who get off on that sort of thing?

Rachel – Monday 16 December, 22.12
Or possibly worn underwear to the wives of virtual lovers who won't play nicely.

Adam – Monday 16 December, 22.12
Rachel? What do you mean???

Rachel – Monday 16 December, 22.13
Lol...maybe I have posted them to your wife...

Adam – Monday 16 December, 22.14
I thought the game was over. Well, it is for me, anyway, lol.

Rachel – Monday 16 December, 22.14
Oh…I'm not playing a game now. I have entered your reality…well, actually your wife's reality.

Adam – Monday 16 December, 22.18
You don't know where we live or where she lives in the week…this is not funny. Rachel, give me your phone number, I need to talk to you properly.

Rachel – Monday 16 December, 22.19
I don't need to know where you live or where she lives in the week. I do know where she works, though. She has a LinkedIn profile. The receptionist was most helpful. I told her I was a florist arranging a delivery from her husband and I just wanted to get directions and make sure I had the right office. Women are such suckers for romance. It wasn't hard to find her at all.
As for the phone number…give me yours first!

Adam – Monday 16 December, 22.24
You wouldn't do that. Are you still in some weird extended role-play? Be you, be normal…it's not funny now.

Rachel – Monday 16 December, 22.26
Perhaps you shouldn't play with people and their emotions…upsetting them may have consequences.

Maybe I am being normal...perhaps you should stop playing safe, because safe doesn't appear to be that safe now, does it? Maybe the real world is safer...come out and play properly, Adam.

Adam – Monday 16 December, 22.29
FFS, tell me you have not done this...I have kids, you wouldn't????? I don't believe you would.

Rachel – Monday 16 December, 22.30
Well, I guess you will just have to wait and see, won't you? Special Delivery! Lol, I really must stop watching Postman Pat. Very special...all black and lacy...and, of course, worn...pmsl.
Sleep well!!!!!

Adam – Monday 16 December, 22.31
Don't fuck with me...this is not fair and not funny. WTF have I done to upset you this much? FFS tell me you are just playing with me.

Rachel – Monday 16 December, 23.56
Oh, and I forgot to mention...I may have included a little photo of the screen with your Facebook profile photo on and just a few of the words where you describe how you want to remove those knickers. I can't quite remember what you said you would also be doing with your tongue...
Looking forward to tomorrow?

Adam – Monday 16 December, 23.59
You are sick and warped!!!!!!!!!!

Adam didn't sleep that night.

Rachel wasn't sure she liked herself any more.

Julia phoned Adam at ten the next morning. He didn't answer the phone; he was in a meeting. At 11 a.m. he saw the message symbol on his phone for both a voicemail and a Facebook message. He decided to face the message from Julia first.

An icy trickle of sweat ran down his back as he dialled his voicemail.

Adam, thank you – the flowers are beautiful! I love you and I'll speak to you later.

Amid the wash of relief was a trickle of fear. Rachel knew where his wife worked: she hadn't lied.

Rachel – Tuesday 17 December, 10.59
I hope Julia liked the flowers ☺

Eleven

Julia read a lot into that one bouquet of flowers. There was no message, just a card that said *Adam x*. The bouquet itself, a mix of white roses, rosehips, lisianthus and lilies, was stunning. It was wrapped in silvery frosted paper, and reminded her of cold wintry mornings looking out on the frost-covered trees that dropped down into the valley beyond at home. Julia sighed at the thought of all those wonderful mornings she had missed, and the times on those dark Monday mornings that she had cursed the biting cold for making her drive more difficult and regretted being up too early to enjoy that view.

Adam used to give her flowers, but he hadn't for years now, and she saw them as recognition of what she had done to keep the family together. She thought of them as a thank-you and an admission of love. She decided the colour choice was his way of saying that the dark days were behind them and that this was a fresh start. Julia read so much into that one bouquet and she glowed inside all day and colleagues commented to each other on the unusual warmth of her smile.

David was worried about Rachel: her behaviour was irrational; her laugh had become loud and excitable. She sang too much and then just as suddenly her mood would dip and she would become sullen and withdrawn. In the last month alone she had spent over £800 on the credit card at various online clothing stores. When he was working from home he had gone through her drawers and wardrobe. There was new underwear, new clothes and, hidden at the back of one of the drawers, a rather elaborate array of sex toys. Rachel wasn't behaving like any Rachel he had ever known. Before everything had gone so wrong and the depression had hit, she had always cared about the way she looked, but this was different: she was out to impress someone.

David presumed it was the Adam he had seen on her screen that day. He took time off work and watched the house. He made excuses to leave meetings to catch her out at times when Jamie was at pre-school. Rachel never left the house alone in the evening or the weekend and he had seen nothing suspicious in her behaviour. He toyed with the idea that she was trying to impress him, that she wanted their old life back but couldn't find a way to say so.

He was confused. He also felt that she had put him through enough in the last few years and he didn't want any more. He hadn't taken solace in Emma, either; he knew that had been the biggest mistake he had ever made, and the resulting sexual failure had left him feeling down and insecure. At least he knew that he could still make love to his wife, but even that hadn't felt right. Life with Rachel hadn't felt right in such a long time…he wanted to just be.

Adam was at a complete loss as to what to do next. The phrase 'keep your enemies even closer' just kept springing into his mind. Rachel knew where to find Julia; what else she knew, he had no idea. She had the capacity to ruin his life and his life had been ruined for long enough. He blamed himself for not listening to those alarm bells earlier, but he had been consumed with desire – not just lustful desire but desire for a time of life that was less complicated.

He couldn't just block her communications; she might go off the rails. All she had done was fire a warning shot and he knew she was right in what she said: he was tempted by her but he had played with her. Except, he'd thought she was a willing party. He guessed that placating her by seeming to agree in theory if not in practice to her demands to meet had been stupid – he had given her hope, and it didn't matter how much he wanted to meet her, there was no way he was capable of driving that far...even the thought of a train made him shudder. He should have been firm, he shouldn't have led her on, but now he had to keep playing her games until she got bored and went away.

Rachel was furious. She was angry at everyone and everything. She hated her mum for dying when she needed her. She hated her kids because they held her contained in this house that felt like her prison. She hated David for letting her down and being a stereotypical male, who had stuck his dick in the first attractive younger female who was willing. Rachel felt sidelined by the world, middle-aged with poor mental health, no job and with nobody who gave a fuck about her. She wanted to scream, but instead she simmered and waited.

Adam – Tuesday 17 December, 12.36
Yes, thanks for sending my wife the flowers. I'm definitely in her good books now.
  Is everything OK, Rachel?

Rachel was confused by Adam's response. She had expected him to spit and bluster, to swear and threaten. She broke down and cried. Jamie hugged her and stroked her back as snot and tears streaked across her face. She curled into a ball on the floor and Jamie tucked himself into her tummy and together they fell asleep. Rachel woke an hour later and Jamie had already moved away from her and was playing with his train set. Rachel sat on the floor and watched him, soured by her own thoughts that she could ever hate her children.

Rachel – Tuesday 17 December, 14.28
Adam, I'm sorry. I'm really sorry. I shouldn't have done that, but I was angry with you. I thought what we had was going somewhere, and when I started to realise that you're not the person I knew and that you are just some weirdo who gets off on wanking over someone typing dirty to them…well, I just felt used and ridiculous. I lashed out. I wanted to let you know that I could hurt you, but you must realise now that I wouldn't.

Adam – Tuesday 17 December, 15.26
You're wrong about me. I wasn't playing with you – I never meant for things to go that far.

Rachel, you have always been in my thoughts. I've obsessed over you for years. None of that was real, though. You were my fantasy…surely that isn't a bad thing? When we started chatting on Facebook I was still in a really bad place after Mum and Dad dying. Understand, I'm not making excuses or looking for sympathy, I'm trying to explain – I just don't know how to. I think we should take a couple of days to cool off. Think about what has happened and calm down.

Then we need to have a proper chat about what we are doing.

Please don't threaten me again, Rachel.

Rachel – Tuesday 17 December, 15.41
I hope I am wrong about you, Adam. I don't think a couple of days is enough time to think and cool off. Have a good Christmas – I'll message you in the New Year.

Rachel needed time to think.

Adam was worried what Rachel was planning

Julia closed the door on her studio flat as a cold icy wind blasted up the stairwell. The van was loaded and gone. She had said her goodbyes at work yesterday. The send-off had been great: lunch in the pub, far too much wine, and she had bought way too much cake for everyone in the afternoon. Plastic bags had been produced and large pieces of cake taken home for children. Julia had cried when she left, but she was drunk and the barriers were down.

She turned the key in the lock and popped it into her bag. She stood for a moment absorbing this day when her life turned the corner and the road to home was a permanent one. The flat would be turned into a holiday let and she had found a company that would manage it for her. Hopefully she wouldn't have to return for a long time.

The wind was raw as it cut though the underground garage where her car was parked, but Julia didn't care. The journey home was treacherous and, still feeling headachy from too much wine the day before, she stopped for coffee twice.

She phoned Adam each time to let him know her progress. He seemed happy, and impatient to have her home; he was cooking a special family dinner – no casserole, he promised. They were going to collect the Christmas tree in the morning and he had planned mulled wine and cheesy Christmas music for decorating it all afternoon. He told her he missed her and couldn't wait for her to be home. So much emotion poured out of Adam in those two brief telephone calls.

Adam hadn't heard from Rachel since the 17th, and at first it was a massive relief. Then he began to feel tense, thinking she was planning something. He found himself dropping back into his old obsessive routine as the panic gripped him. He needed Julia home.

The first few days leading up to Christmas with Julia back were blissful. They were filled with last-minute chores and shopping for too much unhealthy food. They drank too much, they laughed all the time, and they cuddled on the sofa in front of the fire. Christmas was cold and sharp, and Julia's mum and dad joined them for a late afternoon lunch; they too seemed to have overcome their difficulties over the sexting affair, although Adam struggled not to refer to it as he found it so amusing.

Then Christmas was over and the busyness was done and Julia started to annoy Adam and Adam started to annoy Julia. She made Adam feel tense and inadequate, and when he felt that way he thought of how he had failed and the old coping mechanisms dropped into place. Rachel never made him feel like that.

Realising that Adam's old routines had resurfaced was too much for Julia to cope with. This was supposed to be a new start but Adam was still at it: a set time to get out of bed, a set time for coffee, a certain day for a certain sandwich. At first Julia just saw it as teething problems, a period of readjustment, but when a casserole hit the table for the second time on a Friday after Christmas she threw it across the kitchen. The ferocity of her frustration shocked even her, and she spent the rest of the night locked in the spare room, unloading by text to Jim. By 10 p.m. Jim had called her on her mobile, and he had calmed her and reasoned with her and her balance was restored. She had missed talking to him and was looking forward to her return to work. Jim had moved over Christmas and was now living close to Leeds; he said she could drive over and spend the night with him and his wife if she needed some space. She thanked him, but declined with the explanation of the empty bottle of Shiraz that sat on the bedside table.

Julia sighed. She didn't want the Adam of the last four years, she wanted the Adam who had sent her flowers to signify a new start. She realised now that she had read way too much into those flowers.

Those minutes Rachel had spent thinking she hated her own children had sent her into a tailspin. The resulting chaos was an overwhelming spending spree, which left her nowhere to hide the presents. David was furious, until Rachel cried and told him she just wanted to make up for the years of gloom and depression. For once David didn't shy away from her emotion, he just held her and let her sob until his T-shirt was wet. Rachel let it all out; with the kids in bed she just let go of the frustration and the anger. She let David know that she knew about the Bar Tart and he didn't even try to deny it. He cried along with her and they talked for half the night. Later they fell into an exhausted sleep in bed together. Rachel had her head on David's shoulder all night and he never let her go. In the day they carried on with preparations for Christmas, and at night they talked, and they slept holding on to each other.

On the day after Boxing Day David asked Rachel about Adam; and about the clothes, the underwear and the sex toys. Rachel laughed. She told David that Adam was an old college friend and explained that the row of kisses he had seen were just delight that she was in touch with him again after all these years, nothing more. The sex toys she feigned embarrassment about, hinting that sleeping alone had been frustrating. The clothes, she explained, were just her feeling better about herself and wanting David to notice her. These were the things she knew David wanted to hear, so these were the things she told him. But when the sorrys were done and the hugging was over, the arguments started.

The weekend after New Year, while Julia slept in the spare room, Adam opened his heart to Rachel.

Adam – Saturday 4 January, 03.22
I've missed you.

I haven't just missed you, I feel as if part of me has died. Without you, all my old anxieties and obsessive routines have started again. There is so much that I haven't told you.

When I saw your name on Facebook I was slowly piecing my life together, but it had little meaning, and then in the months of chatting to you about everything and nothing I had something to live for. Someone who made me laugh, someone who cared about me. The virtual sex...well, was just virtual sex; it was the communication with you that was important. There is something about you, Rachel...some sort of connection I have to you that I can't explain. All those years ago, after we lost touch, I always felt as though I had lost something.

When you threatened me, I just thought you were turning into a mad obsessive stalker, but having read back through some of our messages I realise now that I led you on – that I acted as if one day we would meet, when until this day I never thought I really would or could.

The virtual sex was addictive – Christ, you just know what to say – but I'm sorry that it sort of took over. There is so much more to you and me...although undoubtedly if we ever did some of those things together that would be amazing too!!

During the time we have chatted I've thought so many things. At times I've thought I would love to meet you. I've also thought I really needed to get rid of you, and please forgive me for that last thought.

When you said we needed to take a break I was relieved – relieved because I thought you were going to ruin my life. Once you stopped messaging me and Julia came home I thought it would all slot back into place the way it was before Mum and Dad died. I thought my life was great, I thought I had it all, but now, when I look back, I realise I was living a life that Julia had set out for me; and, me being me, I just went along with it. The career, the big house and the shit-load of debt that only went away because Mum and

Dad's estate paid it off – I never really wanted any of it. Do you remember the things we used to dream of, the things we were going to do? Well, I never did any of them. So, when we made that connection again, life just became possible.

I'm probably not making sense. There is something I need to tell you. I need to tell you why my life stopped being full of possibilities.

On New Year's Eve four years ago I was driving the car that my parents died in. I did nothing wrong, I understand this now. There was black ice and fog but I was sober, I wasn't tired, and I was driving at a sensible speed. The car slid off a bend at such a perfect angle that only Mum and Dad were killed. I hit a telegraph pole, which caused my dad to have such massive head injuries that he would have died almost immediately. My mum had refused to wear her seatbelt because she had sequins on her dress and she didn't want to ruin it. A combination of the fact that the front passenger seat was shunted into the back and the force of my mum being thrown forward due to the lack of seatbelt caused massive internal injuries and she died at the scene. Julia was with her in her final moments, although she was unconscious and probably never knew. Julia had a broken arm and I had a mild concussion. As my mum died, I sat in a field of cow shit covered in my dad's blood. Julia said she called to me to be with my mum but I didn't go – all I can remember is the feeling of my dad's warm blood as it left his body.

We had been to a party at my brother's house. He turned into such a twat. I blamed myself for the *accident even though everybody told me it was just that: an accident. I also blamed my brother for having the party in the first place. One day he came to the house and I hit him so hard I broke his nose. I locked myself away, I refused to eat or drink; I wanted to die. Julia had me committed. It was only short-term and they released me. They didn't consider me a danger to myself and others, but Julia did. Then, as I slowly limped my way out of the pit of hopeless despair, she left me to take a promotion in Edinburgh. She said it was to keep the family together, that we needed the money. We could have sold the house or we could have just waited for Mum and Dad's estate to be settled. The truth is, Julia got the promotion and didn't want to let the opportunity pass.*

My life after that became a misery: day after day of the same old shit. I created a series of ritualistic obsessive behaviours just to get me through the days. I let everybody down. The biggest fear was driving. Heart-pounding, sweating anxiety barely describes the absolute terror I felt. When I knew Julia was leaving I had no choice but to drive, though, and in the end I could drive set routes locally, but no more.

When you suggested meeting I started trying to drive further, and I knew as well that if I got a job I would have to drive. I drive further now, I'm better, but still I can't just get in the car and go anywhere…in time maybe, but not yet.

The job, I think, was given to me out of sympathy. I had been ready to start a role that was way higher up than this one before the accident…but this is a job, and it is a start.

*The online flirting you once accused me of with
other women…yes, I did that. It was a distraction, but
it was never anything like the intimacy I shared with
you. I'm sorry I lied.*

*I have no idea what you will make of the above.
I should have told you from the start. I should have
trusted that you would understand.*

*It's been almost three weeks since we sent each
other a message and reality has gradually become
more and more unbearable. Without you, as I said at
the start, all my old behaviours have resurfaced. You
are not just a wonderful distraction…you make each
day mean something.*

*I'm still cross at you for threatening me, but, if you
hadn't, I wouldn't have realised any of this.*

*If I never hear back from you again I will
understand.*

*If you do message me back…then let's start over.
Let's get to know each other again. Let's talk on the
phone. Can we take it one day at a time and see where
it goes?*

I miss you, Rach xx

Rachel locked herself in the bathroom and read the long
message over and over. She thought of the kids and she
thought of David. She knew they would never be right
again. The Bar Tart would always get in the way. The fact
that he'd left her to wallow in misery when she had just
needed to be supported would always make her wonder
what if something went wrong again…where would he be
then? Some of the words Adam had said to her were ones
she could equally well have said to him. She shouldn't have

threatened him, she knew that. Sanity and stability were edging their way into her mind.

Rachel – Saturday 4 January, 08.36
There is a lot I need to tell you too, but not today. Telling you today would detract from all that you have told me. You should have told me sooner. It's me, Rachel…you could always tell me anything…

One day at a time, then.

I missed you too. xx

Rachel – Saturday 4 January, 09.22
Adam, I meant to say earlier… If we decide to take this further, well, I just wanted to say …don't worry about coming to me. I can come to you. When I found where Julia worked, I figured out where you live as well. It's really easy to get to ☺

Acknowledgements

Thank you to Cassie, Linda, Vanessa, Gary, Julia, Rachel (neither of whom are anything to do with the characters in the book!), Nina and Fiona: your encouragement has been amazing. You have read for me, given me confidence, kept me sane, talked endlessly with me to the point where my characters became part of us all. I'm sorry for all the conversations I have hijacked with my random thoughts and need-to-knows. Thank you for your friendship and your patience.

Thank you to all the people I have interrogated about your relationships and online dating experiences, some of which are far more bizarre than anything that appears in this book!

Thank you to all of you who have shared your experience with depression – it is still a subject we all need to talk about so much more.

Thank you to the team at RedDoor, who have made the process of publication so much easier than I ever expected.

Thank you to my husband Dean for going out to work every day so that I could follow my dream, and thank you to my kids for putting up with me as your mum. I love you.

My life is full of fantastic people, and I am exceptionally lucky to know you all.

About the Author

Hayley Mitchell spends most of the time writing books in her head and was finally able to put fingers to keyboard and capture some of the words in the form of her debut novel, *Because I Was Lonely*. A law graduate, she has spent most of her life working with people and much of her career as an advice worker for charities. Always fascinated by people and their relationships, she began to write fiction. She is very lucky to live in Wiltshire with her husband, whose support has been invaluable, and their two children, who amuse, inspire and exhaust her every day. She now divides her time between her family and writing her second novel.